BRIDGET WALSH

Daughter of Éireann

Ireland 1847-1848

This book is dedicated to my beautiful granddaughter:
Delilah Belle Walsh

Acknowledgement

With love and thanks

To my team:
Nancy, my daughter and copy editor.
Fran, my daughter and book-seller in Ireland.
Charlotte, my daughter-in-law and marketing editor.

To all of my family for their love and support.

To my Open University Masters Workshop readers and
commentators,
grateful thanks.

Characters

In Galway:

Jane Keating, b. September 1830. She is now just turned 17.

Jane's cousin's children: Sorcha Keating, aged 5, and brother, Jamie, aged 8.

Father Hanrahan, Jane's parish priest; Mrs Flynn, the priest's housekeeper.

Six orphans in the care of the priest and his housekeeper:

Billy O'Reilly, age 12

The Clearys: Shay, 12; Liam, 10, and Maria, 7.

Twins: Lucy and Grace Kennedy, 8.

Other characters:

Michael Fahy, an old neighbour and a friend of Jane's late father.

Niall Smullen, the police officer who murdered Sorcha and Jamie Keating's father, Brendan, in 1846.

* * *

Historical characters in Dublin, Waterford and Ballingarry.

"Speranza" - The pen name of Jane Elgee, Young Irelander, poet and writer.

Thomas Francis Meagher, Young Irelander, Irish nationalist.

Charles Gavan Duffy QC, newspaper owner/editor and Young Irelander.

William Smith O'Brien, the elected MP for Limerick county in the General Election of July - Aug 1847. Young Irelander and Irish nationalist, who led the rebels at the Battle of Ballingarry.

The Widow Margaret McCormack of Ballingarry. https://en.wikipedia.org/wiki/Famine_Warhouse_1848

* * *

Money

I used these exchanges to give an idea of the value of money back in 1848. Thanks to Professor Christine Kinealy.

£1.00 or $5 in 1846 = £100 today

Reference:

Kinealy, Christine. (2013) Charity and the Great Hunger in Ireland. The Kindness of Strangers. (p 14) Bloomsbury Academic, London.

1

Dublin Port, September 1847

H ome. Almost there. The journey from New York had been easy, no storms, just day after day of grey skies and the endlessly moving Atlantic Ocean. By now, docked in Liverpool to discharge the cargo, Jane Keating was a weary traveller after having sailed thousands of miles around the globe.

She stayed in her cabin while the cargo of American timber was offloaded and listened to the thunderous clamour of cranes at work, and the hammering feet of stevedores racing around the deck above her head.

In the early hours, before dawn, she heard screaming, crying, and harsh, shouted orders given. Curious, she put her cloak on and rushed up the stairs onto the deck to see a multitude of people; young and old, being harried up the gangway onto the ship. Some of them could barely walk, and looked ill and exhausted. A few were carried on board by crew members. All were half dressed in rags, most went barefoot and every one of them was filthy, with tangled hair falling around the thinnest, dirtiest faces she had ever seen. A woman on her own with three small children glanced at Jane. The woman looked too old and feeble to be the children's mother, but she had two of them by the hand and the bigger child in front of her. None of the poor souls defied the orders; they all followed, one after the other, down below decks.

Jane stood and watched, but she couldn't make sense of it. 'What's happening?' she asked a crew member.

'They rounded up these Irish. They're destitute and are being sent back to Ireland. England don't want them.'

'How can they do that?'

'The government passed a law. They pays the captain, and he takes them back to Dublin.'

'But why?' She didn't understand.

The crewman had already turned to help raise the gangway. They were getting ready to leave for the crossing to Dublin.

Jane headed back down below decks. On her way, she leaned against the locked door to the compartment that had held the American timber, and now held those poor souls. She heard whispers and weeping. She looked at the brass padlock on the door. When had these people last eaten or drunk anything?

A crew member saw her at the door. 'Best not meddle, Miss.'

'Have they got something to eat and drink?'

'There's a barrel of water in there. I expect they'll be fed when they get back to Dublin.'

She walked slowly back to her cabin. Her mind stumbled over what she had seen. It didn't make sense. Why would they send them back? Only if the famine was over. Was it over? She'd not heard anything in New York or Melbourne.

'They'll be fed when they get back to Ireland,' she assured herself.

2

* * *

She paced the pale, holystoned timber boards and waited until she could just make out the edge of the land, almost hidden by a purple mist shrouding the distant hills. The ship drew closer to the land, the rain fell harder, and she strained her eyes to see some little familiar detail; a cabin, or a field with a few cows grazing. There were only dark shapes in the distance, the mist concealed her first sight of home.

She held on tight to the ship's rail as it turned into the estuary to the River Liffey. Not much further now, then went back to her cabin to collect her few belongings. Two crew members stood to attention beside the doors to the cargo hold. No sounds came through. Jane was within minutes of setting foot on her home soil.

This final journey had been passed in the most comfort she had ever known, but also much sadness. She had her own cabin and had travelled second class from New York to Dublin, thanks to the gift of gold from Sally, her Aboriginal friend. When she had left New South Wales Jane was grieving for her still-born daughter. Her sorrow only intensified when she got to New York to find her friend, Annie Power, lying in her coffin ready for her funeral.

Jane was now almost entirely alone in the world. She clung to the thought of her cousin Brendan's wife and children. Her last remaining family would save her.

She slipped out of her heavy woollen cloak, shook away the fine rain and laid it on the bunk. Then she checked her bag. The gold was still in the woven grass purse that Sally had handed to her two days before she escaped from Melbourne, months before.

She studied herself in the mirror above the wash-stand for a moment or two. It was hard to believe she was looking at her seventeen-year-old self. Not long ago, well, almost two years ago now, she had raced to her cousin's field to help him dig his potatoes. Then, she had dressed as a boy for field work, and had been full of energy and optimism. Now, her face had a drawn look of sadness and grief that she felt sure would never leave her. Was her life to be one of perpetual mourning and regret?

She brushed and smoothed her windblown hair and tied it back with a soft ribbon. The actions allowed her to push her thoughts away, and she checked her reflection in the mirror again. She was tallish, with straight dark brows and a bend in her nose where it had been broken the year before. Her narrow build was accentuated by the horrible dress she wore. She managed a half-smile and made a promise that she'd buy a new dress as soon as she could. This one was a navy-blue, flounced thing that she must have been mad to buy in New York. She had bought it in a rush to have something new to wear to meet Annie, not knowing she'd end up wearing it to her friend's funeral. Thankfully, the jacket she had picked out, a fine wool mix of mauves and dark russets, covered a good part of the dress. At least it hid some of the frills. She sat on the edge of the bunk and retied the laces in her boots. Then she stood and pulled her cloak around her shoulders. She was ready.

* * *

The noises and movement on the deck of the ship had fallen silent. Jane picked up her bag containing the gold and her few possessions and walked up on deck.

The deportees has been off-loaded and sat or lay on the rain-swept quayside. Most had a beaten look about them; no-one went near them.

The captain stood by the gangway waiting to see Jane off. She was the last passenger to leave.

She pointed to the people on the quay. 'Will someone look after them?'

'I expect so. I heard another lot were sent back last week.' His job was done and he clearly was not interested. 'This must be a happy day for you, Miss Keating.'

'It's a blessed day. I thought I'd never see home again.' Her voice stumbled over the words. She glanced across at her fellow passengers on the quay.

'Well, I'm not sure what it is that you've come back to, but good luck to you all the same.' The captain touched the brim of his cap to salute her and held his hand out to help her step onto the gangway, then stood and watched while she walked the last few steps of her long journey home.

Jane stopped as she set foot on the quayside. She wanted to breathe a silent prayer of thanks. Raised a Catholic, she had believed in God and His Blessed Son, Jesus Christ, all her life. And she had prayed all her life. Yet this last year had drained away her faith, for God had not heard her desperate pleas. He had turned His face away from her, and from these poor wretches. She now did the same for Him. She pressed her lips together, left the prayer unsaid, and walked on past the crowd of helpless paupers who had shared her last journey.

She wanted to do something to help, but didn't know what, or even who to speak to.

* * *

She had walked a hundred yards along the quay when she saw another group of people waiting silently under a long eaves beside the warehouses and ticket offices facing the river.

There must have been two hundred men, women and children, of all ages from babies to grannies. They were waiting to embark on the same ship, on its outward journey back to North America. Many of those had a weary droop about them, rather than an air of anticipation ahead of their great adventure. She saw that some were in various stages of dress or even undress. Although, one family, right at the front of the queue, had two trunks of belongings with them, and five children. The mother, father and children were well turned out, and all wore leather boots and oiled topcoats to protect against the rain. Behind them, the next family were bareheaded, and all went barefoot, with just the one small bag. How had they paid for their passage? Jane went over to the father and mother and greeted them in Irish.

'*Dia dhuit*. Where are you off to?'

The mother smiled. 'America, so we are. Off to make a new life. Thanks be to God and our landlord.'

'Your landlord?'

'Ah now, there's a story for you, Miss. Our landlord, Mr Beckett, God save him and keep him, paid for all his tenants to go to America. We're surely the fortunate ones, so we are.'

The woman turned and indicated the other family groups in the queue. None of them wore shoes or boots, although Jane saw one man with a pair of shabby boots, the laces tied together, slung over his shoulder. She had often done the same herself. He's saving them to wear when he gets to America, she thought.

Jane nodded. 'You don't have a cloak or boots?'

'We'll get everything on the ship. It's all there waiting for us,' the woman assured Jane. Then she peered at Jane's face and looked over to the ship, and the offloaded souls further along the quay. 'Where have you come from?'

'I've just come home from New York. Those poor people over there have been sent back from Liverpool.' She reached into her bag and took out a silver dollar. 'Here, take this. It will help you.'

The woman clutched the coin in her filthy fingers. 'Thank you. Sure, you're a good woman, may the Lord bless you and look kindly upon you.'

Jane left them standing in the rain, waiting to embark. Strangely, despite her new lack of faith, she felt comforted by the woman's blessing. If that woman, who had nothing, could bring her family into the unknown, then she, Jane, could rejoice about returning home, surely?

Yes, she decided, but not until she had spoken to someone in charge about these returned immigrants. She'd do that first.

* * *

She spotted the Port administration buildings spread out along the pier. She went in and asked to speak to the manager.

'What is your business with him?' the clerk asked.

'I've come about the people sent back from Liverpool. I want to find out what will happen to them.'

The pasty-faced clerk blinked, then shrugged. 'I'll find someone to speak to you.'

Jane waited a few minutes until the clerk came back with an

older man.

'Are you the manager?' she asked.

'No, I'm his assistant. Timmy here told me that you've come across from Liverpool with a group of deportees.'

'Yes, that's right. I want to know what will happen to them. A lot of them look in a bad way. They can't spend much more time out in the rain. And I don't think they've had anything to eat today.'

The manager's assistant nodded. 'We know they're there. They'll be taken care of, don't you worry, Miss.' He was a stocky man, with shaggy greying hair and a yellowed moustache.

'So, tell me, how will they be taken care of?' Jane persisted.

'We're getting several groups of these, every week for the last month now. They'll go to the Dublin workhouse.' The man turned away to leave.

'Wait! They've not eaten today. Will you see they're fed?'

'Leave them to us and don't you worry your head about it.'

The clerk held the door open for Jane to leave. She could do no more.

What had she come back to? She glanced around the docks. There were shabby stevedores working on and around the ships, loading and unloading. The place appeared to be busy, but there was none of the urgency about the work that she remembered when she had worked here in Dublin more than a year ago. Now there were only a couple of ships lined up on the glittering Liffey waiting to dock. And shambling all around her were the poor, wherever she looked, ragged men and women with thin, desperate faces, dirty and unkempt hair and bodies, and their half-dressed gangs of children. Was she wrong to have come back? Should she have stayed away? She shivered in the warm, damp air and walked on.

* * *

The walk into town along the quays allowed her to get her balance back after being on board the ship for weeks. Low clouds drizzled on everything below, and she pulled the hood of her cloak tighter around her face.

She passed the Custom House, with its columns and cupola, a great stone monument to the British Government's grip on her sister, Ireland. The building itself was open. Horse-drawn cabs dropped off well-dressed gentlemen to go about their business of importing and exporting Ireland's agricultural produce. Maybe things weren't that bad. She tried hard to persuade herself, but the poor *crathurs* she had seen on the docks suggested a different tale. One lot paid to leave by their landlord, another lot sent back from England, all unwanted.

Jane walked right into the heart of the city, across Carlyle Bridge and glanced back at Nelson's Pillar. The statue towered over the crowded streets and the multitude of beggars lining the sides of the bridge across the Liffey. She knew then, in her heart, that the deportees from Liverpool would still be on the pier at Dublin docks. Nothing had changed since she had left last year. She only hoped that she could find the remnants of her family in Galway. Then everything would be better. Everything must be better.

She turned the corner into Fleet Street and stopped at the door of the Fleet Inn. She had to step over a poor *divil* to get through the door, stopped, found a coin in her pocket, gave it to him, and went inside to book herself a bed for the night.

In her room, she took her clothes and the gold out of her

hold-all. She transferred the gold nuggets into the small leather satchel she had bought in New York. Right at the bottom of the hold-all, swathed in a black silk scarf, were her memories of Annie Power. After the funeral, Finn, Annie's brother, had given her a copy of Annie's Commonplace Book. It had been published shortly before his sister died.

Jane held the small book in her hands and smelled the soft brown leather cover. She flipped through the pages and felt a puff of air against her cheek. She had read it on the ship and had seen her own name in it. She shook her head and replaced the book, then picked up the thing she had been looking for: a copy of The Sun, a New York newspaper. She folded it into the satchel.

She added the last of her money and fastened the buckles, then put the satchel strap over her shoulder. The bag was now secured across her body. She wrapped herself in her cloak, stopped at the reception desk to make a request, then left the inn and headed back out into the rain to see about her first bit of business.

2

The Nation Newspaper, Dublin

I
t was noon and the air was full of the sound of church bells as they rang the call for prayer. Almost every person Jane passed slowed to bless themselves and recite the Angelus. Without thinking, she began to whisper. 'The Angel of the Lord declared unto Mary.' Then she stopped. The whole of heaven, all the angels and saints, didn't worry a jot about faithful Irish Catholics, and had left them to starve since the potato blight struck two years ago. This was beyond Jane's understanding. Maybe the British government in London was right when they said Almighty God wanted to smite the Irish people for their sins of ingratitude and rebellion.

By then she was only a couple of streets away from The Nation newspaper offices, and stepped up her pace. Jane had spent a few months working there before she was transported to New South Wales and now it felt almost like a homecoming. But who would be there? Perhaps she'd see Thomas Francis Meagher again. She smiled at the recollection of the look on his face when he realised that she was really a girl and not the boy, Jack, she had impersonated to get a job at the newspaper.

The man she really wanted to see was the owner-editor and barrister, Charles Gavan Duffy. She imagined him at his desk in his cramped, wood-panelled office, writing up another polemic about the state of Ireland. But for all his strong views, he had a softer side. Mr Duffy had been like a second father to her when she had turned up at The Nation, penniless, with just a letter of introduction from Annie Power, the Waterford poet.

He had offered her a job at the newspaper and she was soon training as a typesetter. She found out later that he had been orphaned at a young age himself and he tried to help other orphans whenever he could.

In the months she had spent working at the newspaper, she met some of the Young Irelanders, men and women who wanted to see Ireland freed from British rule, including Tom Meagher, and the famous poet, Speranza.

She hoped they hadn't forgotten her, and the day she had taken Annie's place on board the transportation ship. She knew that Speranza saw her as a hero back then. It wasn't true. Jane owed her life to Annie and was simply repaying her debt.

Would Annie have died if she had gone to New South Wales and served her sentence instead of going to New York? That thought had kept Jane awake at nights on the ship back to Ireland. She sighed, and put it to the back of her mind, for she had arrived at the newspaper.

* * *

She opened the door to the smell of newsprint, and felt the floorboards rumble beneath her feet. The air trembled with the clatter from the press and she heard the hiss of the steam engine used to power the press. The first edition of the week must be underway. The front office was empty so she walked along the hall and pushed open the door to the printing room. And there he was, the owner-editor, standing by the window, holding a freshly printed newspaper up to the light.

Charles Gavan Duffy's spectacles glinted in the lamplight. He was a tall, well-built man in his early thirties. His dark auburn hair and green eyes, strong nose and full lips marked him out. He had married young, but his wife had died, just before Jane arrived in Dublin, the previous year. He was still in mourning when Jane had first met him. Although he had only discovered that his young apprentice was not a boy, when Speranza and Annie had explained, with much laughter, that Jack was, in fact, Jane Keating.

He looked up from examining the newspaper when the print-room door opened.

'It's me, Mr Duffy, Jane Keating. Do you remember me?' She held her breath. Dressed now as a woman, with her hair grown down past her shoulders, she wasn't sure if he would recognise her.

Gavan Duffy took off his spectacles and tilted his head while he considered at the stranger at the door. Then he laughed. 'No! I don't believe it! You're back. But you were transported to New South Wales. How is it possible you're back?'

By the time he had finished speaking, he had walked over to her. 'Yes, it's you alright, Jane.' He shook his head, then he smiled. 'Let me shake your hand.' He turned to his assistant. 'Ciaran, finish checking this draft, there's a good man. I have to go and talk to my friend.'

He held Jane's hand and studied her face again. 'Why, I never thought to see you again, Jack. Forgive me, Jane! It's surely a miracle. Come. You must tell me all about it.'

* * *

Jane and Gavan Duffy left the newspaper offices and walked to a coffee house on College Green. The rain had eased and they strolled together past the grey stone walls of Trinity College. They didn't speak, but Jane caught Gavan Duffy glancing at her as they crossed the road and turned a corner into Saint Stephen's Green. 'I can't understand how I ever took you for a boy.' He shook his head and smiled wryly.

The editor was a well-known customer of the coffee house and an elderly waiter led them to a table in the back of the room, nicely tucked away, where, Jane thought, the sight of a woman wouldn't cause shock and horror to the male patrons. After ordering coffee for both of them, he sat back to listen to Jane give her account of her travels since the last time they had met.

'I've been travelling for months. When I got away from New South Wales, I went to New York to see Annie Power. You published some of her poems, if you remember.'

'I do, of course. And some of the articles she sent me from New York. But I've not heard from her for a while now. How is she?'

Jane swallowed hard. Her voice broke as she spoke about her best friend. 'I'm truly sorry to say this, but she died a few days before I got there. I arrived in time for her funeral, in August.'

Gavan Duffy sat back in his chair and stared at Jane for a few moments. 'No! Sure, that's desperately sad news. She was so young. What did she die of, do you know?'

'I was told she had the consumption. Then there was a fire at the refuge she had set up. She was caught in the fire and her lungs were damaged. It was a disaster. She didn't recover.'

'And what of her brother and sister? I don't remember their names.'

'Finn and Katty. They're just brokenhearted. But they live with their aunt, so they are settled, at least. I still can't believe she is dead, and I'd say they can't, either. But it's true, I saw her with my own eyes.' Jane had cried all her tears for Annie and was left with just her broken heart.

The waiter brought the coffee and they sat in silence while the old fellow fiddled with the cups and poured the coffee from a silver jug. When he had finished he left them to their drinks and Gavan Duffy put his hand over Jane's.

'And what about you, Jane? Are you going to tell me how you managed to get out of New South Wales? I sincerely believed there was no escaping that place. Sure, it is at the end of the world!'

'I had a lot of help, Mr Duffy.' Jane felt the warmth from his hand on hers and it reminded her of Owen, her friend, the British soldier. 'Two friends helped me get on a whaling ship. It was an American ship that had stopped into Port Phillip Bay. The captain needed a woman to support his wife who was due to have her baby. There was no one else around, so he took me with them to Nantucket. And a woman friend gave me a precious gift before I left.'

Gavan Duffy smiled. 'I wouldn't put it past you to try your hand at delivering a baby.'

She attempted a crooked smile in return, but his words only brought back the pain and despair when she delivered her own stillborn daughter in Melbourne. She sipped the bitter drink and decided that she hated coffee. It made her heart beat too fast, and she really didn't like that. It reminded her of those other times. Her breathing became shallow. The air in the coffee house was full of smoke from pipes and cigars and the place stank of old tobacco. Deep voices in the room echoed around the walls; men doing business deals, the occasional loud laugh, or cough, the chink of china. She felt dizzy, and the smells made her feel sick. She heard Mr Duffy's voice. 'Jane?'

She focused on the sounds until the dizziness receded. Her heartbeat began to slow down. It was a hard thing to talk about her escape and Annie's death, but there was no getting away from it.

'I'm sorry.' She took a deep breath. 'Will you tell Speranza and Tom, please, Mr Duffy? I find it really hard to talk about Annie.' She picked up her bag and rooted through it. 'There's an article here in a newspaper I bought in New York. It's lovely. It tells all about the work Annie did for young women emigrants.'

Gavan Duffy took the folded newspaper from her. The article was on the front page, towards the bottom. 'Thank you. I'll read it now.' He put his spectacles on and gave the newspaper a shake to straighten it out. 'Ah, Bishop Hughes, took the funeral. He's a famous man, from a neighbouring county in my own part of Ireland, I believe.' He said no more and read quietly. When he had finished he folded the newspaper again and placed it on the table. 'Annie was a great young woman, by all accounts. She'll be much missed.'

'You'll show it to Tom and Miss Speranza?'

He nodded. 'I will, and I'll be sure to let you have it back.'

Jane glanced through the window at the front of the shop and saw a group of people on the move. A man carried a heavy bag on his back, the woman next to him held a baby in one arm and a small child by the hand. They were followed by four other children of various ages, all young, the oldest was no more than eight or nine years.

She pointed to them. 'Are they heading for the docks?'

Gavan Duffy sighed. 'They could be. More likely they have just arrived here from the south or the west of the country. The potato blight is still in the ground. But there's hope that this harvest will be sound. At least the Government in London seems to think so, for they have declared an end to the famine, and have started to close down the soup kitchens. Only the Quakers are still operating on the Quays. I see them there every day. I'd say that family is going there.'

They sat together for a few more minutes. Gavan Duffy finished his coffee and glanced at Jane and her unfinished drink. 'Come on. Let's get out of here. We'll take a stroll, and see what the Quakers are doing.'

* * *

The nearer they got to the river, the thicker the air became, and grey water roiled sluggishly between the banks of the Liffey. Jane covered her mouth with her hand. 'The smell is worse than I remember.'

'That's because the city is full up and the river is the only place for waste. Whatever you do, don't fall into that water!'

They found the soup kitchen up on Grattan Quay and spotted the family they had seen earlier eating bread and drinking cups of soup. There must have been more than a hundred people crowded together while they ate the bread and drank the hot broth.

17

The two Quaker women were almost finished packing away their utensils and the boiler onto the back of the cart.

Gavan Duffy hailed them. 'Mrs Bingham. Good day to you, and Miss Bingham.'

Slim, in a dark grey dress with a shawl crossed over her chest, the older woman wore a matching grey bonnet. Her daughter, a young woman in her twenties, wore similar somber colours, but a white frilled cap peeked out from under her bonnet and black hair gleamed around her handsome face. They stepped away from the cart to shake hands with Gavan Duffy.

'Let me introduce you to my friend, Jane Keating. She's just back from America, and further afield.' He looked at Jane and smiled.

'Good day, to you,' Jane said. 'How long have you been doing this work for?'

The older woman spoke first. 'Good day to you both. We're here every day, with soup and bread, and we have been doing this for more than a year now. But it's getting harder to buy the makings of the soup. People are tired of hearing about the blight, it seems.'

'Do you not get money from the Government?' Jane asked them.

'No. The Quaker Central Relief Committee gets donations and pays for all of this.'

Jane looked across at the family who handed back the tin cups. They nodded to Jane but did not stop, the mother grasped the youngest child by the hand and they continued on their straggling walk.

Jane and Gavan Duffy said goodbye to the women and headed back towards the newspaper offices.

'So what is the government doing?' she asked.

18

'They're feeding the paupers in the workhouses. And many of those are full up. That's the situation here, at least.' Gavan Duffy stopped in mid-stride, as if a thought had just occurred to him.

'Forgive me, Jane, but I didn't ask you about your plans. Do you have a place to stay? You're welcome to stay at my house.'

'Thank you. But I have a room in the Fleet Inn tonight, then I'm going to Galway. I made a promise to find my late cousin's family as soon as I got home.'

'You must be weary from all that travelling, without putting another journey on yourself. At least come for supper this evening. I'll invite Tom and Speranza. They'll want to catch up with you. I must tell you, I married again, since you were last here. My wife, Susan, would like to meet you, I'm sure.'

'Thank you, I'd like that, and congratulations on your marriage.' She smiled. 'If you have time, I do need your help with one thing.' She lowered her voice and looked to see if anyone was listening. They had stopped at the top of D'Olier Street. It was busy with people going about their business, and a few poor souls sitting with their hands out begging. Gavan Duffy dropped a sixpence into the hand of one beggar, then they walked on towards the newspaper office.

' I told you I have money,' she whispered. 'I need to put it into a bank, but I don't think a woman can open an account. Will you come with me?'

Gavan Duffy laughed. 'What other surprises have you got for me, Jane Keating?' He saw she was serious and asked. 'Where is it? Your money.'

'Here, in my satchel.' She pulled back the edge of her cloak to show him her satchel. 'I have a few dollars, but most is in gold.' Still whispering, Jane looked up at him and smiled. 'I need to change it into sovereigns.'

Gavan Duffy frowned and looked at her. 'Gold? How did you come by it?'

'It was a gift. Given by a woman friend I helped.'

'Right so. Then we'll go to my bank. It's not far. You can't be walking around with . . . You didn't say how much.'

She whispered again. 'I have three dollars and six gold nuggets.'

The number caused Gavan Duffy to stop walking. 'Six gold nuggets! But they must be worth . . .'

'Shh, Mr Duffy!' Jane frowned.

Gavan Duffy looked around him. Several people had stopped on hearing his shout. He raised his hat to them and smiled. Then he crooked his arm for Jane to link hers. They walked on.

'What help did you give your friend? To be given gold nuggets?'

'I helped save her son's life, and her life, too. I'll tell you about it one day,' Jane promised.

'And how did she come by the gold?'

'She didn't steal it, Mr Duffy. Whatever she had, she came by honestly.' Although Jane had no knowledge of how her friend, Sally, had come across the gold, she was confident it had been found and not stolen.

They arrived at the bank. Before they went inside, Jane and Gavan Duffy agreed on the story they would tell the bank manager. Jane had come into an inheritance from an American relative and Gavan Duffy would confirm that. An inheritance would be more believable than the true story that Jane thought even Mr Duffy might wonder at.

* * *

The editor of The Nation was an important customer and there was no need to stand in line. The bank clerk, ensconced behind the high mahogany counter, spotted the newspaper owner and Queen's Council, Charles Gavan Duffy, and hurried over to escort the two of them to a railed-off seating area.

The clerk went through a door into the rear of the bank and came back a moment later. He lifted the oak flap of the counter and invited them through.

They followed him to the bank manager's office. Jane said nothing, just listened to the two men, the bank manager and the barrister. Gavan Duffy explained his request. Jane smiled at the look of surprise on the bank manager's whiskered and jowly face, and his glance in her direction.

In the end, they had no trouble opening the account in Jane's name, with Gavan Duffy, as a guarantor. The bank had branches in Galway and Waterford, so Jane would be able to withdraw money when she needed it.

The bank manager weighed five of the gold nuggets. He told them the value, then changed her dollars into shillings and she put the coins and ten sovereigns into her purse. The balance was added to her new bank book. Soon afterwards, they were back out on the street.

Jane slipped the book into her bag and touched Gavan Duffy's arm. 'Thank you. I think he might have had me arrested if you hadn't vouched for me.' They both smiled and nodded at the same time.

'You could be right. They're a suspicious lot, bankers,' her friend said.

They walked back towards Fleet Street and Jane's hotel.

Gavan Duffy stopped at the doorway.

'One more thing, Jane. About the money. Don't forget that you were destitute when I met you last year. Remember what it feels like. There's plenty of desperate people around these days. If some of them find out you've got money, then they'll have it off you. Or they'll sell you a sad story to get it off you. I want you to promise me you'll keep it to look after yourself. At least until you get settled and can decide on who and what to spend it on. Will you do that?'

Jane nodded. She had been thinking about the money and how she could use it to help other people. 'I'll wait a while, until I get settled and see where I can spend it best. I promise I'll not be destitute again, Mr Duffy. And thank you for suggesting I keep one of the gold nuggets.'

He pushed the door open for Jane. 'You'll come for supper later?

'I'm looking forward to meeting Speranza and Tom. Will you remember to tell them about Annie? I can't explain it all again, really.'

'Don't worry, I'll tell them. I'm still at the same address. Be sure to get a cab and come after seven. The children will be in bed and we can enjoy a quiet supper.'

They shook hands.

Jane had things to do before meeting her old friends. One of them involved buying a new dress. And she'd have a bath and wash her hair. She made arrangements for the bath. The inn had a bathroom on each floor and would provide hot water and towels later. Then she went back out to spend some of her money on a dress.

3

The supper, Dublin

Charles Gavan Duffy lived in a fine, brick-built three storey house just off Merrion Square. The evening sun cast long shadows as Jane passed the handsome buildings of Trinity College. She crossed the Square and was soon at the Duffys' house. Steps led up to the wide front entrance and a fanlight above the door glowed with a warm light.

Tom Meagher opened the door and put his hand out to shake Jane's hand. 'Welcome home, Jane. I see you are all grown up, too!'

Thomas Francis Meagher was the son of the Lord Mayor of Waterford and a nationalist, a Young Irelander, as opposed to the Old Irelanders, who had followed the late Daniel O'Connell. He was also a terrible flirt. Both handsome and charming, his fair hair curled in thick sideburns along his jawline right down to his collar. Tom's brown eyes sparkled as he shook hands with Jane. He was fashionably dressed in a dark, fine wool suit, with a starched white shirt, and trousers that narrowed at the ankles and just reached the tops of his gleaming leather boots.

'I can't wait to hear how you got away from Australia. I wasn't expecting to see you again for seven years!'

Jane smiled. 'I didn't think I'd ever see Ireland again, to be truthful. But it's so good to be here in Dublin.'

Gavan Duffy came out to the hall and caught Jane's hand. 'You got here. I'm glad you came. And you look rested. Susan will be down in a few minutes, she's just settling the children.' He turned to his friend. 'Give me a minute, will you, Tom? I have something for Jane that she'll want to see right away.'

He took a letter out of his pocket. 'Forgive me, Jane, I absolutely forgot all about this. It's addressed to you. It arrived at the newspaper a couple of weeks ago and I was in two minds whether to open it. I only remembered it when I got back to the office this afternoon.'

She took the envelope from him, read the postmark and knew instantly who had written it. 'It's from Melbourne, New South Wales.' The letter must have travelled in a British army ship to arrive so quickly in Dublin.

'Listen, go into the parlour and take a few minutes to read it.' Gavan Duffy opened the door into a small sitting room overlooking the back garden. 'Join us when you're ready.'

* * *

Jane sat on a low settee and closed her eyes briefly. Owen. He had not forgotten her.

She opened it and read it, she could almost hear his soft Wicklow accent.

Melbourne 2nd July 1847
Dearest Jane, I'm writing to you in the hope this
letter will find you safe and well and back home in
Ireland.
There was a big hue and cry after you left. Colonel
Johns was outraged by the posters we put up. I think
a lot of people believe what you said about him
being a rapist. It'll be a while before that is
forgotten.
And I have good news to tell. I've just had word
that my unit is to be reassigned to Dublin. The
British Government is transferring troops to
Ireland, in advance of a winter rebellion, they say.
We leave Melbourne in two weeks' time and should be
in Dublin by the end of December.
It will do my heart good to see you again, dear
Jane. If you get this letter, leave word for me at
The Nation. I'll call in there when I get back.
Your affectionate friend,
Owen Doran

Jane read Owen's words over again, then kissed his handwriting. She'd see him in a few months.

They had first met on board the transportation ship to New South Wales, when she had been attacked during the night by one of the crew. Owen, an army sergeant accompanying the convicts on their journey, had been called to sort out the hullabaloo. They had remained friends in Melbourne and she had slowly come to love him.

She tucked the letter back into the envelope and her spirits lifted as she went through to the drawing room.

The sound of her footsteps became muffled when she moved from the dark wood flooring of the hall onto thick-piled, scarlet and cream carpet into a room filled with warm amber light. An elaborate chandelier hung in the centre of the ceiling and crystal lamps were set on gleaming, dark wood sideboards. Long, cream silk curtains were drawn across the windows to keep the heat in and the night out. The drawing room was furnished with two pale blue silk covered settees and matching chairs. They were grouped around a fire of logs and turf in a wide marble grate. The whole scene gave a picture of warmth and comfort.

A flame sparked in the grate and a sudden image of her cousin's burning cabin flashed through Jane's mind. She blinked, and the image vanished as suddenly as it had come. She cleared her throat. *Don't!* she commanded herself. She tensed the muscles in her neck and face, and forced a smile.

'This is lovely. Thank you for inviting me, Mr Duffy. You have a beautiful house.'

The last time Jane had been in a drawing room was in Melbourne when she had cleaned out the fireplace and polished the furniture, as the housemaid in the Colonel's house. Here she was now, a guest of the famed barrister and newspaper owner.

Susan, Gavan Duffy's wife, joined them. She was a young woman who appeared to be not much older than Jane. She had a lively face with thick glossy hair swept back from a high forehead. Her blue eyes seemed to sparkle in the lamplight of the room and she had the confident air of one who lived a comfortable life and managed her household and children in her beautiful Dublin home. Jane knew that disease hadn't reached the wealthier parts of Dublin, and hunger probably never would touch them.

After the introductions, Susan led her over to sit on one of the settees and sat next to her while Gavan Duffy poured wine into glasses.

'How on earth did you get away from New South Wales?' Susan asked.

'I had help to escape. One of those is a sergeant in the British army, Owen Doran. He's a Wicklow man and he wrote to tell me that he's coming back to Ireland soon.'

Jane smoothed the sleeves of her new brocade dress. It fitted perfectly around her shoulders and flared out from her narrow waist into a bell-shaped skirt, that stopped at her ankles and showed off slim leather shoes.

'That's great news, Jane.' Thomas had overheard and came over with a glass of sherry to perch on a dainty armchair. 'So tell me, now you're home, what are your plans? Are you staying in Dublin?'

Jane shook her head. 'No. I'm going back to Galway tomorrow.'

The lace edging around the neck of her new dress gleamed in the lamplit room. Her dark hair hung loose down her back and her shoulders and chest, usually covered, were exposed to the gaze of her companions. She adjusted the lace at the front of the dress. She had checked in the mirror before she left the hotel, and the neckline wasn't too low at all. Nevertheless, she was unused to being the centre of attention.

The door opened again and Speranza, Annie Power's friend and mentor, came in. She rushed straight over to Jane, knelt down and put her arm around her. Jane breathed in a light citrus scent from the young woman's dark hair.

'Jane, welcome home. Charles told me that you escaped from Melbourne. What a brave girl you are.' Speranza's lemon silk dress billowed out around her as she knelt on the carpet in front of Jane.

'I can't wait to hear how you did it. I never thought to see you again.' Her face darkened. 'But you brought news about Annie. Charles told me. I just cannot believe she is dead!' Speranza leaned on the edged of the settee and stood up to straighten her skirt. 'She was so young and strong. I know that you don't want to talk about this, Jane, but are you absolutely sure? There can be no mistake?'

'I was in Manhattan for the funeral, Miss Speranza. It was so sad. There were hundreds of people there, at Saint Patrick's Cathedral. The Bishop said the mass. Annie did such a lot to help young women immigrants.'

'Charles said she was caught in a fire, and that she had consumption?' Speranza's brow creased and she shook her head. 'How did that happen?'

'That's what I was told. She had a longstanding lung complaint, and the arson attack, at the refuge she had set up, was the end of her.'

'She was such a lovely poet. I was proud to get her poems published. And her brother and sister, how are they?'

'They are both heartbroken, but they have their aunt Bridie. She's very good to them, like a second mother. And Annie's brother, Finn, has started up a small business, so they'll not be short of money. But they were all in shock at the funeral. I left straight afterwards. Sure, there was no point in staying.'

'Here, come and sit with us,' Susan said to Speranza, and moved up to make space on the settee.

Susan laughed. 'I've just realised, you're both Janes! I shall call you by your pen-name, Speranza, so we don't get confused. I'll get the supper brought in soon and we can eat here informally.'

Later, a maid brought in a supper of cold meats, bread and cheese and fruit cake and laid it out on a small dining table beside the curtained window. They helped themselves to the food.

Gavan Duffy poured more wine and Jane told them about her escape from Melbourne. She made no mention of the stillbirth of her daughter. It felt like a part of her was in shadow, a hidden part that no-one saw. Then she thought of Owen. He, and only he, knew everything about her.

* * *

When the plates and dishes were cleared away, Charles lifted his glass, and the lamplight slanted through the ruby wine and the sharp-cut edges of the crystal.

'To Jane Keating. *Cead mile failte!* Welcome home!'

'Thank you. It's wonderful to be back in Ireland.' Jane took a sip of the strong wine and put her glass on the side table. Now it was time to find out about the situation she had come back to.

'May I ask what is happening now, with the potato blight? I had hoped that it was coming to an end. But I've not seen anything to give me cause to think it's over.'

Gavan Duffy nodded grimly. 'You are correct, Jane. The government has stopped the soup kitchens. The ones we saw earlier today? They're run by Quakers. The main soup kitchens finished at the end of August. Everyone has to go to the workhouse if they are destitute. And if they want to get in, they must give up their bit of land. It'll be a disaster by the end of the year. Sure, the workhouses are already full. And now we're hearing tales of evictions.'

'In his letter,' Jane said, 'Owen wrote that his regiment were being recalled back to Ireland. The government thinks there is going to be a rebellion here. Is that true?'

Gavan Duffy and Thomas Meagher shared a look. Tom spoke. 'Sure, it would be a miracle if starving labourers were able to fight a war when they're dying in their thousands from hunger and disease. And more so out in the south and west of the country.'

'Did you see the article from Lord Dufferin and Mr Boyle?' Susan asked. 'It was published in all the newspapers. They came over from Oxford University in the summer and went to Skibbereen. It was a hard thing to read.'

'Can I see it?' Jane asked.

'Yes, it was in The Nation, wasn't it, Charles, darling?'

'Yes, my love. We have a copy in the house, and I'll get it for Jane before she goes,' Gavan Duffy promised.

'So it's not over yet?'

The two men shook their heads.

'Tell me, what of the bigger farmers, and the gentry, with businesses and money?' Jane asked. She could see the people in this room weren't short of money.

Gavan Duffy took a cigar out of a box beside him, leaned over to the fire and lit a taper. He put the flame to his cigar and puffed until it glowed. 'I've heard that lots of the wealthier farmers are just up and leaving. They're taking their savings, their rent and the rates money and heading for America. There's free farmland to be had there. And no rent to pay. Why wouldn't you go?' Silence settled over the gathering. 'And others keep their heads down and wait for this to end.

'As for people like me, Jane.' He shook his head. 'Well now, we seem to spend all our time bickering about what's to be done. You have the Old Irelanders, and now our lot, they call the Young Irelanders. All at loggerheads. We'll never get a rebellion at this rate. And without a change of government, the poor will always be liable to starve. We do our best to help, we publish articles and give money to charity, but it makes very little difference.'

'We need a revolution,' Thomas Meagher added in a low voice. 'That's why we set up the Irish Confederation, to gain independence.'

Jane wanted to ask what the Irish Confederation was, but Gavan Duffy spoke first. 'Enough of politics and death and sorrow. Let's try to enjoy the rest of this evening. I want to welcome you home, Jane. Sure, you were so brave to escape! And on an American whaling ship. You're some woman! Everyone, let's raise our glasses to Jane Keating! Good health to you!'

'Good health, Jane!'

She lifted her glass and took another sip of the wine and smiled. They had invited her among them and made her welcome, and for a few moments, she was happy.

'Right so, who's for another glass?' Gavan Duffy asked. 'Susan, my love, will you play us a tune on the piano? And you, Thomas, you're to sing us a song. Then we'll see if we can persuade Jane to tell us more about life on a whaling ship.'

* * *

Later, Tom offered to escort Jane back to her hotel. Gavan Duffy returned the newspaper article about Annie's funeral and added the Nation's report on the situation in Skibbereen written by Lord Dufferin. She had both newspapers safely in

31

her bag and, after saying farewell to her hosts, Tom hailed a cab and they set off for the drive back to Fleet Street.

Night had drawn in and gas-lighters were busy lighting the street lamps around Merrion Square.

'They look new, since I was here last,' Jane commented.

'Yes, they were installed last winter. They got rid of the old whale oil street lamps. These are gas powered.'

'There's money for gas lamps, then? How can that be?' Jane asked and her voice sharpened.

Tom turned to her, his expression grim. 'I meant what I said earlier, Jane. We need a rebellion, or we'll be living like this for another generation, if not more. Daniel O'Connell, God rest his soul, said Ireland needed the English government to help them through this famine. And that if they don't get help, then a quarter of the population will die. He was right. I think O'Connell, the poor man, died of a broken heart. That won't happen to me. I'll fight for a free Ireland.'

In the confined space of the cab, Jane looked at her companion's face. This time, Tom looked serious and determined.

'I'll join you in the fight, Tom. I'll do whatever I can.'

* * *

Earlier that day, when Jane had paid for a night's lodgings, she enquired about booking a ticket on the post carriage to Galway the next morning. She was advised to catch the steam train on the newly opened line from Dublin to Enfield. This would shorten her journey by several hours. A messenger boy had been dispatched to buy the tickets. Jane only had to get up early the next morning.

Before she went to sleep, she re-read the letter from Owen.

His homecoming was something to look forward to. And what could she do to help in a rebellion? More to the point, where were the rebels?

The only working people, apart from the stevedores at the docks, she had seen since coming home were either starving and dying, or on their way out of the country. Middle class, educated men, like Charles Gavan Duffy and Thomas Francis Meagher had no experience of fighting. Jane had seen the British army, and the power it held in Melbourne. Her Irish friends were no match for them, of that she was sure.

Speranza, bless her, had highlighted the conditions of the poor in her poems and articles. Susan was a home-maker and a mother. There seemed to be no raging will to fight, to risk everything, to throw out the British government.

Jane thought that neither Mr Duffy nor Tom Meagher would cause much of a problem for the British government in Ireland. Maybe Owen could help. She drifted off to sleep and dreamed of her friend. Maybe. He'd have to give up his British uniform first, though.

4

Late September 1847, Galway

J ane left the hotel early the next morning and loaded her
bag onto a waiting cab for the ten minute trot along the
Quays towards King's Bridge and the newly built railway
station of the same name. It looked like a palace, with long
windows, nine of them across the second storey, with carved
stone swags and curlicues below the top floor eaves.

They have money to build all this, and put up new gas lamps,
while people starve. She wondered how that could be, but
in her heart she knew the value put on her countrymen and
women by their government.

She walked through to the platform and the waiting train.
The narrow chimney on the engine billowed dark smoke and
a short, sweating man stoked the furnace for the twenty-five
mile journey. She had seen trains in Melbourne and New York
but had never set foot on one. The gleaming black engine
had two carriages attached. The one nearest the engine, First
Class, was covered and looked very much like the horse-drawn
carriages that were common on Irish roads. Jane stepped up
into it and sat on an upholstered seat. The second carriage

was open to the elements and the passengers were huddled down on wooden benches to avoid the fine rain that drizzled onto them from a sullen sky.

The train was due to leave at eight o'clock and shortly after she had boarded, the station master raised his flag to indicate all clear to the train driver. Two long whistles sounded from the engine and the train slowly pulled out of the station. She watched as the city was left behind and they moved into open countryside. The engine began to puff and the train whistle squealed again as they built up speed.

Sitting beside the window, the whole carriage moved and swayed as the engine accelerated. Soon, the hills and fields outside began to blur into a pale cloud, now green, then purple, as they reached higher ground. The man sitting opposite Jane warned her that they would soon be travelling at a speed of forty miles an hour. Jane was unsure how he might know this fact, but held on tight to the arm-rest of her seat. She was terrified and excited at the thought of what it would be like to travel all the way to the west coast at this speed. It might take only a few hours to cover the whole journey. She felt nauseated, with the constant motion of the carriage swaying side to side and the forward, thundering race across the miles, almost as if sea-sick.

After a short while, she relaxed her grip on the seat and looked around at her fellow passengers. Some of them sat reading newspapers, oblivious to the speed and motion of the train. With a sudden squeal of brakes, the train began to reduce speed and now she could make out the fields; some with sheep and others with cattle grazing. Then empty fields which must have grown crops of wheat or barley that were already gathered in. She saw no potato crops anywhere on her journey.

Screeching iron on iron sounded as the brakes were applied with more force and the engine and carriages shuddered to a stop. They had arrived at Enfield in County Meath. Jane's legs felt unsteady as she stepped down from the train onto the gravelly path beside the railway line. The line ended at this point. Up ahead she saw gangs of labourers digging furiously. She assumed they were working to lay the next section of the line.

A stagecoach waited beside the station house. After a stop to use the privy, the passengers climbed on board the coach. Jane had paid for an inside seat and squeezed in between two large men. As soon as the coach driver finished securing the luggage, he checked the doors were secured, then climbed up onto the driver's seat and they went on their way to Athlone. They halted there to change the horses and eat a quick dinner at the post inn, then set off again. The coach crossed the bridge over river Shannon. Once they reached Ballinasloe, Jane relaxed, for they were in County Galway and almost home. The coach trundled past the new workhouse and the police station. She had seen the two things; workhouses and police stations in all the towns she passed through. The bigger towns, like Athlone, all had army barracks, too.

The further west she travelled, they passed more and more groups of people on the roads. All seemed to be heading east to Dublin or further afield.

She looked forward to finding her cousin Brendan's wife, Aoife, and her two small cousins, Jamie and Sorcha. Then she could really begin to feel at home, surrounded by family. She decided that she would confide in Aoife about Margaret, her lost baby. She had to find someone to talk to about her loss.

They arrived in Galway late that night. Jane hadn't spoken to a soul all day apart from the man on the train that morning. And she was hungry after eating nothing since her dinner in Athlone.

The moonless sky was black with a sprinkling of shimmering stars when she finally stepped off the coach in her home town. It was too dark to see anything so she followed the rest of the travellers into the dim hallway of the Coach Inn. The proprietor locked the front door as soon as the guests arrived, and checked them in. Jane was stiff and tired, but felt blessed to hear Irish spoken. She knew then that she was home.

She hauled her bag up two flights of stairs to the women's attic bedroom and found that she'd have to share the only bed with two other women. The mother and daughter told her they were catching the early coach to Dublin the next morning. She spent the night tossing and turning in the bed, was sure there were lice in the straw mattress and tried not to roll over into the back of the older woman in the middle of the bed. Jane lay perched on the edge of the mattress and faced out into the room, for it seemed to her that the old girl was quite happy to lie with arms and legs splayed, while snoring and farting her way through the night hours.

* * *

By morning, the chamber pot was close to overflowing and the bedroom stank of must, mould and piss. There was nowhere to wash, so Jane, who had slept in her clothes, put her boots on and laced them up. She collected her bag and went downstairs to use the filthy privy at the back of the inn. After she had paid her bill, she nodded her farewell to the mother and daughter, who both gawked at her from the dining room while they ate their breakfast. Jane shuddered at the scraps of half-cooked food on their plates. If the kitchen was anything like the bedroom, then she'd eat elsewhere, thank you very much. She reminded herself to look for another inn to sleep in that night, then went out to revisit her home town.

Most shops were closed. It was still early, but she expected to see some business being transacted. She passed the baker's shop that she remembered always had a line of women outside, gossiping and waiting for the just-baked loaves and pies. This morning, the shutters were pulled across the window; she peeped through the glass in the top part of the door and saw only empty shelves behind the bare counter. The interior of the shop was hazy, as if white flour stood in the air, but there was no movement, just the fleeting glimpse of a tiny grey mouse that scurried across the floorboards.

In the eighteen months since she had left Galway, the town seemed to have shrunk in on itself. The quayside was almost empty of cargo ships that usually docked to collect bacon and wheat for the English market. Instead of business being transacted, she passed throngs of people, milling around the streets. To Jane, they all looked homeless and starving. A bit like herself, at that very moment. In truth, she reminded herself, she was hungry, not starving, and had the one thing they all lacked. Money. In her purse and in the bank.

From the look of them, these Galway folk had few possessions; she guessed most of their belongings might have been sold or pawned. Also, unlike Jane, who had eaten a dinner in Athlone the day before, most of these poor, ragged *crathurs* had a haggard and grey-faced look about them. She was sure that if she asked any of them, they'd tell her they hadn't had a decent meal for quite some time.

She decided to do just that, and stopped by a couple of girls her own age, with dirty hands and faces, not to mention their bare, muddy feet and a chilled look about them from the thin rags they wore. They were sitting together in a shop doorway, and both glanced up at Jane.

'*Dia dhuit*, God be with you,' she greeted them. Neither spoke. They glanced at each other.

Jane tried again, still speaking in Irish. '*Cad es ainm duit?* What are your names? I'm Jane Keating. Do you live here in Galway?'

The dark-haired girl shook her head. 'No, we've come across from Inishmore. We thought there'd be something here.'

'Have you tried the workhouse?'

'Yes,' the other girl replied. She was the smaller of the two, but they looked like sisters, both had large teeth and wide mouths in long faces, thin grey skin stretched over hollowed out cheeks and sharp bones. Everything about them was dirty, their tangled hair, their skin, and the rags they wore. Yet Jane saw something of herself in them. A light in their eyes that showed they were determined to survive this, to live to the end of it, whenever that was. Unfortunately, they had reached the mainland, only to find it was as bad here as on the island.

'Do you want to get something to eat with me?' Jane asked them. She had her tasks to complete, to find her cousin's wife and children, and to get a headstone on her father's grave. But the tasks would keep for an hour until she, and they, had eaten.

Both girls nodded, and their sudden smiles transformed their dirty faces.

'Come on then, we'll look for a baker's shop. And tell me your names. I'm Jane.'

'I'm Ellen Foley and she's Nancy. We're sisters. And there's a bakery just along the street,' the smaller girl said.

They soon reached the shop, which was open, and sat on a bench underneath an awning outside the bakery to eat and drink in the cool, bright air. The round cobs were still warm from the oven, crusty on the outside and soft inside, with golden butter melting into the bread.

A small woman, on her way past, stopped and stood in front of the three of them. The woman had a threadbare shawl covering her head and shoulders and stood silently with her hand held out. Jane swallowed the bread she had just been chewing and looked at the woman who just stood and stared at the crusty bread in Jane's hand. Jane, no longer hungry, slowly reached out and put the rest of the bread into the woman's hand. She opened her purse and took out a coin. 'Here, get some more bread in the shop,' she said. The woman still didn't speak; she went into the shop, came out a few minutes later with a bag of bread and went on her way.

Jane waited while the two sisters finished their food. They ate and drank at speed. When they had both finished eating, they sat back and Ellen wiped her mouth with the back of her filthy hand.

'Thanks be to God and his blessed Mother!' Ellen sighed. 'Thank you. You're a good Samaritan.'

The sisters hugged each other and Jane saw that both had tears in their eyes.

* * *

It was still early morning, with only the groups of homeless people on the move through the drizzling autumn rain. To

Jane, most of them looked as if they were just one or two steps away from falling down dead to the ground out of sheer exhaustion. When an old ass or donkey was on his last legs, the farmer would put it out to grass. Here, these poor souls just had to go on and on. Had they all been evicted? All of them? There seemed to be dozens on the move, and it was still early.

Mr Duffy had told her that the government soup kitchens were coming to an end, and the Quakers in Dublin, God bless them, had told Jane their organisation had run out of money to keep their voluntary soup kitchens going. Their donors, too, had run out of compassion and funds, it seemed.

'When did you get here?' she asked the girls.

'A few days ago,' Nancy said.

'And you slept?'

'In that doorway, where you found us.'

'So, now the workhouse is full, where'll you go?'

'Sure, we don't want to go into the workhouse. We were looking for work there, so we can send money back to our mam and dad and brothers,' Ellen, the younger girl said.

Jane looked at the two of them. Who would employ them? 'What work can you do?'

'We can gather seaweed, and shear sheep and spin wool,' Nancy told her.

'I can knit, too,' Ellen added. 'And we can both fish, but Daddy had to pawn the nets last winter.'

Jane smiled wryly. There'd be work for them shearing sheep, fourteen thousand miles away, outside Melbourne in New South Wales. Much good that would do them here.

She found herself in a quandary. She had taken it on herself to speak to the two sisters. She'd bought them some food and now she needed to get on and go to the workhouse to look for Aoife and the children. Yet she had made a connection with these two girls, as if a gossamer thread had passed from their souls to hers. She tried to pull away and break the thread and get on with her tasks, but felt the tug at her heart, and sighed.

'Well, even if there are any jobs, you'll not get taken on looking like that. You'd better come with me. I'll see if I can help you, somehow.'

The sisters smiled at each other, then stood together and waited for Jane to decide where they were going.

* * *

Jane led the way back to the inn she had just left, then remembered that she had vowed not to spend another night there, and walked further along the street to the next hotel.

'Wait here,' she said to the girls, and stepped inside to take a look at the place. The reception area had been swept and the floorboards gleamed dully in the light from the open window near the desk.

The woman at the reception desk was clean and tidy in her person, which boded well for the rooms. The woman greeted Jane. *'Dia dhuit.'*

'Dia is Muire dhuit,' Jane returned the greeting. 'I want a room for me and two friends, for tonight, to start with. Would you have a room we don't have to share with anyone else?'

The woman smiled and glanced at Jane's bag. 'You wouldn't have come from the Coach Inn, by any chance?'

Jane returned the smile. 'Yes, I had to sleep in a bed with two other women. The coach got in late, and it was either that or sleep outside. I've not even washed my face today!'

'Well, you've come to the right place. We have plenty of rooms.'

'My friends are sisters. They came over from Inishmore and have fallen on hard times. I'm going to give them some money to buy clean clothes. Will you be able to send up soap and hot water and towels for them to wash themselves and their hair?'

'There's a bathroom on the first floor. I can send up hot water in an hour or so.'

'I don't know if they . . .' Jane was sure they had never used a bathroom.

The woman smiled again. 'I'll show them, don't worry.'

'That's very kind of you,' Jane said.

'I'll put the cost on the bill. You can pay in advance?'

'Yes, of course, *go raibh maith agat,*' she thanked the woman. 'And I'll pay you for a dinner for them, too. My name is Jane Keating, and my friends are Nancy and Ellen Foley.'

Jane put her bag down, paid for the room and board, and went to the door to call in the girls. To the woman's credit she did not pull a face when she saw the state of the two barefoot and ragged girls.

The three of them followed the woman up a flight of stairs. She pointed out the bathroom and unlocked the door to their room, which was clean and had two beds as promised, and handed Jane two keys.

After the woman had gone, Jane sat on one of the beds. 'You two can share that one by the wall. I'll be gone for most of the day, but I've paid for a dinner for you.' She pulled her satchel out from under her cloak and took out some coins and handed over five shillings to the older girl, Nancy. 'Here, buy yourselves some clean clothes and shoes, and have a wash and sort your hair out. And you need to decide if you're going back to the island or what you'll do. Make your minds up. I'll see you later.'

She left them in the room, and started out for the workhouse. She made a promise to herself not to stop and speak to any more waifs, or she'd have a line of them tagging along behind her, like a row of orphaned chicks. Somehow, Ellen and Nancy had touched her heart. They reminded her of herself and Annie Power, when they had both lost everything.

* * *

It had started to drizzle fine rain again, so she pulled the hood of her cloak up around her head and kept walking in the direction of the workhouse. There was something about a Galway cloak that Jane had missed when she was a convict in New South Wales. The drape of the hood, wide and deep, around your face, like an embrace, kept the wind and rain out, and the warmth in. The fullness of the body of the cloak covered her skirt to below her knees. She held her satchel underneath the cloak with one hand and pulled the edges of the cloak together with the other hand as she moved along the footpath. She stepped lightly around wet and ragged country folk. Desperate people.

'Don't look, and don't stop,' she bade herself.

On the way, Jane passed a stonemason's sign outside a yard full of grave monuments. She reminded herself to call in and speak to the owner after she had found Aoife and the children, then she hesitated. The mason was right there, working on a piece of granite in the open workshop. It would only take a few minutes to find out about a headstone. She'd do it now. She stepped into the yard and greeted him. The stonemason put down his hammer and chisel and pulled a scarf away from his nose and mouth. He came over to speak to her.

'Can I help you, Miss?' he asked. He was a young man, strongly built with wide shoulders and a friendly face. Jane was unsure what colour his hair was as it was coated with fine white dust from working the stone.

'Is this your business?' she asked.

'Yes, that's my name on the sign there. John O'Malley. Would you be looking for a headstone, or a monument?'

'I want a headstone for my father's grave out at Saint Vincent's chapel on the Salthill Road. Do you know where it is?'

'I do indeed. Come and take a look at the monuments I have.' The stonemason pointed to the piece he was working on.

'This cross is in granite. You can have the plain cross or the Celtic version, whichever you prefer. Or I have some in marble, but they are more expensive. Like that one.' He pointed to a white headstone with a mournful angel leaning on the side of the stone.

'A granite cross will be lovely. I want to put the names of my family on it.'

'That's no problem. I can add a brass plaque with their names, right on the centre there. Look, that one has a plaque already, and it's for sale.'

Jane looked at the tall cross he pointed to. It was made of granite, with grey, white and black speckles. It stood about six feet tall. 'I like it. How much will it cost?'

'Come inside and we'll talk about the money,' he said.

Jane smiled. He saw a sale. She saw a bargain.

'You must be busy these days,' she commented, as they walked into the shed. In the corner there was a table made of

45

wooden planks. A pen and inkwell sat on it, covered in a layer of the same pale dust that coated the stonemason's hair.

He swept the wooden work table clear of dust and grit and pulled a sheet of paper out of a drawer. 'You would think that I'd be busy, but it's not the case at all.'

He glanced at her as if expecting her to ask. She had a good idea why that was, but asked the question anyway. 'And why is that?'

'Because if you die in the workhouse, they bury you there. No headstone is needed.'

Jane nodded. 'My mother and brothers died in there last year. I want their names on the headstone. But, tell me, surely not everyone dies in the workhouse?'

'That's true. But there's no money anywhere. They all go into paupers' graves. Sure, if you're from around here, and by your accent you are, then you know that.' He looked at Jane, as if puzzled.

'I've been away for a while. I've just got home.'

'Ah, right so. Let's agree on a price for this cross. You'll have change out of ten pounds for the cross, the plaque, and the installation. What do you say to that?'

Talking about her mother and her brothers, hearing her own voice state the facts of their deaths had brought to mind the last time she had seen her mother alive. She remembered her father's promise. 'I'll find work, *a stor,* my darling. Hold on for a few weeks and I'll come and bring you and the boys home.' Her father's promise went unfulfilled. He had died around the same time as her mother and brothers, leaving Jane alone in the world.

'Miss, are you alright, there?' The stonemason touched her arm.

Jane started, a tear trickled down her cheek. She shook her head. 'I'm sorry. I got to thinking.'

'Tell me the names for the plaque, and I'll make up the bill. Then it'll be done. I'll take care of the rest for you.'

She appreciated his kindness. 'Thank you, how long will it take?'

'The cross is out there and ready. I can have the name plate on and the cross installed in two days.'

She took a deep breath. 'The first name is my father, Dara Keating, then my mother, Margaret Keating, and my brothers, Joseph and Seamus. They all died in March, 1846.' She paused while he wrote down the names and dates. 'Then baby Margaret Keating, she was born and died on the 16th April, this year, 1847.' She saw his flicker of a glance, then he continued to write. 'And my cousin, Brendan Keating, who died in January, 1846. I want you to carve on the stone, that they will never be forgotten.'

Jane didn't think she had more tears left in her, but they came nevertheless. The stonemason left her to cry while he totted up the bill which came to eight pounds, ten shillings and sixpence. He must have felt sorry for her and given her a bargain, so she didn't haggle.

She was pleased to have the job done and handed over the money in return for a receipt. The stonemason promised to call in to see Father Hanrahan at Saint Vincent's church to get directions to Jane's father's grave.

* * *

She walked on up the town towards the workhouse and passed a small boy selling newspapers and paid him for one of the broadsheets. She was about to continue on her way when she spotted a man in police uniform coming around the corner towards her. She had to look again to be sure, but she'd know him anywhere; she'd seen him enough times in her nightmares.

The same heavy build, the same age as her cousin, Brendan, had been, so he must be well into his thirties. The policeman's low brow and squinting eyes were unchanged. He took no notice of her and continued walking until she stepped up to him, then he had to stop.

'I know you, Niall Smullen,' she said in a voice that was more of a hiss than a whisper.

The man looked sideways at Jane. He seemed to search his memory for who she was, then shook his head.

'I think you must have mistaken me for someone else. I don't know you, Miss.'

'Oh, but you do. Nearly two years ago, at my cousin's cabin on the road to Salthill. You murdered him.'

He blinked, lifted his chin then stepped back from her. 'Keating. You're one of those Keatings. We evicted the family. I don't recall his name.'

'Brendan! His name was Brendan Keating! Don't pretend you've forgotten.' She shook her tears away, angry at showing weakness to this murderer.

Out of the corner of her eye, she saw the newspaper boy scuttle off along the road.

'Yes, Brendan Keating.' Smullen nodded, he seemed to be thinking back to that winter's day. 'But you're wrong. I didn't murder him.'

'You're a liar. I was there, right in front of you.' Jane's body trembled from the top of her head to the bottom of her feet. She could barely speak the words. 'He was trying to save his home, that's all.'

The constable put his hand out as if to calm her, but didn't touch her. His forehead shone with sweat. 'I say again. You're wrong. It was the bailiff. My gun went off, but I shot into the air. The bailiff killed Brendan Keating.' He stammered over the last sentence.

Jane couldn't breathe, felt herself about to fall to the ground, like the last time, but she leaned against the wall. She was trapped again in the nightmare and relived the shot, and the fall. Her cousin had fallen back on top of her and they were both covered in his blood. By the time Jane's father had helped her up, the bailiff, and this man right in front of her, the constable, had turned away to set fire to Brendan's cabin.

'You're a liar! Get away from me!' Jane shouted again.

Smullen shook his head. 'I'm no murderer.' Then he turned and walked off down the road. Jane watched him go and tried to steady her breathing.

She pictured the two men on horseback, and the guns. It was freezing that morning in January 1846, snow all around. Their landlord had sent the bailiff and the constable to evict the family into the winter snow. Jane and her father would not be able to bring Brendan's family home with them to their cabin. *Dare you give shelter to anyone evicted, you'd be for the road, too.*

She couldn't remember if she had heard one shot or two shots. She was sure of one thing. *Smullen is a rotten liar.*

5

The Union Workhouse, Galway

I t was getting on for afternoon and the sky had closed in over the town, like a grey cap that darkened the day. Jane breathed in the sodden air as she hurried along the road towards the Union Workhouse on the edge of the town. She hated the place. It held only heartbreaking memories for her, of her mother and brothers and the terrible way they had died.

After a while, her feet dragged, and she slowed. Each step on the way brought her closer to the answer to her journey. She had hardly slept after the long trek from Dublin the previous day and, this morning, her unexpected meeting with Niall Smullen had dislocated her thoughts. His denial went round in her head. She was so sure of what she had seen back then, had dreamed of that moment, over and over. The pistol shot and Brendan's body, his blood, warm on her face, and in her eyes and mouth. Smullen had knocked a crack in her memory with just a few words. No! He was a liar and a murderer. Her heart pounded in her chest and her head ached.

By then she had arrived at the workhouse. She'd been here before with her father, when her mother and brothers had fled to find safety. It was either that or they'd all starve. Jane had then stayed at the cabin with her father, Dara, trying to find work, to earn some money to get them through that hard winter and praying not to be discovered by the authorities. It was only permissible to go into the workhouse if you had first given up any land you had.

She recalled her final visit here, only to find her mother and brothers dead from fever. Brendan's wife, Aoife, had been there at the time with the children, but she hadn't seen them. Now Jane had money and could help the last members of her family.

The workhouse was set well back from the road on a large parcel of land. She passed a few people sitting beside the gates, and walked towards the main building. What were they waiting for? She looked back at them. An older man didn't seem to have the energy left to even sit up. He just lay on the wet ground, his jacket was open and showed a ragged vest, and the lower half of his legs were bare from the knees down. He must have been freezing, but he seemed to be asleep for all that.

The double front doors were shut. Jane looked up at the top floor where long narrow windows with small glass panes glittered in the autumn sunshine. There was no sound from within. She lifted the iron knocker. banged it down and waited while the sound echoed inside.

After almost two long years, she was only moments away from finding Aoife, and her little ones, Sorcha and Jamie. She willed them to be on the other side of the door. Picturing their smiling faces, she could almost hear Aoife's soft voice.

* * *

A low-sized, stocky man in uniform opened the door. He had thin hair, balding on top, and his beard had the yellowish tinge from smoking a pipe. Even his eyebrows were a mix of grey and tan.

'I'm here to look for my cousin's wife and children. They came in last year. Can you help me?'

'Well, you'd have some chance if you could tell me their names, young lady,' the man replied.

Jane closed her eyes briefly and pressed her lips together. Have patience, she urged herself.

'My cousin's wife is Aoife Keating and her children are Sorcha and Jamie. Sorcha would be four now, and Jamie is six, I'd say. They came here in January of last year, 1846.'

'I'm well aware of the year, thank you. I'm the Master here,' the man interrupted her.

'Do you know them. Are they here?'

The man opened the door wider. 'And who might you be?'

'My name is Jane Keating. Aiofe was married to my cousin, Brendan. They lived on the Salthill Road until they were evicted and Brendan was . . . he died.'

'You had better come in, then. I know the name. Come in and I'll tell you.'

Jane rested her hand on the lintel of the doorway. 'What do you mean? Are they here or not?'

'I'll not discuss this on the doorstep. Come in, if you're coming.' He made as if to close the door in her face, and she put her hand out to stop him.

'Wait, I'll come in.'

After he had closed and locked the front door, she followed him along the empty hall to an office with just one window that overlooked the back garden. A high stone wall surrounded the perimeter of the garden, and herringbone paths criss-crossed the enclosed space. There was no-one out there. Where was everyone?

'Here, sit down.' The Master pointed to a chair beside his desk. His tone had changed, he almost looked sorry for her. She tried and failed to shrug off a sense of dread. What was he going to say?

He turned to the bookshelf at the side of the desk and took down a large, blue, cloth-bound book. He opened it and started to leaf through the yellow, lined pages. From where she sat, Jane could see each page was filled with ruled columns of lists. There appeared to be names and dates. She leaned towards the table but couldn't read any of the details, for the script was tiny.

She waited as the Master ran his finger down the first column, then watched as he turned to the next page and did the same. She breathed in tobacco tainted air while he searched the book. Her neck ached from stretching to see. What could the lists be for? Only of the people, the paupers in the Workhouse, surely?

'She's here somewhere,' he said, without taking his eyes off the page.

Jane wanted to grab the book and look for herself. She smoothed her skirt, pushed her hair back from her face and fidgeted with her cloak, all in a vain attempt to try and stay calm. She shook her head to get rid of the image of Niall Smullen's pale, square face in her mind. *The liar.*

Although the sun shone outside and the rain had cleared, it was chilly in the room and the fireplace was empty. It had the look of a place unlived in. The only sound was that of the rustle of the pages as the Master turned over the next page, then the next, in his search for a name. She blew out slowly. Would this ever end? What is he looking for?

Finally, his finger stopped, halfway down a page. 'Ah, there she is.' Then he scanned further down, paused, and looked across the table at Jane. He nodded.

'I have Aoife Keating's name here in the book. She presented in January of 1846, as you say. Unfortunately, she succumbed to the fever, in the Infirmary, in April, of this year.'

Jane let out a sigh. 'No!'

He continued. 'Her name is right here. Aoife Keating, aged twenty-nine, died on the sixth of April, 1847, of typhus fever. But there's no mention of the son or daughter. They're still here, then.' He swung the book around on the table. 'Take a look for yourself.'

The dread that had settled on Jane's head, now turned into an ache behind her eyes. She wiped her nose and brushed away tears, then read the name. 'Ah, Aoife.' She reached out and touched the name on the page, ran her fingers over the date of death. 'How did she get the fever?'

'We're overcrowded and short of money. We've rarely been clear of fever. Sure, half of the workhouse has been turned into an infirmary.'

'Where is she buried?'

'There's a grave site, out the back there.' He turned and pointed through the window. 'Just beyond that wall.'

'A cemetery?'

'Yes.'

In her heart, she knew. The stonemason had been correct, the dead were thrown into a mass grave. Her own mother and brothers had died in this place. Their precious bodies were there, too.

'What about Jamie and Sorcha, her son and daughter?'

'They're here. Do you want to come and meet them?'

Jane was stunned into silence. What did it mean? Her cousins lived. She shivered. They were orphans in this place.

He closed the book and replaced it on the shelf, then stood and waited for Jane's reply.

'Yes, I do.' She had to force the words out. 'Are you sure they're here?'

'I don't have much to do with the children. They're kept together on the children's wards. Let's go and find them.'

Jane stood up and adjusted her cloak and bag. She was about to meet her lost cousins, Brendan and Aoife's children. She hadn't dreamed this might be the outcome. She always saw Aiofe and her little ones together. It was all wrong, and somehow it changed everything.

* * *

Their footsteps echoed along the wooden floorboards. They passed the women's ward and Jane caught a glimpse of girls and women all in the drab workhouse uniform, all with their heads down. No-one spoke. At that moment, Jane saw the reason for the silence in the building. The women, young and old, sat around long tables, working at what looked like lumps of knotted rope.

'What are they doing?' she asked the Master.

'Working hemp. Earning their keep.'

'Did Aoife do this work?'

'She would have done, yes. The children would have been in school or on the babies' ward.'

'Are they not allowed to speak?'

'They're not here to gossip. Plenty of time for that later,' the Master replied.

'And the men. Where are they?'

'Out. Breaking stones in the quarry.'

* * *

The babies' ward, on the first floor, was full. There must have been more than twenty young children and babies, none above the age of three or four. They all wore the same clothes, both boys and girls. One child, a small boy, Jane guessed from his shaven head, sat on his own in a corner. He wore a woollen dress to just below the knee with knee-socks and soft shoes. All looked to be fairly clean. Those who could not yet walk, sat or lay in cots, two or three together. The older children sat on the bare floor. A few looked up as the two visitors came in. The little fair-haired boy in the corner, looked at Jane out of wide blue eyes, then stuck his thumb in his mouth and sucked it. No-one took any notice of him.

Two women, matrons, Jane guessed, sat in armchairs by the fireplace. Each had a baby in their arms.

'Mrs Bourke,' the Master said. 'I have a visitor for you. This is Jane Keating, she's looking for her cousins, Jamie and Sorcha Keating. Are they here with you?'

The woman stood, still holding the baby, and smiled at Jane. 'Little Sorcha is here. She's in her cot, having a nap. Sure, she woke with the crack of dawn, and now she needs a rest. Come and see her.'

And there she was, the beautiful daughter of Brendan and Aoife Keating, one of Jane's only remaining family, lay asleep on a striped mattress. Sorcha clutched a small blanket in her hand, and her soft cheek rested on the blanket.

Jane watched the child sleeping. Yes, this was Brendan's daughter. Her father's black curls framed her face and Jane caught her breath. 'Ah!' She closed her eyes against the flash of crimson, then she looked again. The child's skin was fair and unstained by Brendan's spilt blood.

Sorcha was a Keating, alright. Just like Margaret, her own lost baby. Jane shook her head to clear the image of her still-born child's face. She took another breath and looked at the matron. 'I'm sorry.' She couldn't speak, or explain the nightmares she still endured.

Jane pressed her lips together and felt them tremble. 'And Jamie?'

'He's in the schoolroom, with the other children. I'll take you to him in a minute.'

Jane was entranced looking at Sorcha. 'Thank you, and thank you for saving them,' she whispered to the matron.

'She's not been well lately, but I'll wake her now and you can play with her, while I get her things together. There's just the few bits belonging to her poor mother.'

'No, please don't wake her. Let her sleep.'

'What do you mean? Did you not come here to fetch them? Will you not be bringing them home with you?' Mrs Bourke's tone sharpened. She glanced at her companion and the Master, who both turned to look at Jane.

'With me?' Jane asked, as if she did not understand the language used, although she spoke Irish as well as anyone in the room. 'Where to?'

'Sure, you'll be wanting to take them home with yourself.' The matron repeated the words slowly.

'I can't. I can't take them. I don't have a home,' Jane replied and shook her head. 'I've just got back to Ireland. I have nowhere to take them. I thought their mother, Aiofe, would be here. I wanted to help her.'

She couldn't say that she was suddenly afraid of this four-year old child and her brother, wherever he was, and the bloody nightmares they might bring with them, for they had witnessed their father's murder, too.

The matron narrowed her eyes, then looked from Jane to the Master. 'Why did you bring her here? Just to look?' The matron turned away from Jane and went and sat down by the fire without another word to either of them.

* * *

Outside on the roadway, Jane slumped against the low stone wall. There was a crowd of paupers gathering, as the damp day wound to its close. Maybe they were hoping to get in out of the weather and get a bite to eat. They would have another hard night if the workhouse couldn't find room for them. The poor man she had seen earlier was still on the ground. No-one went near him, there was nothing any of them could do.

She had left her little cousins with strangers. Was it that she was afraid they would replace her own dead child? No, that wasn't it. Her head ached from trying to make sense of it. One thing was sure, as soon as she saw Sorcha, her cousin's bloody face had flashed before her eyes. Was she afraid that she would see Brendan every time she looked at his children?

'I don't know,' Jane muttered. 'Maybe they're better off in the workhouse. Not with someone who is haunted and homeless.'

You're not destitute though. You can save them! The words echoed in her head.

'No. I can't do it!' She half-walked, half-ran along the familiar road past the edge of the town out towards the plot of land where their old cabin had stood.

The day changed as she walked, and by the time she arrived, the sun had dropped below the horizon. The sky had turned a deep mauve and was streaked with swathes of gold and russet light that flared through the dark green leaves of the trees on the edge of the road. Her ghosts were at her shoulder, and there before her, in the ruins of her family home.

6

Saint Vincent's Chapel, outside Galway

The tree was the only feature she could identify; an old hazel tree just along from the ruins of her family's cabin.

She walked on, then turned into the lane where her cousin had lived. The hedgerow that delineated his field was still there. Thorny and stunted, the hedge was a darker green than the grass that covered the field; a sprinkling of tiny white blossoms peeked through the thorns. At the top corner of the field she knelt and touched the ground where Brendan's body lay secretly buried. The grass was cool to the touch and damp from the rain that morning.

She felt her cousin's spirit around her and recalled the January day, almost two years ago, when this very ground had been covered in a foot of snow. She and her father and their two neighbours had dug through the soft snow to make a grave for Brendan's poor, murdered body.

'Rest in peace, cousin,' she whispered. 'Sorcha and Jamie are alive. They'll look after them in the workhouse. I'm truly sorry, but I can't do it.'

She had been kneeling too long and her skirt was wet at the knees. 'I'll keep a look out for Sorcha and Jamie, Brendan. I promise. And I'll make Niall Sullivan pay for what he did to you. He's a liar and a murderer. Fahy was there, too. I'll find him. He knows, and he'll tell me I'm right. '

Jane stood and looked around her at the empty fields, and the sheep, the only living creatures she could see. This was the place she had once called her home. She must have walked about five or six miles that day, but the long walk with her ghosts had somehow helped her to focus. Her goal had been to get home, and she had achieved that. But home was different. Everything had changed, including her.

Now she had money, and she'd find Fahy. Together they would get justice for Brendan. The questions in the back of her mind nagged at her. *And justice for Brendan's son and daughter? What will you do about them, Jane Keating?*

* * *

Saint Vincent's chapel was just a quarter of a mile further on. All the land around had been cleared. Here and there, there were piles of jumbled sticks and stones, where cabins had been knocked down. Where had everyone gone? She recalled the queues of people waiting to board the emigrant ship just the other day in Dublin. The graves of her father and cousin, and the mass grave outside the workhouse, and in it, her own mother and brothers. And Sorcha and Jamie in the Workhouse. *What have I come back to?*

She reached the top of the hill, saw the chapel and the cemetery ahead, and turned along the lane to the cemetery gate.

Apart from a few elder trees, heavy with their hanks of tiny black berries among the glossy dark leaves, the only structure still standing was an ancient ruins of a small, stone chapel.

The old chapel had been replaced, years ago, with the larger Saint Vincent's church built nearby. The ruins were covered in ivy, with tendrils running through the narrow arched window spaces. Whatever the roof had once been made of was long gone, had fallen into the aisle of the chapel and was now overgrown and unrecognisable, just a shadow of a holy place guarding the souls of the dead.

She shivered as a breeze built and rustled through the hazel trees, and whispered along the lengths of ivy on the chapel walls, like some long dead souls, woken by the breeze. The bell in Saint Vincent's church behind her, tolled the Angelus. It was getting on for dusk, the sky had faded into pale grey, with just a cold sliver of the moon high above her head. She walked straight to her father's grave, beneath the elm tree in the corner of the cemetery. 'I've come home, Daddy.' She stood in silence for a few minutes, unable to pray, then she stretched and looked out across the valley to the bay below, where a few fishermen hauled in their nets. The silvery sheen on the water glittered, like the scales on the fish they were netting. Some lucky souls would eat a fish supper tonight. Her stomach rumbled and she realised she hadn't eaten anything since the mouthful of bread and butter that morning.

She left the graveyard and called to the priest's house. It was empty, but the door stood open and a kettle steamed on the hob, so Father Hanrahan wasn't too far away. She walked next door to the church. Out of habit, she dipped her fingers in the holy water font on the wall and blessed herself, then stepped back as three children pushed past her to run inside. 'What's this?' she asked, of no-one in particular. She hadn't heard children's laughter, lilting and musical, for many months.

Inside the church itself, there must have been half a dozen or more children, all on the move. She guessed they were aged from around six or seven years up to eleven or twelve. Father Hanrahan looked almost unchanged from the last time she spoke to him on the day she left Galway eighteen months ago. He was perhaps a little thinner and greyer, as he stood on the steps leading to the altar. He seemed to be trying to get the children into some sort of order and was failing badly at his task.

The boys and girls were playing a game of tag, they jumped over benches, hopped along the kneelers and chased each other around the two huge statues of saints, which threatened to topple over onto them.

Jane laughed aloud at the sight of the elderly priest in his black cassock, his white hair tousled and standing almost on end, as he held his hands out beseechingly to the small devils.

The priest heard her and waved her over. 'Why, it's young Jane Keating, come home. Sure, I'd know you anywhere, and still the image of your poor father, God rest his soul. Here! You're just in time to help me with these ruffians. Get them to sit down in one place, there's a good girl.'

Jane found that she, too, was outnumbered and outrun by the 'ruffians'. The children's bare feet pattered along the aisle of the chapel, as they skipped off ahead of her. She got two of the older children to sit down but they soon jumped up to join their friends, and Jane had to begin again.

It took ten minutes to get them in order and sitting on the one bench. They turned their faces towards the priest and inspected the newcomer beside him. She counted them. There were only six of them, but on the move, they had seemed like twice that number.

'Now then, children. Mrs Flynn is in the kitchen. I want you to stand in line and walk quietly out to get your supper. Billy, you're the oldest, you can lead the way.'

When the children had left, the priest sat down on the steps of the altar.

'Ah, Jane. The dear Lord knows what I've let myself in for with this lot.'

'Who are they, Father?'

'Well now, where to start? They're local children. There's three little families among them. Billy O'Reilly, then the Clearys, three of them; Shay, he's the oldest at nearly twelve, his brother, Liam and sister, Maria.' The priest stopped for breath. 'The most recent additions are poor Lucy and Grace Kennedy. Sure, God help them, they're twins, and all that remains of their family, too.'

Father Hanrahan lowered his voice and gestured to Jane to come and sit beside him.

'I buried Lucy and Grace's mother and father only a month ago. Then I tried to take them into the workhouse in Galway. Sure, t'was still full to the brim! The Master told me they were fast running out of food for the inhabitants. So what else could I do, but bring the poor *crathurs* home here?'

The priest clearly wasn't expecting an answer, for he continued. 'And now here we are, with six orphans and just me, sixty-five years of age, and Mrs Flynn, who's fifty if she's a day, but don't say I said, to look after them.'

Jane looked around the church, at the few sticks of benches and not much else, other than the two garishly painted plaster statues of saints, one standing at either side of the altar.

'And is there still no room at the Workhouse for orphans?' she asked.

'That's my understanding.' The priest put one hand on the step and heaved himself up to stand in front of the altar. He genuflected and blessed himself. Facing the altar, he still spoke in a low voice, as if the children could hear him. 'You might say I'm in a quandary, Jane. I've almost no money left to keep them. Sure, they don't eat much, but I try to give them milk and oatmeal twice a day, to build them up a bit. They've been half-starved for going on two years now. Then I had to buy clothes for every single one of them. You should have seen them when they got here, half-naked and filthy dirty.'

'I've just come from the workhouse, Father. I went to look for my cousin's wife and her two children. They had to go in there last year, after they were evicted. You remember what happened, don't you, Father, to Brendan Keating?'

He nodded. 'I remember, girl. What are the times come to? God help us all. And did you find them?'

'Aoife died last April. There's only the children, Sorcha and Jamie, left.'

'And what'll you be doing with them, then?' the priest asked.

'Well, they'll stay there, in the Workhouse. They'll look after them. I can't.'

'What do you mean, Jane?' Father Hanrahan turned his head as if to study Jane's face while he waited for her reply.

'I don't know what I'm going to do now, Father. I just wanted to come home to my family, but with Aoife gone, there doesn't seem to be a home or a family for me anywhere.'

The priest nodded. 'Then you'll need to make one. But don't leave it too long, girl. Here, let me bless you.' He held his hand up and laid it on her head. 'May the Lord bless you and keep you safe, and help you find home. Amen.'

The gentle touch set tears rolling down her cheeks; she brushed them away and wiped her nose. 'The stonemason from Galway will come here in two days' time. Will you show him my father's grave? He has a cross to put on it.' Her voice trembled and she cleared her throat.

'I will, to be sure, Jane. I'll be here. Sure, where else would I be with that lot of ruffians. I've been a priest for forty years and never thought I'd have a family. It is a blessed wonder how things turn out.'

Jane pulled out her purse and handed over her last gold sovereign to the priest. 'Here, this will keep you going for a while, Father. I'm staying at an inn in the town. I'll call out again to see the cross.'

The old priest's eyes glistened. 'Why, thank you, Jane. You have your poor mother's kind heart. Go in peace. And don't be a stranger. You are welcome here. I seem to have a knack for orphans.' He chuckled as he walked her to the door of the chapel and stood while she headed up the path towards the road.

* * *

By the time Jane got back to the inn, Nancy and Ellen were asleep in the second bed. The air in the room smelt clean and soapy. Ellen half-woke as Jane got undressed, but didn't speak.

That night, although hungry, she slept straight away and dreamed, not of Death, but of Father Hanrahan's gang of laughing ruffians and Sorcha's soft dark curls. She woke in the early hours, and remembered that she had not yet seen

Jamie, her cousin, who must be seven or eight now. She must not forget that he, too, had witnessed his father's murder.

7

Jane meets Fahy, end of September 1847

She was woken early by Nancy, the older of the two sisters, who shook Jane's shoulder. 'Wake up! We have news!'

'What?' Jane sat up in the bed and stared at the two girls. She hardly recognised the young woman sitting on the side of the bed, and she struggled to understand what she was seeing. It was Nancy, but transformed from the homeless girl she had been just yesterday. Nancy's dark hair now gleamed and Ellen's was a mass of auburn curls around her face and shoulders.

'We're after finding work here, in the town,' Nancy said.

Their rags were gone and replaced with clean dresses and stockings and leather shoes. They must have crept out of the bed to get dressed and surprise her. She pushed back the blanket and got up and hugged them. 'You both look lovely. Tell me all about it.'

She sat and listened as they took it in turns to tell her about their transformation. Yesterday, with the money Jane had given them, they had bought second hand clothes and shoes and came back to the inn to wash and dress. 'We had a bath!'

Afterwards, the innkeeper suggested they go and visit the nearby convent of the Sacred Heart and ask for advice from the nuns. As luck would have it, the sister in charge of the convent kitchen needed another helper. Nancy had talked her into offering the one job to the two of them.

'We'll only get paid for one of us. But we can live-in and get our food as part of the wages. We'll be able to send the money we earn home to mam and dad. What do you say to that?'

'It's a miracle, that's what I say.'

'And we'll repay you the money you gave us to buy clothes and for our stay here. Just as soon as this is over.'

Jane shook her head. 'You don't need to repay me. If you can, then help someone else. That's all I ask.' She hugged both girls again. 'I didn't know you were such beautiful young women.'

Jane got dressed and they ate breakfast together, then said their farewells. She watched the two sisters head off, arms linked, to start their new job. She booked the bedroom for another night and asked for some hot water to be sent up to the bathroom. She stripped and washed herself, towel-dried her hair and left it to dry in the air. She put on the grey brocade dress that she had bought in Dublin earlier that week, but decided that she'd need a couple of changes of clothes. The Dublin dress was lovely but it felt out of place here in this hungry town.

* * *

After a visit to the bank in the town where she withdrew some more sovereigns, she found a pawn shop and had a root around the unclaimed clothes now for sale. She bought two woollen skirts, one black, the other a deep russet. They fitted her for length and she found a leather belt to hold them in at the waist. The two white cotton blouses looked a bit worn, but they were clean and would go nicely under a knitted grey wool jacket that was in surprisingly good condition. On the same street she went into a haberdasher's and bought some drawers and knee stockings and another cotton night-shift. She had enough clothes now to see her through the autumn and winter. It seemed that some shops had stayed open through this disaster.

* * *

It was milling rain again, so she waited a couple of hours for the weather to clear before setting out to find Fahy. He'd know about Constable Smullen and he'd tell her she was right.

On her way down the stairs, she saw another guest with a small child, just leaving. The small girl had a look of Sorcha about her. Jane recalled Father Hanrahan's comments about fever at the workhouse. But the Master hadn't mentioned fever when she was there. What if Sorcha or Jamie got sick? She slowed in her descent. 'You can't bring them to live here with you. They're better off in the workhouse.' She gritted her teeth. 'Don't think it!'

She hauled the door open and stopped outside to compose herself. After a few deep breaths, she started to walk.

* * *

She took the road south and followed the coastal path that overlooked Galway Bay. After walking for more than an hour, she made her way down to the beach at Salthill. She took off her boots and stockings and pulled the hem of her skirt above her knees. The first touch of sea water on her toes made her shiver as she waded out into the shallows and looked towards the horizon. Sea and sky misted together and hid the Atlantic Ocean she had sailed on, first as a convict, then not long ago, as a free woman coming home.

She bent and caught a handful of cool sea water. She imagined her baby in her icy coffin in the Southern Ocean. Drops of water fell onto her skirt, not salt water, but tears for herself and all the lost souls belonging to her.

'You have to go on,' she whispered. 'You have some family left alive. Thank God for them.'

The sky clouded over and a breeze pushed the sea water around her and threatened to topple her.

On the way back to the beach she looked up at the cliff edge and the sky beyond. 'I'll try. That's all I can do.' She dried her feet and legs off with her cloak and set off in search of Fahy.

* * *

She turned north, away from the bay and saw the small cabins in the distance. She'd find her old neighbour there, and question him about the shooting. He would confirm that she was in the right: Niall had murdered her cousin, Brendan. She tried to focus on just the one thing: to find Fahy.

She had to stop thoughts of Sorcha and Jamie, her lost baby, Margaret, and her mother, father and brothers from roaming around in her mind. Instead she looked at the cabins ahead and walked on.

Jane was glad of her leather boots along the stony path

between the green fields, although she had walked and run barefoot along these roads in the past. Most of the land was surrounded by low stone walls. In some places, spindly trees leaned alongside the walls, and dark berries gleamed on a blackthorn bush. She looked out across the fields towards the river where the tide was out and the mud banks reflected glassy light from the sun. It all seemed so peaceful until she heard shrill voices on the air. Yet she couldn't place them.

In the time it took to walk the couple of miles to the settlement, the sunlight fell behind the hills to the west, taking its light and with it any last heat there was in the day. The noises she had heard in the distance, the shouting, banging and hammering, had ceased. Silence lay thick on the air, just the breeze on her cheeks, with a few spots of drizzle from a shower cloud overhead.

A woman's cry, low and muffled, was abruptly cut off. Horses' hooves clattered, cartwheels rattled, an ass sounded his complaint. Jane stepped over the low wall at the side of the lane and crouched down beside scrubby hawthorn bushes. She pulled the hood of her cloak up around her head and face, leaving only her eyes uncovered, to witness a parade of men and horses along the road. They halted a few yards away from where Jane hid. The ass and cart with its driver soon caught up with them. Jane had seen a similar contraption on the back of a cart before. It was a wooden crane, and it was used to knock down homes.

The gang of men, animals and their equipment turned onto the road. They were heading for the bridge then back to Galway town. It seemed their work was done, for this day at least. Jane waited until the last sounds had disappeared on the evening air. She hitched the strap on her satchel up onto her shoulder, hopped back over the wall and walked into the village.

It was as if she had travelled back through time. She knew that evictions happened for a number of reasons: tenants unable to pay their rent, being the most pressing. In the last few years, even before she had left Ireland, as she well knew, eviction had become an easy method for landlords to clear their land of unproductive peasants and their huge families. Nowadays, it seemed to have become a more acceptable way to remove the problems caused by the potato blight. Her cousin, Brendan, God rest him, had tried his best, but he and his family had been evicted in the winter of 1846. He had been one of the first on this estate.

Jane came to the site of the tumbling. Two cabins had just been knocked down, leaving heaps of stones and broken walls. It looked as if everyone who lived there was gathered around the rubble.

The two families who had been made homeless stood in separate groups with their children around them. One of the women was of an extreme thinness, with deep sunken eyes and jutting cheekbones. Her husband had his arm around the woman's shoulders and their four children stood beside them. All looked to be in a state of frozen disbelief. The other woman stood alone with her children.

Other villagers waited silently, a little apart. To Jane, they all appeared cowed and fearful. She stepped forward and raised her hand, spoke the Irish greeting. '*Dhia dhaoibh.* God be with you all.' She hoped that someone would recognise her for she had gone to school with some of these people not so many years ago.

Her hope was answered when a girl of her own age stepped

out of the crowd. 'Is it you, Jane Keating?' The girl spoke in Irish and Jane replied in the same language.

'It is. You're Susannah.' Jane nodded to the girl she remembered from school.

'Yes. I heard you went to Waterford last year to look for your uncle.'

'I did. Then I went further afield, across the ocean. I'm home now. I've come looking for Fahy. But I see you have troubles here.'

Susannah nodded. 'Two cabins tumbled. God help the families, because we can't.'

Jane heard sobbing from the lone woman as she tried to calm her youngest, a child of three or four years of age. Jane counted the woman's children, six of them. Dear God!

Someone pushed through from the back of the crowd of neighbours. She knew him straight away.

'Jane Keating. I heard you say my name.' It was her old neighbour, her father's friend, Michael Fahy. For as long as Jane had known him, he went by his last name.

Fahy used to be a well-built man, and strong around the shoulders. Now, after just eighteen months, he seemed diminished. His hair had thinned and greyed, and he was bearded, a thing he had never been.

'Fahy, it's good to see you. I have something to ask you, but it will keep. Why are they evicting?'

'It's the landlord. We've heard he is intent on getting rid of all of us before winter sets in. Then he won't have to pay the rates to keep us in the workhouse.'

'Why? Because you have not paid the rent?' She asked the question and heard mutterings from the crowd gathered around.

'The rent is neither here nor there.' Fahy stopped speaking as the thin woman beside one of the tumbled cabins stepped forward.

'Our rent was paid up to last June,' the woman said. 'Sure, we've gone without food. I've sold our clothes, the bedding, my cook-pot, all to pay the rent. As soon as we couldn't pay, the eviction notice was issued. Now, we are as you see us. We have nothing left, not even a roof over our heads.' The woman's hair was damp from the drizzle and the lack of a cloak to cover her head. Her four children crowded around her, all in rags, barefoot and dirty.

'But you should know this, Jane,' Fahy said. 'Where have you been and why have you come back now?'

'I've been away, and now I'm home. I want to help, if I can.' Explanations about where she had been and how she got home would keep for another time.

'Can you make potatoes grow in the ground?' Fahy asked. 'That's what's needed here. Potatoes we can eat, pigs and grain we can sell to pay the rent. And if we can't do any of it, what makes you think you can?'

She heard the bitterness in his voice. 'You're right. I don't know what I can do.' Jane spoke to the lone woman standing in the ruins of her small home. 'Maybe you can tell me how I can help.'

'We need to get in, out of the weather, and we need food. I haven't eaten for three days now. The children are not far behind me, but they were fed yesterday at a soup kitchen in the town. They had the last of it.'

The woman's voice was barely above a whisper. Jane leaned forward to hear her. A sharp, rank smell rose off the woman and Jane turned her head away.

She knew those two simple things, food and shelter, were beyond all of them, at that very moment. The rain had eased, but night had fallen.

In only the recent past, evening was the time to gather around the turf fire and tell stories and sleep until the morning came. But now there was no turf fire, no pot of potatoes, no walls or even a roof.

'Will anyone take in these families until morning?' she asked.

No-one spoke for a moment, then Fahy put his hand up. 'Orlaith, you can come with me. Bring the children.'

A woman at the back spoke up. 'Jimmy and Nuala, there's room in my cabin for youse.'

Jane heard sounds of disagreement.

'You shouldn't have asked that of us, Jane.' Susannah spoke clearly so everyone could hear her. 'We'll all be put out on the road when the bailiff comes back. It's against the law to offer shelter to anyone who has been evicted. They have to go to the workhouse. You, of all people should know that.'

'I'm sorry, please forgive me. I forgot. I was there only yesterday. I met the Master. I heard it's full, but I'll walk with you into town.'

'We'll go there,' Orlaith said. ' I don't want to be the one to get my neighbours into trouble. Jimmy and Nuala, will you come, too?'

The couple stepped forward. 'We'll go together, Orlaith,' the mother said. At this moment they would probably do anything to get themselves and their children inside, out of the cold, damp air.

'Fahy, I need to speak to you. It's about Brendan,' Jane whispered.

'I'll walk with you. We can talk on the way,' Fahy said.

76

They set off along the road back to town. Orlaith turned and looked over her shoulder, as if to take a last look at the ruins of her home, then put an arm around her smallest child, and began the long walk to the workhouse.

* * *

A little way further on, they passed the remains of another cabin that had been reduced to blackened lumps of debris. It looked as if it had been burned to the ground.

'What happened there?' Jane asked Fahy.

'The whole family, the mother and father and the five children, one just a baby, died of the fever. We think it was dysentery. No-one dared go near them for fear of spreading the disease. They died, all of them. A couple of the men pulled the roof down over them and set fire to it.'

'Their bodies are still in there?'

'Well, there was no-one to bury them. What would you have done?' Fahy seemed to be impatient with Jane's questions.

Jane had no idea what she would have done. But she would not have walked past that charred mass of turf and timbers every day, that was for sure. She kept that to herself. There was no knowing what a person would do if they were desperate enough.

They walked in silence together. 'I came here to ask you about Niall Smullen. Do you remember him?'

Fahy stopped and turned to look at Jane. He shook his head. 'I'll never forget that day. I still dream about it.' His eyes filled with tears.

'I spoke to him yesterday morning, in Galway. Have you seen him since?'

77

'No, he left right after Brendan was killed. Well, I wonder what brought him back?'

'He didn't know me at first, until I called him a murderer. Then he swore he hadn't shot Brendan. Said it was the bailiff's gun. He made me think I was wrong. But I'm not wrong, am I? You were there, you saw it, too.'

She held her breath and waited for him to speak. He looked down and seem to search his memory. Then he sighed. 'Jane, I'm not sure, what happened, it was all so fast. I think there was only the one shot. I saw Niall aim and shoot his pistol.'

'I don't understand why we didn't call the police on him.'

Fahy laughed, a harsh sound, almost a sob the way it caught in his throat. 'Jane, he was the police. Who were we to call?'

* * *

By the time they arrived in Galway town, they were all soaked through. The women, Nuala and Orlaith, had no cloaks and their arms were bare and slick with misty rain. Their skirts had been worn to the end of their limits; the hems, tattered and dirty and now almost stuck to their legs. Jane wondered how Nuala managed to stand, let alone walk. But the woman walked up the hills with her husband and children and kept on going until they reached the workhouse door, and shelter. The two families were taken in and Fahy and Jane watched the door close behind them. 'They must have found some space,' she whispered.

She arranged to meet Fahy the next week. She had to find a room in a lodging house, it would be cheaper than staying at the inn in the longer term. And she needed to go back to the stonemason and get Aoife's name added to the plaque.

8

Repeal Association Meeting, October 1847

It was evening, and winter seemed to have arrived early. Jane had been home for a month and the nights had drawn in. Most days rain clouds came in from the Atlantic Ocean and dropped their burden of rain over the coast and the west of Ireland. The air, when breathed in, was chilled and damp.

Jane had found a room in a boarding house near the bridge. She had left word with Father Hanrahan of her address and Fahy found her there.

Fahy was the only friend she had in the town and the two of them would talk about the village. By now, mid-October, it had been completely cleared. The cabins knocked and any garden walls levelled. Often their talk would turn to Smullen. Strangely, he seemed to have vanished again, for she hadn't seen him since that meeting near the workhouse.

One morning, they strolled towards the Spanish Arch and along the Long Walk. The slate grey waters confined between the banks of the River Corrib raced past, ragged white tops visible where the waves broke, and in the distant sky, dark clouds scudded towards the town.

'There's a storm coming,' Jane said. The air felt heavy, and a thin flash of lightening streaked on the horizon.

'How are you getting on in the boarding house?' Fahy asked her.

'Only for you, Fahy, I'd not speak to a soul all day. There are only four other lodgers, and they are men. They go off to work early. That's all.' She turned to him. 'To tell you the truth, I'm not sure why I came home.'

'These are hard times for everyone, Jane. Listen, I want to thank you for the money. It has paid for my lodgings. But I must find work soon. If not, I'll be sleeping on the streets.' Her friend clenched his fist. 'Ah, sure, I don't know.'

'I have money in the bank, Fahy.'

'I don't want any more of your money, Jane. You need to keep it. You've helped me enough. I get my dinner at the Quaker soup kitchen. I've been thinking about offering to help them. I doubt if they can pay me, but it must be a lot for them two women to do on their own. That'll be something.'

'I haven't seen it, where is it?'

'Up by the National school. That's where they pitch up. They have a cart with a boiler on the back of it.'

'Well, good luck. I'd say they won't turn down a fine strong man like yourself.'

Fahy laughed. 'My days of being a fine strong man are far behind me! I'll head over there now and see if they'll have me. I'll call in to you tomorrow and tell you if I have any news.'

She went on a little further, to the end of the Walk and looked out over the bay.

If Michael Fahy had glanced back, he would have seen a

solitary figure, dark hair blowing in the sea breeze, her hand shading her eyes as if searching the horizon for a lost soul.

* * *

The next day they sat together in the downstairs parlour to talk. The door remained open on the instructions of the landlady.

'I got the job!' Fahy shook his head, as if in wonder at his luck. 'Mrs Smith offered me the job as soon as I mentioned it.'

'How much will they pay you?'

'Nothing. They have no money to pay me, but I'll earn my dinner. And it's a start.'

'You'll find something, Fahy. Keep looking.' He still had his rent to pay and it must be due soon, but she knew he'd sooner sleep on the streets than take any more of her money. She stared at his worn boots and sighed, was about to tell him how much she had in the bank, when he asked a question.

'Have you heard the latest news?'

'News about what?'

'There's been seven shootings, all around the west coast. One of them was what you might call a good landlord. He paid for some of his tenants to emigrate. But he also evicted those who wanted to stay on their land.'

Jane nodded. 'Yes, I read it in the Star. Have there been any arrests?'

'Not so far. They think it's different groups doing it.'

'It's a pity they wouldn't shoot Smullen.'

'Oh, I forgot! I saw him, just this morning, up near the soup kitchen. He's not in uniform though.'

'Where has he been?'

'I don't know. But he's back in town.'

'So, tell me, what'll we do about him, Fahy?'

'I know someone who has a gun that I could borrow,' Fahy said, and smiled as if at a joke.

Jane glanced at him to see if he was serious.

Fahy blessed himself and frowned. 'What am I saying, Jane? We can't murder him. Sure, we'll be as bad as he is. Don't you see?'

She thought of the Colonel in Melbourne. He'd have dropped down dead if she had hit him a bit harder with the smoothing iron, but she'd hit him to save her life, to stop him from murdering her. Then she remembered her relief when she saw him breathe. She was not a murderer, either.

'How do we make him pay, then?' she asked.

They sat together and each pondered an answer to that question.

'He's a Catholic. Let's ask the priest to denounce him from the altar.' Even as she spoke, she shook her head.

Fahy laughed. 'He'd sue the priest, girl, or complain to the Bishop. No, that won't work.'

'Did I hear you say he has a business in the town?'

'His wife runs a pawn shop.'

'We'll ask people to shun him. Take their business elsewhere. It's common knowledge he's been involved in evictions, and we'll tell them about Brendan. But sure, everyone knows that.'

'It's worth a try.' Fahy was silent for a few moments. 'I tell you what. Come with me to the next Repeal Association meeting, I heard there's one on next week. We'll put our case to them. If they like the idea, then we'll have a chance.'

* * *

Fahy and Jane found the meeting in a small room at the back of a public house on Cross Street. Unfortunately, there were only half a dozen men in attendance. The death of the Irish Repeal Association's leader, Daniel O'Connell, earlier that year, had left the nationwide Repeal Association movement foundering. Here in Galway, just a few small businessmen and tenant farmers remained as members. They had more important things to discuss than the alleged murder of a poor tenant farmer, almost two years ago.

'Any one of you might be the next to be evicted,' Fahy explained. 'Please God, that won't happen. But if we combine together, then we might make the likes of Constable Smullen think twice before he shoots another innocent tenant.'

It was to no avail. The farmers were adamant they were not going to be evicted. Sure, hadn't they paid up their rent? The shop owners stayed quiet. Anyhow, the meeting was to discuss how to get hold of more Indian cornmeal from the government. Food was the main worry. Not that any of these men went hungry, it was the ability to sell it and make money.

One of the men, a heavy-set man, with a bulbous drinker's nose, had been staring at Jane while she spoke.

'So, you're a relative of Brendan Keating, then?' he asked.

'I am. I'm his cousin. Or I was until he was killed.'

'I'm sorry for your loss. I heard about the shooting, right enough. Your cousin pulled a gun on the bailiff, so they say.' The man's eyes glittered in the dull light of the room.

Jane shook her head, as if she hadn't heard right.

'So they say? Who says that? Brendan was unarmed, he was murdered.'

The man whispered something to his neighbour, then turned back to Jane.

'You want to be careful about throwing around accusations of murder, and by a police constable, at that. There's no knowing who might report you to the authorities.'

Jane felt herself begin to shake, her hands trembled and her breath shortened as if she had just come upon danger.

The man stood up from the table. 'I didn't come here to listen to this.' He turned to the chairman. 'Let me know when you want to talk about business. I'll come back then.'

'Joe, Joe, sit down, man. We'll get on to it right away.'

Before the chairman could say any more, a sharp knock came at the door and it opened. Jane was sitting with her back to the door and saw the men's faces. They showed no surprise, nodded and one pulled a chair out for the late arrival.

Beside her, Fahy laid his hand on her arm and held it there. She turned to see Niall Smullen step into the room. He took his hat off and spoke to the chairman. 'Sorry I'm late. I got held up at home.'

He sat down next to Fahy and looked across at Jane. 'Good evening to you, Miss Keating.'

Jane went to rise, but Fahy's hand on her arm stopped her. 'Wait,' he breathed. Then the chairman spoke.

'Niall, glad you could make it. We're about to start the business at hand. We're worried about the attacks on local businesses, there's a lot of lawlessness about lately.'

'I can't help you with any news on that. Since I resigned my position, I don't know anymore than you do.' It was cold in the room, yet Smullen had a light sheen of sweat on his face. He rubbed it away with a large stained handkerchief. 'As I explained to you, Jim, my wife has a shop in the town and I want to join this association to find out how we can stay in business, now that I'm not in work.'

'Why did you resign?' Jane asked.

'Not that it's any of your business, Miss Keating, but I got tired of being on the wrong end of my countrymen. Eviction is perilous work, as you well know, and I have a family to raise.'

There was silence in the room. Jane was the only woman there, and it felt as if she was being pulled to sympathise with him. A thing she would never do.

'T'is dangerous times we're living through,' Fahy said.

The chairman turned to Jane and Fahy. 'Considering what you said before Mr Smullen got here, I'm asking you both to leave now. We have business to attend to.'

Jane and Fahy stood. Jane would have the last word. 'You're all afraid that you'll be the next to go hungry or get evicted.' She pointed at Smullen. 'And you've been one of our oppressors for long enough, Niall Smullen. If you want to get on the right side of your neighbours then stand beside them at the next eviction. You're cowards, the lot of you!'

She felt dizzy and she staggered by the time she got outside the door of the public house.

* * *

Fahy followed her out. 'Jane, wait for a minute. Sure, girl, you're trembling. Here, come and walk with me as far as the bridge. We'll stop there till you get your breath back.'

He held his arm out for her to link his and they walked together.

Jane's legs felt as if they would give way under her. She leaned on the stone wall of the bridge and looked down at the dark water rushing beneath her feet.

Somehow, the way the light fell on the water, or maybe it

was a twig that had gotten caught up by the flood tide, but for an instant, she saw the small wooden basket, the coffin that held the body of her daughter, bobbing and turning on the waves. She blinked, then it was gone.

'Ah,' she sighed heavily. 'Margaret.' She bent her head to her hands and sobbed. Fahy stood silently by her side and patted her shoulder.

Some passersby looked at the girl crying as if her heart would break, and others glanced at the man beside her. Fahy tipped his hat to them, and turned his attention back to Jane.

After a few minutes, her tears eased and she straightened up and wiped her face with her hand. 'I'm sorry.'

'Who is Margaret?' Fahy asked. 'You seemed to see her in the water. What is she to you?'

Jane shook her head. If she began to speak about her baby, then she would have to tell about the rape. If she told about the rape, she would certain that she would break in two and never be able to heal. Silence was her only cure. 'It's nothing, I'm sorry. Walk me back to the boarding house, will you?'

She avoided looking at Fahy, for fear of seeing disappointment in his face. But he held his arm out again. 'Here, take my arm.'

They neared the street where Jane lodged. 'Why did that man say I'd be reported, Fahy?'

'People love a good gossip. And they have to make sure they are on the right side of the constabulary. Especially if they are in business. Sure, the army and the police are their best customers.' He didn't mention Smullen, or his tale at the meeting. Did he believe that Smullen was no longer in the Irish Constabulary, Jane wanted to ask.

'Listen to me, get yourself some supper and a good night's

sleep. You'll be grand in the morning, so you will.'

'I'm going to see Father Hanrahan tomorrow.' She tried her best to sound positive. 'When do you start work on the soup kitchen?'

'Tomorrow, but I'll be finished by early afternoon. I tell you what, I'll walk out the road with you. I could do with a change of scenery. Would you like some company?'

Jane smiled. 'I would, Fahy, and thank you. I'll wait for you.'

* * *

Once inside the boarding house, Jane let her smile drop. Her body felt heavy as she climbed the stairs to her attic room. She couldn't eat the supper the landlady had left in the kitchen, for her throat was still raw from crying. Another long night lay before her. She prayed she'd get some sleep. Even an hour would give her some relief from the constant, shifting images in her mind. She didn't undress, used the chamber pot, blew out the candle and lay on the bed to wait until morning.

She closed her eyes and watched the basket containing her child's body swirl on the dark waters, felt the weight of her rapist as he pinned her to the floor. She opened her mouth to breathe or cry out, but was stifled, suffocating, then forced a scream and woke up, sweating. She put her feet on the floor and grabbed hold of the side of the iron bed-frame. Her heart beat as if it would come out through her chest. Then she heard a knock on the door,

'Are you alright in there?' The landlady had heard her.

'Yes, I'm sorry. Just a bad dream.' Her voice cracked and she coughed.

'If you're sure. Good night, then.' The stairs creaked as the landlady made her way downstairs. Jane moved over to the chair by the window and pulled back the shutter. She flinched at the sound of a dog barking on the street. Then she picked up her boots and went downstairs quietly. She pulled the boots on at the door and let herself out of the house. She walked through the town and ended up outside the workhouse. It was in darkness. 'Keep safe, little cousins,' she prayed. She made a decision, then turned and walked back the way she had come. She'd visit them at least, and tell them she was family.

* * *

Early the next morning Jane went back to the workhouse. She explained her quest and the Master escorted her to the nursery. He left her with the matron.

'I need to speak to Sorcha and Jamie,' she said.

'Jamie is in the boy's dormitory. And you needn't think you're coming in here to upset Sorcha.' The matron's expression was stony as she faced Jane.

'I want to explain, so she'll understand.'

'She's four. What will she understand. And just to make you feel better?'

'The Master said I could speak to her.'

The matron sighed. 'Suit yourself. She's over there.'

Jane turned and saw her little cousin. She was playing with a tattered doll. Another child ran up to Sorcha and grabbed the doll by the hair. 'It's mine!'

Sorcha's face creased into a frown and tears streamed down her cheeks.

Jane knelt down in front of her cousin. '*A stor*, do you remember me?'

Sorcha looked at Jane through her tears. 'Niamh took my doll. I want it back.'

But the other child had by now started a game with a small group of children. The doll was at the centre of the game.

'I'll get you a doll, *acushla*. Don't cry.'

Jane's little cousin wiped her nose with her fist. 'Did my mammy send you?'

Yes, she told me you're here. But the words stuck in Jane's throat and she swallowed them whole. She glanced around and saw the matron watching the interaction.

'Do you know where Jamie is?' Sorcha asked.

'Can I sit down next to you?' If Jane didn't sit down, then she'd fall in a heap on the floor in front of her little cousin.

Sorcha nodded and her short curls bounced and gleamed around her face.

'Your brother is in the boys' dormitory. And I'm your cousin, Jane. I've been away for a while and I heard you were here. I've come to say hello.'

'What's a cousin?'

'Family,' Jane replied. The word hung in the air like the white seed-head of a dandelion. One blow and the seeds would disperse in a puff of air. She held her breath.

'Did my mammy send you?' Sorcha asked again.

Jane blew out and the seeds dispersed. 'Yes, she did. I have to go now, but I'll come and visit you again. I'll bring you a dolly.' She reached to touch Sorcha's hand, but stopped, as if in fear. She couldn't do it.

She walked past the matron without speaking and let herself out of the nursery. Her steps echoed on the stairs as she raced down to the front door and out onto the path. She kept running, away from her cousin and Jamie, the cousin she was yet to meet. If asked, she would not have been able to explain why she ran, for her devils were not chasing her, they were inside her head.

* * *

Later that day, Jane and Fahy walked through the town towards the road west. She looked across the river, at the high stone walls of the workhouse. Jane was almost sure the children were safer in there, better off with the Guardians, than out here. She looked away and caught a glance from Fahy.

'Did you speak to Sorcha and Jamie?' he asked.

'Just Sorcha. Jamie was in the boys' dormitory.' Jane pressed her lips together and swallowed.

They turned on to the road towards the Silverstrand beach. The rutted earth on the road stretched out between the gently sloping tilled fields. The crops had been harvested earlier that month. Only last week, Jane had stood on the quayside in Galway and watched as full-to-bursting sacks of grain were loaded aboard British ships, and sold out of the country.

'Why can't they keep the grain here in Ireland, Fahy? We could live on bread until the potatoes come back.'

Fahy shook his head. 'The small farmers still have to pay their rent. There is no getting around it. To pay the rent they must sell the crops. The British government is a big buyer, and the grain goes to England and the colonies, so I hear.'

'It's just not right. Leaving people with nothing.'

They passed small stone-built cabins, their roofs pulled down, with just the broken stone walls left standing. The work of destruction looked to be recent. She caught a glimpse of a bent figure under a scrap of shelter in the ruins of the cabin.

'Tell me, why did those men at the meeting call it the Repeal Association? And Repeal of what exactly?'

'I don't know much about it. We used to have a parliament here, in Ireland, but then it was united with the parliament in London. Daniel O'Connell wanted to get that law overturned, repealed, and go back to a Dublin parliament. That's what I think it's about.' Fahy pushed his hand through his hair, as if his head ached. 'Sure, t'won't make much difference. The parliamentary seats are bought and paid for by the gentry. They probably like a jaunt across to London every now and then.'

* * *

Jane had promised Thomas Meagher that she would help him if he started a rebellion. If those men at the last meeting were all who were interested, then her attempt to get people to join the Irish Confederation was doomed. The same went for her hope of shunning Smullen. She was determined not to give up on that. She must think up a way to make him pay for his crime.

9

Jane and her cousins. Mid-October 1847.

The situation at the church was much the same as she had left it on her last visit. Today, the three older boys, Shay and Liam Cleary and Billy O'Reilly were playing outside. She stepped onto the ditch as they raced up the muddy lane in pursuit of a small leather ball, a *sliotar,* using their hurleys to balance the *sliotar* and run with it, or bat it along the lane.

The younger girls, Maria Cleary and Lucy and Grace Kennedy, were inside the presbytery with Mrs Flynn. 'Ah, you're back. Come in, Jane. And Mr Fahy, you're welcome. How are you keeping?'

'Well, thank you, Mrs Flynn. How are you these days?' Fahy asked.

'Now that you ask, I think I'm getting too old for this,' the housekeeper said.

'It's not an easy job, I'd say, looking after all these children.'

Jane smiled at Lucy, Grace and Maria, pleased that she remembered their names. Sorcha and Jamie would be better off here, she thought, until she caught the end of Fahy's comment.

'What did you say, Mrs Flynn?'

'I said, it's been hard, with all these to feed and mind. But I do my best. I just can't see any end to it.'

The housekeeper's face was deeply lined and her white cap accentuated her lack of colour, almost as if her skin had been bleached to the bone beneath. She wiped a tear away.

'Don't mind me. It's just the worry for these children. And they should be in school, but we have no way of getting them there.' She paused for a moment and whispered. 'I worry if anything should happen to Father Hanrahan.'

'Girls, come outside and play with your brothers.' Fahy led the way and left Jane with Mrs Flynn, who finished what she had started to say.

'I suppose then they'll have to be taken into the workhouse. But it feels like a death sentence, with the fever in there. I'm sorry, I don't mean to frighten the children. I'm not thinking straight.'

'What fever, Mrs Flynn?' Jane knew there had been fever early last year, before she left Galway. Her mother and brothers had died of it.

'Typhus. They say it's deadly. Have you been to see Sorcha and Jamie lately?'

'I was there on Sunday. I didn't see Jamie, but no-one mentioned typhus fever.'

'Well, you might want to go and check on them.' The housekeeper's voice had a worried edge to it as she spoke. Fahy had come back in at that moment.

'Mrs Flynn,' Jane said. 'I don't have a home for them.' It seemed so simple to everyone else that she would take them

93

out of there.

'Then, you had better make one, don't you think? You've been mooning around for weeks now, since you got back. Not doing the one thing you say you have the money to do. Either that or give up on them. Because I tell you this, one or both of them poor *crathurs* will get that rotten disease. Then where will you be?'

Jane bowed her head, then turned and walked out of the presbytery. She kept going past the children. Fahy followed her.

'Jane, wait!' He caught up with her. 'I'll walk back to town with you.'

They walked together in silence until they were halfway to town.

'She's right, isn't she?' Jane asked.

'Why did she say that to you? About making a home?'

'There's fever in the workhouse. I need to get them out of there.'

'And how do you intend to go about that?'

'I don't know. The only thing I do know is that they can't stay there. Mrs Flynn is right, I'd never forgive myself. I thought they were safe in there, Fahy.'

'Will they stay with you at the boarding house?'

'They'll have to. For a few days at least. I can't see Mrs Flynn taking in more children, can you?'

Fahy smiled, then stopped and reached to touch Jane's arm. 'Do you want me to come with you to get them?'

'No. I need to do this myself. But thank you.'

By then, they had reached the edge of town.

'I'll leave you off here,' Fahy said. 'I have a message I want to do. I've an idea about school for the children. I'll come and find you later. God be with you, girl.'

Fahy turned off and walked up the town, leaving Jane outside the gate of the workhouse.

* * *

She stood at the edge of a huge crowd of paupers and tried not to breath in the smells from their unwashed bodies. It was the children she found hardest to look at. All the children, boys and girls, whatever age they were, shivered in the cold air and had a thin, sad look about them. It must be heartbreaking for their parents to have no food to give them, not to mention a warm home.

Jane dreaded going inside that place again. The only thing that forced her on was the thought that Sorcha and Jamie might be in danger from the fever. She didn't want the responsibility of her cousins, but nor did she want them to suffer any more than they must have already.

She waited and watched, but the front door remained firmly shut. Just then, voices in the crowd at the gates called out, and a horse and cart pulled up nearby. A man and a woman hopped down from the cart and hitched the horse's reins to the gate. The man climbed on to the back of the cart and lifted the lid on a huge pot. Steam rushed out and filled the air with the smell of onions and cabbage. It was another soup kitchen.

People jostled forward but quickly got into line. They knew what to do. The woman put on a white apron and picked up a tin cup and began to ladle in the soup, while the man sliced off chunks of bread. Each man, woman and child got a cup of soup and a piece of bread.

Jane didn't stay to watch them devour the food. She slipped

95

off along the road and turned the corner to follow the wall around to the back of the workhouse. When she and her father had last visited her mother and brothers, they had gotten in unnoticed through the back gate.

This other gate, the one for deliveries, was unlocked. She pushed it open and waited to see if anyone came to investigate. A path led straight to the door of the kitchen, and beside it, steps down to the basement. She caught up the hem of her skirt and stepped quietly down the steps to the storage area. The basement door was open, like the last time.

There was no-one around so she walked quickly past the bins and coal storage through to the stairs and made her way up to the main corridor, then she followed the hallway to the nursery she had visited a few days ago. She walked purposefully as if she was supposed to be there, until she got to the door.

The matron and a nurse that she had seen before were busy feeding the children. Those aged between three and four, sat around a low table and spooned their porridge into their mouths. Both of the women had a baby each on their lap and held bottles of milk for them to drink.

The matron looked up. When she spotted Jane, her face hardened. 'She's not here.'

'Where is she then?'

'On the fever ward, in the infirmary. She's sick.'

'I need to see her.'

'Why? You don't want her. You said as much.'

'I've changed my mind.'

The other nurse nodded. 'Oh, there's the fine one!'

'You don't know anything about me.' Jane shook her head, she stayed dry-eyed and gritted her teeth, to not shout at them.

96

'You had better hurry.' The older woman said.

'Where is it? The infirmary?'

'Go on down the hall, all the way. Then you'll come to an archway, the infirmary is beyond that.'

The two nurses looked at each other, both with grim faces, and returned to feeding the babies.

* * *

Jane ran, under the stone arch, around the corner and stopped. The infirmary was newly constructed. It was built in stone like the rest of the workhouse, but looked like a single storey barn, as if it had been thrown up quickly and cheaply, with a flat roof.

The first thing that struck her was the noise. Calls from sick patients, for water, or the privy; nurses rushed from one patient to the next, their shoes hammering on the wooden floorboards.

The second thing was the smell. Jane gagged as she stepped into the wide room. This was a ward for women and children. The smell came from the privies at the far end. She spotted about a dozen metal cots, pushed together in one corner. Each cot had two or three babies or young children, all of them listless and sick.

Jane went over to the cots and searched for Sorcha. She was in the last cot, lying down beside another sick child. Jane leaned in to stroke her cousin's hair and felt the fever in her face and neck. Her little cousin blinked slowly.

'Jesus, Mary and Joseph,' Jane whispered. 'Sorcha, your daddy and mammy sent me. I'm going to take you home with me.' A hand touched Jane's shoulder and she turned to see one

97

of the nurses.

'Who are you, and how did you get in here?'

'They sent me here from the nursery. Sorcha is my cousin. I've come to take her home.'

The nurse shook her head. 'You can't just come in here and collect a child. Take yourself off. Speak to the Master and get his permission.'

The nurse waited for Jane to move away from the cot.

'I'll be back.' She hurried along another corridor, found the Master's office and knocked at the door. He recognised her.

'Miss Keating.'

'I need to speak to you. It's urgent.'

'Come in and sit down.'

She didn't want to sit, she wanted to take his hand in hers and run back to the infirmary. But he was in no hurry.

'Tell me, how did you get in? The whole place is locked down.'

'There's a way in around the back, and the gate is open for a delivery. I got in with my father, when my mother and brothers were here.' She clenched her hands for a moment, then straightened her fingers to smooth the fabric of her skirt. It was chilly in the room. 'My cousin is sick. I need to take her home with me. And I'll take her brother, Jamie, too.'

'Ah, so you've made arrangements.' He nodded. 'But you're right, we're not in the best condition to be looking after sick children. Or adults for that matter. I'll give you my permission to take them. Tell me where they'll be, so I can put it in the record book.'

'I'm at the King Street lodging house in the town.'

He wrote the information in his ledger and laid his pen down, then took a deep breath and stood. 'Let's go and get your cousins, then.'

They walked past the women's section of the workhouse. The double doors were open and Jane saw up to a hundred women and girls sitting at the long tables she had seen the last time. All of them were picking at lumps of hemp with their bony fingers. It was cold on the corridor and she saw an empty grate at the far end of the room and guessed it wasn't much warmer in there.

She thought of the orphans that Father Hanrahan and Mrs Flynn had in their care at the chapel, and realised how hard it was to keep them warm and fed.

'Do you get government money to feed all these people?' she asked. They had reached the end of the corridor and turned under the arch.

'No. It's from the rates paid by farmers and businesses in the town. But lately there's not enough rate money coming in, so we've been operating on credit for the past three months.' He was silent for a moment. 'I suppose I shouldn't be telling you this, but lately some of our creditors have stopped supplying us.'

'Supplying what? Food?'

He nodded. 'We're trying to get other food suppliers, but I think the next step will be for the bailiffs to come in.'

'What do you mean?'

'The creditors want to get the money they are owed. They'll get a confiscation order from the court and send in the bailiffs.'

Jane stared at the man before her and hardly heard his next words. She looked around at the bare rooms, the cold walls and floors. There wasn't much here to confiscate.

'You're a good soul to come back for your cousins. We've a hard winter ahead of us, that's for sure.'

They had arrived at the infirmary. The Master greeted the nurse in charge and gave permission for Jane to take Sorcha and Jamie home with her.

One of the assistant nurses lifted Sorcha out of the cot. Jane's cousin wore a threadbare, long-sleeved dress that finished well above her knees. She had a stained nappy tied around her bottom. The nurse left it on and gave a woollen blanket to Jane, who held out her arms to take her cousin. Sorcha felt light and small, like a three-year-old, not a child of almost five.

'Sorcha, I've come back for you.' The child lay limp in Jane's arms.

The Master went upstairs to the schoolroom to fetch Jamie. She looked at the small boy in his workhouse uniform. Brendan's son was dressed in rags that were only fit to be burnt. She swallowed back a sob and knelt down to greet her cousin. 'I'm your mammy and daddy's cousin. My name is Jane Keating and I've come to take you home with me.' Tears overflowed her eyes and wet her cheeks. Why had she left this day so long?

Jane held her hand out to Jamie and the Master escorted them to the door. 'You need to bring back their clothes and shoes when they get others to wear.'

Then she stopped, as she remembered the bailiffs were due to come in here. This man had his own troubles. She nodded. 'I'll bring them back. Thank you for taking care of them when I couldn't.'

Jane walked past the waiting crowds with Sorcha in her arms and Jamie, at her side.

She stood on the road. They were a good quarter of a mile away from Jane's lodging house with no cab at this end of the town. She glanced down at Jamie, shivering beside her.

'Where are we going?' he asked, and turned his worried face up to Jane.

'We're going away from this place. It's not good for you or Sorcha,' she muttered. 'What have I done?' she asked herself, and grasped Jamie's small hand tightly. 'Let's get on then.'

10

Homeless

Half an hour later, at the boarding house, her landlady had taken one look at Sorcha, another at Jamie in his workhouse garb, and told Jane to get her things and leave. The landlady helpfully hailed a cab for Jane while she packed. It only took a few minutes to load her bag and the two children inside the waiting cab and jump in to join them.

While Sorcha drowsed beside her, Jamie tugged at Jane's sleeve. 'Where are we going?'

'To find somewhere nice to stay.' She looked at the boy. 'Do you remember me?' He shook his head.

She said the same as she had told Sorcha all those weeks ago. 'Your mammy and daddy want me to look after you.'

'Mammy and daddy are in heaven.'

'I know. And I'm going to look after you.' Her heart lightened as she faced up to it, and it was done; not as she had feared at all.

Their cab passed the fields at a slow trot. Jane prayed that Mrs Flynn would not take the same attitude as the lodging house landlady. If that happened then then they were surely in trouble.

The cab caught up to, and began to overtake a walker. It was Fahy. Jane shouted to the driver to stop and her friend jumped in.

He nodded to Jamie and frowned at Jane. 'I thought you were taking them to the lodging house?'

'I did. She threw me out! Said she wasn't running a hospital for sick children.' Jane hugged Sorcha close to her. 'I'm hoping Mrs Flynn will let me stay for a few days until I find us somewhere else in town.'

'Well, I have some good news for her, so she might be inclined to be generous,' Fahy said. 'After I left you, I went to the National school and asked them if they'd take the children from the presbytery. They agreed, if I can arrange some transport for them, and books and slates.'

Jamie spoke for the first time since Fahy had gotten into the cab. 'I'll go!'

Jane and Fahy looked at each other and both laughed.

'I can help with the books,' Jane said. 'And I'll have a think about transport.'

* * *

By the time they arrived at the chapel, Sorcha's body was damp with sweat. Her dark curls were plastered to her forehead, but she was awake. Jane paid the driver and stepped down into the church porch.

Sorcha wasn't a heavy child, in fact, she was just skin and bones. Jane hitched her cousin up onto her shoulder, took a deep breath, and pushed open the door.

A hush fell on the children inside as they watched Jane carry in a sleeping child, followed by Fahy and the boy.

Mrs Flynn and Father Hanrahan were watching the children. 'Dear God!' Mrs Flynn said.

'Father, Mrs Flynn. We need your help.'

* * *

In the end, Mrs Flynn had no choice. Father Hanrahan gave over the small box room to Jane for a few days. There was one bed and Jane lay Sorcha on the bed. Mrs Hanrahan said Jamie could sleep with the other boys in the vestry at the back of the church.

Jane knew that bringing a sick child back here was a risk to the other children, but she would keep Sorcha away from them, safe in this small bedroom until she was well again.

The first thing she did was strip Sorcha and wash her small body from head to toe. She used three jugs of warm water, then got another jug of water and rubbed a soapy flannel through Sorcha's dark, curling hair. Then she rinsed out the flannel and used it to take off the soap. Sorcha made no sound while Jane towel-dried and combed her hair.

Mrs Flynn cut up a soft towel and Jane used the fabric as a nappy for Sorcha. Until the diarrhoea cleared up, Jane would keep her in nappies. Jane saw she would have to get back into Galway and buy some supplies for the children. She had not thought to do this before she went to get them. Sorcha was now asleep on the bed and her fever had lessened a little.

While Jane was taking care of Sorcha, Mrs Flynn washed Jamie and dressed him in some clothes borrowed from the other boys.

Jane needed a sit down and something to eat, so she went

downstairs to the kitchen and cut a slice of bread and helped herself to a bowl of the evening soup. Jamie was already sitting at the table with Fahy. Everything she did, everything she touched or used or ate must cost money.

Another thing that also gave her pause for thought. She had been reluctant to take on Sorcha, partly because she would be somehow betraying her own daughter. But today she hadn't thought about her baby when she had held Sorcha, and washed her. Maybe, just maybe, she was healing.

* * *

The next day, Mrs Flynn agreed to keep an eye on Sorcha while Jane went back into town. Jamie had already made himself at home with the other children. She was thankful for a lift on a cart heading in the direction of the town. She walked the last mile and arrived in time to find a haberdasher's shop was open and bought new clothes for the two children. Two sets for Sorcha; cotton shifts and knickers; one navy dress and another in pale grey wool and a couple of knitted jackets. She had no idea what shoes to buy her, so settled on a pair of black leather lace-up boots with woollen socks, and hoped they would fit. Then she bought two of everything for Jamie: one black pair and one brown pair of knee breeches, cotton shirts, underwear, socks and a pair of boots . The woman in the shop asked how old Jamie was and wanted to sell her a dress for him. Jane was having none of it. That old belief that you needed to disguise young boys as girls was well gone. Sure, why would you worry about the fairies stealing a boy-child when typhus fever or hunger would do it?

Next, she called into a doctor's office and asked him to come and examine her cousin.

He came that evening and diagnosed Sorcha with dysentery, and he added, to no-one's surprise, that she was malnourished.

'Thankfully, it's not typhus. I was in the workhouse this week,' he said. 'The poor souls in there don't have enough food to eat. It's no wonder they are sick.' He gave her an emollient to put on Sorcha's sore bottom and Jane paid his bill gladly.

She washed, dried and folded the children's borrowed clothes and cleaned the shoes ready to take them back to the workhouse when she was next in town. She held the small items of clothing and felt the coarse fabric, knobbled on the inside where the dress would have rubbed against Sorcha's little neck.

Why had she left them in that place for so long? What had she been so afraid of that she risked her cousins' lives so recklessly? She knew the answer to that question. Her heart and soul were broken from the loss and pain she had endured over the last two years. Poor murdered Brendan, the children's father, and their mother, Aoife. Then her own mother and father, her brothers, Joe and Seamus. Her friend, and almost-sister, Annie Power, and just six months ago, Margaret, her still-born daughter. One more death would finish her, she was sure of that.

But she took courage from Mrs Flynn and Fahy, who helped her to nurse Sorcha.

Fahy got hold of a truckle bed and bedding and arranged for it to be delivered. They set it up later that week, next to Jane's bed, and Sorcha slept in it. As soon as she was better, Jamie would join her, as the beds in the vestry were full. Mrs Flynn tempted Sorcha with bowls of sweetened porridge and soft boiled eggs.

By the end of the month, both children were calling Mrs Flynn, Nan, like the rest of them. There were now eight children at the presbytery.

The turn of the month brought *Samhain*, the ancient festival to mark the start of winter. At the same time, the feasts of All Saints and All Souls were celebrated at the church. Jane said a quiet prayer at her father's grave. The plaque on the new headstone was filled with the names of her dead.

After the mass for All Souls was celebrated, Father Hanrahan lit the bonfire the children had built in the church garden. Mrs Flynn baked small cakes and they ate them, as they stood around the bonfire in the dark early evening and watched the flames leap into the sky. It was the welcome to winter and to the ghosts of their dead.

11

School and work, November 1847.

It was a fine and bright winter's day; the river was full and water splashed under the bridge on its way out to the bay. Jane walked up the town to The Star business premises on Saint Augustine Street.

Today was a good day, and she marvelled at how many times in the last two years she had visited or worked in newspaper offices. Her training as a typesetter at The Nation newspaper in Dublin had stood her in good stead as a pardoned convict, and she had loved her work at The Melbourne Odyssey in New South Wales. And now, here she was heading to another newspaper, The Galway Star.

This time, she needed to check up on an advertisement she had seen for a pony and cart for sale. The perfect transport to take the orphans at the presbytery to school in Galway town.

She smelt newsprint as she opened the door. There was no sound from the printing press, but she knew The Star was a weekly publication, sold on Fridays, so the presses would most likely run on the Thursday. It was a small business premises and she spoke to the woman clerk sitting at the front desk.

'Good morning. I saw an advertisement in the newspaper, a pony and cart for sale. It said to enquire here. Can you help me?'

The clerk squinted through her gold-rimmed spectacles. Jane smiled and hid her surprise, for it had been a while since she had seen anyone with fat on their bones. The young woman looked like a plump hen, a russet fringed shawl lay around her shoulders and arms and emphasised her soft curves. She replied in Irish.

'Good morning. Take a seat while I check. I think it's for Mr Lynch.' The woman pulled out a ledger and riffled through the pages, then nodded. 'Yes, Mr Fergus Lynch is selling a pony and cart. Did you want to go and look at it?'

'I do. I'm in need of some transport. Where does he live?'

'Go out the Salthill Road, a quarter of a mile past the lighthouse. You'll see the farm at the crossroads.'

'Ah, I know it. Thank you. I'll call out that way this morning.' Jane was about to leave when the woman added.

'Although, I wouldn't be surprised if you went there today and found an empty house.'

'Oh, why is that?' Jane asked.

'He may already be gone. The whole family are away to America.'

Jane understood, after hearing from the Master of the workhouse. Farmers like Mr Lynch would be the ones liable for the increased rates to pay for the upkeep of the Union workhouse. Anyone with a little money put aside would think twice before pauperising themselves and their families and ending up in that very place before too long. Many of them preferred to take their chances in America.

'I'll get along and take a look.' Jane paused as she noticed a pile of corrected proofs on the woman's desk.

The woman waited.

'Sorry, I saw the proofs on your desk and it reminded me of a job I had in a newspaper. I was a typesetter.' There was no possibility that she could mention Melbourne, so she added. 'In Dublin, at The Nation.'

The woman looked surprised. 'Oh, I didn't think women were employed in the print room.'

Jane smiled. That would surely be a tale she could tell one day.

Business must have been slow that morning, for the woman said. 'Would you like to take a look at our new printing press?'

'I'd love to see it, thank you.'

'My name is Una, I'm here for a couple of days until my father gets back from Dublin. My brother has gone back to university and Papa has taken him. I'm taking the messages and the advertisements. What's your name?'

'Jane Keating.' She followed Una along the corridor towards the back of the building. She guessed the brother might have been the clerk until he went off to University, or maybe the father?

Una opened a door into the back room. The typesetting area was set up next to the large rear window and the printing press took up most of the rest of the space.

Una held the door for Jane and called to the man at the press.

'Paddy, come and meet Jane Keating. Would you believe, she's a typesetter? She worked at The Nation in Dublin.'

The older man wiped his hands on a cloth and came over to shake hands with Jane. He had a strong grip that belied his whippet-like build and bony face.

'Good-day to you, Miss. What do you think of our little

set-up here?'

'It's a nice looking press. Steam powered?'

'To be sure. It's only five years old. What do they use in Dublin? Something very like this one?'

Jane nodded in response. 'Yes, it's a Koenig, too, but a bit a bigger.' She put her hand on the cold metal flatbed. 'This is a well kept machine. Who does your typesetting?'

'Me. I do it all, printing and typesetting. We only have the one edition a week.'

'Ah,' Jane said. 'All of it?' She knew how much work was needed for even a small print edition. The man nodded. Jane caught his eye. They both knew printing a newspaper was a two person job as a minimum. The typesetter and the printer were a team.

'We're only a small business,' Una said, then she glanced at Paddy, who nodded again. 'But if you're looking for a bit of work, then let us know.'

'No, I'm not.' Jane stopped herself. 'Well, sure, I am, I think!' She laughed. 'It's time I got some work. I've been back home for a while.'

'I'd have to talk to my father. He'll be back by the end of the week. But we've been thinking about getting a bit of help in here, haven't we, Paddy?'

'Only for the last three years, Miss Dwyer.' The printer smiled as if to take the sting out of his comment.

Jane understood. 'I didn't come here looking for a job, but if there's a few hours going, I'd love to keep my hand in with the typesetting, or even a bit of clerking at the front desk. I'm staying at Saint Vincent's Church, out past Barna Woods, until I get settled. But I have a reference from the owner of The Nation.' Jane held her hand out again to the printer. 'It's been grand to meet you, Mr . . . '

He shook her hand. 'Call me Paddy. And don't forget us!'

Una walked Jane to the door. 'I'll have a word with my father when he gets back. Do call in next week. There might well be some work here for you.'

'I surely will, and thank you, Una.'

* * *

An hour later Jane found the fork in the road, and the farmhouse right on the corner. It was a sturdy stone built house with a barn on the end of it.

Una was right. Steamer trunks and bags were stacked at the open kitchen door, although there there was no sign of any family, just the farmer, sturdy like his house, who stood and watched Jane walk up the path towards him.

'Mister Lynch?'

He nodded and tipped his felt hat to her.

'I've come about the advertisement for the pony and cart.'

'Good day to you, Miss. Well, you're just in time. Come and take a look.'

The ass, for it wasn't a pony at all, was enjoying his free time in the garden at the side of the house. His head was down and he munched away on the stubbly grass.

She went over and patted the side of the ass's neck. 'Hello, old fella.' He snorted as she interrupted his grazing, but let Jane check his teeth, and his feet. All looked to be sound. He was in good condition, his short dark hair gleamed and he had a bit of muscle on him. She rubbed his upright ears and he nodded as if he liked it.

The farmer patted the ass. 'He's a strong animal. He'll pull the cart all day long. Just keep him fed and watered. And he's no good if you beat him. He's a bit of a stubborn *divil*.'

'And the cart?' Jane pursed her lips together to stop a smile. She knew the feeling of being a stubborn *divil* when beaten.

'It's over this way.' Mr Lynch led the way back to the house and the barn. Tilled fields of rich dark earth surrounded the farmhouse and homestead. It was a fine day and the pale stone walls reflected the low winter sunlight. 'You have a lovely place here, Mr Lynch.'

The farmer nodded. 'You heard we're leaving?'

'Yes. Are you sorry to go?'

'No.' The farmer's broad face smiled. 'T'is our time to go. There's a saying in the Bible, "To everything there is a season, and a time to every purpose under the heaven." This is our time to cast away. And we're the fortunate ones, wouldn't you say?'

Jane had never heard those words before. She whispered them. 'To everything there is a season,' and stopped.

'And a time to every purpose under heaven. A time to keep and a time to cast away.' Mr Lynch finished.

'Thank you, Mister Lynch. Yes, we are the fortunate ones.' She blinked. 'Show me the cart, please.'

* * *

The wooden cart had recently been used to gather in bales of hay and was well-made in pale wood. It was old, but everything, including the shafts and the two wheels, looked sound. There was a narrow bench up front for the driver to sit on. It would do the job nicely. Fahy could fit a couple of side benches for the children.

Jane and the farmer haggled until they agreed a price. She knew the farmer had to get rid of the ass and cart. He was ready to be on his way and they soon settled on a bargain.

'There's just the one condition,' he said. 'My family are already in town, but I have some work to finish off here. Then I need to bring the bags into Galway tomorrow. I'll drop it off to you then.'

'That's fine. Tell me where to meet you and I'll pay you tomorrow.'

The farmer spat on his hand, and they shook on the deal and arranged to meet up the next day.

* * *

Jane saw Fahy later. He had good news. Because of their situation, the Headmaster at the National school had agreed the children could all start the next week, and he also said that Sorcha, who was not quite five, could start, too. 'I told him none of them could read or write, they've not been to school. The Headmaster said they'll be taught in English as it's a state school, but sure that'll be no harm to learn.' Fahy paused. 'As long as they don't forget their Irish.

'Will Sorcha be well enough to start, do you think?' he asked her.

'The diarrhea has cleared up and she's playing with the others now. I'd say she'll not want to be parted from Jamie.'

Fahy had a list of books and equipment the children would need.

'I'll buy the books and slates,' Jane said. She silently thanked her mother and father for insisting she attended school until she was twelve, where she had learned to speak English and read and write in the language.

She went to the bank and withdrew more of her money. This would cover the cost of the ass and cart and buy the schoolbooks and new clothes for the children. If there was any left over, she planned to give it to Father Hanrahan to see them through to the spring. She asked Fahy to meet her the next day to buy the books, clothes and schoolbags.

Jane remembered the promise made to Mr Gavan Duffy. She'd be careful with the rest of her money, but she still had to pay her board and lodging at the presbytery.

However, she had an idea, and for that, she needed to write a letter. She headed to the Post Office in the town and bought some writing paper and an envelope. She stood at a desk in the centre of the Post Office and took a deep breath, then began to write a letter to her friends in New York.

```
Dear Finn, Katty and Mrs Foley.
I hope my letter finds you well. I am sending my
love to you all, and, of course, my sincere
condolences. I miss Annie.
```

She paused to dip her pen and watched as the black ink ran down the metal nib and dropped back into the inkwell. Better just say it.

```
Since I returned to Ireland, I've been helping the
priest in my old parish, a few miles outside Galway
town. He and his housekeeper have taken on six
orphans who lost their parents in this terrible
time. Nothing much has changed since I left in '46.
If anything there is more hunger and disease. More
and more people are leaving this blighted land.
```

When we met at the beginning of August, I remembered
you told me that the Aid for Ireland Committee had
sent money to Mr Gavan Duffy to help with the
distress over here.

You may begin to guess the reason for my letter.
From what I have seen, there is still no work
anywhere, either in Galway town or on the farms
around. The whole place has come to a standstill.
Hundreds, if not thousands, are destitute and living
by the side of the road. I've heard it is the same
all over the west and the south. I have no idea how
many have died, but there is Typhus fever in the
workhouse now.

I have some money and I've already spent a good bit
of it. I gave some to Father Hanrahan to help him
with the orphans. Now I have the care of my two
cousins and must keep what I have to look after them
and myself.

I am writing to ask you to help Father Hanrahan. As
you can imagine, six children are not cheap to feed
and clothe. There are hardly any parishioners left
here, and those who are, have no money to put in the
collection plate. The problem is that I truly don't
know how long this situation will go on for. Father
Hanrahan is adamant the children won't go into the
workhouse. It is full of disease.

A thought occurred to her. What if these children had family
somewhere? She added another sentence to the letter.

I will try to find out if the children have any
family in Galway town who could take them in. But in

the meantime, they will stay at the presbytery.

If Annie had been alive, she would have sent money. Might have even brought it herself. Jane did not really know what Finn's situation was or their aunt Bridie's, but she had to try.

If you can help, with even a small amount, then send it to me in care of the Post Office in Galway. I will understand if you cannot help us, as life is hard for everyone, but these children are a special case.
I will ask Father Hanrahan to say a mass for you and anyone who donates money to help. Please keep us in your prayers.
Yours truly
Jane Keating

There, it was done. She folded the page and wrapped it in the envelope, then stood in line to pay the postage. 'How long will it take to get to New York?'

'Four weeks depending on the weather,' came the reply.

They'd have the letter by Christmas. In the meantime, please God, Jane would get that job and start earning some money. The last gold nugget she possessed was sewn into the waistband of her old skirt and was safe, for now.

* * *

Fahy cleaned up the cart and put in two side benches. He had

117

the job done in a single afternoon and was ready to start taking the children to school on the second Monday in November.

Early that Monday morning, the eight children stood in a row on the altar steps, dressed in their new school clothes and boots, and waited to be blessed by the priest.

Father Hanrahan touched each child on the forehead and sketched the sign of the cross. 'May the Lord bless you and keep you safe, my children.'

And they were off. Fahy and Jane walked beside the cart and took it in turns to lead the ass. They listened as the children chatted all the way in the road.

Fahy squinted at the clear sky; there were just a few clouds in the distance. 'I'll keep a look out for some oiled gabardine to make a cover for the cart. It won't be this fine every day, would you say?'

Jane smiled. 'We're in luck today. And we both need a gabardine cloak if we're to walk this twice a day, too.' She put her hand on the asses neck and patted him. 'He's the only one the weather doesn't bother, aren't you?'

The Headmaster met them at the school gate and congratulated Fahy and Jane on the well-turned out children.

Jane went off to The Star to enquire about an advertisement for the children's relatives. Fahy took the cart and joined the Quaker ladies to make the soup.

* * *

At the Galway Star, Jane wrote up the advertisement. She was in two minds as to whether she really wanted to find family for the three sets of children. They seemed so settled and happy with Father Hanrahan and Mrs Flynn. 'It's for the best. They

118

should be with family.'

```
Search for families.
Six orphan children are being cared for by the
Reverend Father Hanrahan and his housekeeper, Mrs
Flynn, at Saint Vincent's Church near Barna, County
Galway.
They are:
Billy O'Reilly, aged 11. Parents: the late Pat and
Elizabeth O'Reilly.
The Clearys. Shay, aged 11. Liam, aged 10. Maria,
aged 7. Parents: the late Seamus and Ethna Cleary.
The Kennedys. Lucy and Grace, twins, aged 7.
Daughters of the late Tomas and Grainne Kennedy.

The children are all from around the Barna area.
Their parents and other siblings died last winter.

If you know anyone who is related to these children,
then please get in touch with Father Hanrahan at the
Presbytery so they can be reunited with family
members.
```

There, it was done, and it was the right thing to do.

'How much will it be to keep the advertisement in until Christmas?' she asked.

'I'll put it through at half price,' Una said. 'I hope you get a few answers, but there's been a great scattering of people away from here.'

Una took the piece of paper from Jane and worked out the cost per word. 'There, that's done. At half price, that'll be seven shillings and sixpence.'

Jane paid the asking price. It was a bargain and she knew it. Yet her money was being eaten up.

'I spoke to my father, Jane. He said I can employ you to help me here on the front desk. I don't want to be tied here every day. I can offer you two days a week. What do you say?' Una looked very pleased with herself.

'Well, thank you, but I said I want to do some typesetting, too. Do you remember?'

'Sorry, I forgot to say. There's one day a week there, too, on Thursdays. Paddy rolls the press on Thursday night and the newspaper is out on Friday morning. The two jobs can go together. What do you say?'

'Thank you very much! What's the pay?'

'Not a lot, unfortunately. The newspaper barely pays for itself. But it'll help towards the upkeep of those children, that's for sure.'

They discussed the money. Jane agreed to start the next day. She'd work Tuesdays and Wednesdays in the front office and in the press room on Thursdays .

She'd walk in the road, with the children on the cart, each morning, and finish when they finished school. That way she could be around for Sorcha and Jamie at the end of each day. She made her mind up to look for somewhere to live in town. The presbytery was full to the brim.

12

Gifts for the children, Christmas 1847

The weeks flew by into December and it would soon be Christmas. Jane had spent the last couple of months living at the church. She had made no progress with finding a place to live in Galway, and the presbytery was overflowing with children and adults. Fahy slept in the outhouse, but the nights were now getting frosty and Jane worried that he'd need the spare room that she was camped in with Sorcha and Jamie. Both children seemed to have forgotten all about their time in the workhouse.

She knew that she must think about moving out, but she needed the companionship of Mrs Flynn and Father Hanrahan and the children. Above all, Sorcha and Jamie thrived in this environment. They loved going to school and had made friends with the other orphans. This week the school would shut until the New Year.

One day Jane walked the road into Galway town. The market place was busy for a change. She tried a few shops; a haberdasher's and a pawn shop, on the lookout for something to give as a gift to Sorcha and Jamie, but none of them seemed to have much in the way of children's toys. She recalled the doll that a child had taken from Sorcha in the workhouse. Yes, a doll for Sorcha. Then something for Jamie. She walked around the town and saw nothing suitable, and had no idea what a boy might like. She remembered seeing the boys playing with a *sliotar* and hurley, as her own brothers had. But they had plenty of those already.

Eventually she reached the market place. There were food stalls and a couple of second-hand clothes stalls. At the edge of the market, a small, raggedy old fellow had a table piled high with stuff. Jane barely gave it a glance; it all looked like rubbish. The old man called to her in a high.cracked voice. 'What are you looking for, Miss?'

Jane sighed and shook her head. 'I'm looking for a doll.' She kept walking. And heard the wizened little man, call her. 'Miss! Miss! Come back!'

She looked over her shoulder, to see him holding up a floppy rag doll, with ginger, plaited hair and wearing a yellow checked dress.

She laughed. 'Where did you get that from?' She went back and took the doll from him. It was about twelve inches tall, and stuffed with horsehair from the feel of it. The doll's dress was grubby, but it opened at the back and Jane saw that she could take it off and wash it, and the doll's knickers for that matter. It would make a nice gift when it was cleaned up.

'I have all sorts here, Miss. And what I haven't got, then I'll find it.' He wore fingerless gloves and the ends of his fingers and his nails were filthy. He was missing quite a few of his teeth and had a small clay pipe stuck in the corner of his mouth. He took a puff on the tiny pipe and blew out white smoke.

'Well, tell me now,' she said. 'I'm looking for something for a small boy to play with. Would you have anything?'

'I have the very thing! Wait there,' he said, and bent to rummage in the back of his stall.

What else was he going to say? He has a customer in front of him and he'd sell anything. Still, she waited, and held the doll. It was a soft little thing, about the size her own baby had been. It fitted nicely into her hand. She closed her eyes and pressed the doll's body close to her chest. Heat surged through her and she bent over the doll and put one hand out to lean on the edge of the stall. *'Acushla!'* she whispered to the ghost of her still-born child.

She shook her head to clear out the thought and took a step away from the stall to wipe sudden tears from her eyes.

'Hold on there, don't go off with that doll.' The old fellow came around the front of the stall with another, similar, doll in his hand. 'Here's another one. And I have a train set in the box here.'

The second doll looked as if it had been chewed by a dog, its clothes were filthy and torn and its hair hung off in strings. Jane handed it back to him with a wry look.

The box held a miniature steam engine and some wooden, open topped carriages. Iron rails were jumbled in the bottom of the box. All the same, it looked as if it could be salvaged.

Trains were still a novelty for Jane, and most people in the west of Ireland, as train lines had not yet reached the west coast. She looked at the old fellow.

'I'll take this and the doll. How much do you want for them?'

'Five shillings,' he said, with a bold look on his face.

Jane laughed. 'Five shillings! One shilling would be a good price. How about that?'

'Now then, Miss. I'm only a poor peddler, sure what would

I know about how much a lovely dolly and a train set like that would fetch? I tell you what, you can have them both for three shillings and sixpence.'

Ah, so that was his game. 'And I'll tell you what,' said Jane, who loved to haggle. 'I'll buy the dolls and take the broken train off your hands.' She picked up the engine to show him the crack in the chimney. 'I'll give you two shillings for the lot and not a penny more. Because I don't have a penny more.'

He took his glove off and spat on his hand, then held it out for her to shake on the deal. 'You have me there, Miss. Take them, take them, and take the broken doll, too. Pay me two shillings and thruppence, and we have a deal.'

Jane gritted her teeth, and shook his hand, thankful she had her gloves on. It was agreed. She opened her purse, made sure he didn't see the sovereigns, and took out two silver shillings, then rooted in her skirt pocket for a thruppeny piece and dropped the coins onto his outstretched hand.

She put the two dolls in the wooden box, pushed the lid down and held her hand out to shake again. 'Thank you. I know where to come if I need any more toys.'

The old man waved her off. He seemed to enjoy the haggle and he had money in his hand. Not a bad morning's work.

The ragged doll gave her an idea. Jane had never owned one, but remembered Sorcha cuddling the little doll in the workhouse. It occurred to her that she needed to get a gift for the other girls, if she was intending to give Sorcha a Christmas gift.

She went back to the haberdasher's shop she had tried on the way up the town. She pulled the ginger haired doll out of the box and put it on the counter. 'Can you sell me the makings of three more like this, please?'

The woman behind the counter brought over a basket of fabric remnants. 'I have just the thing you need here. You'll find some pieces to make the dolls' bodies and the dresses and knickers.'

The woman helped Jane pick out some fabric and then sold her a couple of sewing needles and threads to stitch up the dolls' bodies. 'And you'll need some stuffing. And some embroidery threads for the eyes and the mouth.' The woman smiled at Jane. 'There's yarn here for the hair. Have you done this before?'

'No,' Jane laughed. 'I think I'm going to need a bit of help. But I know just the woman.'

She walked the road out of town back to the chapel, with her purchases wrapped up in a brown paper parcel under one arm, and the box with the train set and dolls under the other arm.

A good morning's work. Now she only had to persuade Mrs Flynn to turn her hand to doll making, and Fahy to repair the train set. The boys could share it.

* * *

It took the best part of ten days to get the dolls made, working in secret when the children were in bed. One each for Lucy, Grace and Maria. Jane had to turn her hand to sewing, a thing she had never done, but she was a fast learner.

Jane had washed the first doll and its yellow dress then re-dressed it for Sorcha. Mrs Flynn was in the kitchen, putting the finishing touches to the new dolls. They each had a different coloured gingham dress, their bodies were soft, with lengths of coloured wool for hair. One had two long black plaits, another had a ponytail, the third had yellow pigtails.

'Ah, Mrs Flynn. They are just lovely!'

'I just need to stitch their eyes and mouths in place, then they'll be ready.' Mrs Flynn put the dolls down. 'This was a good idea, Jane. The girls will love their dollies. They need something to cuddle.'

Fahy announced that the train set was mended. He had taken the engine into town to the blacksmith's and brought it back as good as new with a spot of solder on it.

* * *

Then it was the week before Christmas. One night Jane had just tucked Sorcha and Jamie into bed. Sorcha, sleepy after the day, asked the same question she asked almost every night. 'Are you our mammy now, Jane?'

'No, I'm your cousin.'

'Have we got a mammy?'

'Yes, *acushla.* Your mammy had to go to heaven.'

'So, will you be my mammy now? Don't I need a mammy?'

Jamie sat up in the bed. 'No! We already have a mammy and a daddy. Father Hanrahan says they are in heaven.'

'Darlings, you have me and Nan and Father Hanrahan to look after you, and uncle Fahy.' Jane felt as if the children were walking her into a corner. Sorcha needed a mother, while Jamie remembered his mother and didn't want a replacement.

What was Jane going to do about it? She shook her head. These children were her last blood relatives.

'Come here and give me a hug.'

The child wrapped her arms around Jane's neck and hugged tightly. Sorcha's body, light and narrow, pressed against Jane's breasts. She rested her cheek on Sorcha's dark curls and closed her eyes, then put an arm around Jamie. 'Shush now. It's time to sleep.' I'll never forget you, Margaret, she vowed silently.

Jane had not been able to save her own child, and she would try her best to save her two cousins. But her heart still ached for all she had lost.

She rested against the bedstead and held the children. They sat together, the warmth from Sorcha and Jamie's bodies, the light weight of them, their slow breaths as they dozed, all helped to calm Jane's own breathing and she closed her eyes. The words of Mr Lynch, the farmer, flitted through her mind. 'And a time to every purpose under heaven.'

* * *

A noise woke her. Mrs Flynn tapped on the door and pushed it open.

'Jane, I'm sorry to wake you, but I'm worried about Father. Will you come and take a look at him?'

'What is it? Is he sick?'

'He has a fever. Come and see for yourself. But he won't lie down. He says the children need him.' Mrs Flynn twisted the end of her apron and her hands shook. They both knew that the fever could be deadly.

Jane moved carefully and tucked both children in under the blankets.

She went downstairs and crossed over to the chapel, now turned into a play-room for the orphans, when Father Hanrahan didn't need to say mass. Fahy had set up a small stove by the wall and kept it going with a bucket of turf to keep some heat in the place.

The priest sat in his chair beside the altar and watched Billy, Shay and Liam at their homework. The younger girls, Maria, Lucy and Grace, were already in bed.

Father Hanrahan mopped shining beads of sweat from his brow with a crumpled white handkerchief then tucked it into a pocket in his cassock.

Jane knelt in front of him. 'Father, Mrs Flynn tells me you are not well.'

'I think I have a little fever, but it will pass. Don't you worry about me, Jane.'

'Will I get the doctor to come and see you?'

'You'll do no such thing. You can get me a cup of water, that would be very nice.'

'I'll get it now. Then I'll give Mrs Flynn a hand with the supper.'

The priest refused all offers of a doctor that day and into the next. He sat stubbornly in the chair, wrapped in a blanket, said his prayers and read his breviary, got the children to sit around him while he read them stories from the gospels. He ate nothing, just sipped tea and water. He left the chair only to use the privy at the back of the presbytery. When the children were all in bed, he went to his own bed.

By the Friday, his fever had eased. Mrs Flynn thought the Lord had worked a miracle, thanks to all the prayers said that week.

* * *

Christmas was a time of peace for them all. The mass on Christmas morning was sparsely attended, for there weren't many people left in this part of the county. There were no other children apart from the orphans.

Jane had last attended mass in Melbourne, back in April. She had been pregnant and in labour, and had come to understand that the church would not baptise the child of an unwed mother. She refused to utter the name bestowed on such a child.

This mass was different. Father Hanrahan would have welcomed Margaret, of that Jane was sure, but she still didn't receive Holy Communion. Instead, she prayed for the repose of the souls of all her dead and remained in her place when the bell rang for the Eucharist.

The children spent most of the day playing with the gifts Jane had bought and made. Jamie and the older boys invented jobs for each of them to manage the train and the tracks. At one point, the dolls sat on the coaches as the train took them off around the tracks laid along the aisle of the church. She sat and watched as they played together, all focused on the new toys.

There had been no response at all to the expensive advertisement she had placed to search for relatives of these children. What would become of them? Please God, these hard times would soon pass. But if anything were to happen to Father Hanrahan, or to Mrs Flynn. She flicked a glance at Fahy, who was watching the children play, then went to the presbytery kitchen to help Mrs Flynn with the supper.

13

Work and family, January 1848

I t was early January and Jane was working her three days at the newspaper. Business was usually slow at this time of year, so Una told her. But there were still advertisements to be sold and the newspaper to print.

A cast iron stove stood in the corner of the office and Jane kept it alight with blocks of turf stored in a basket beside it. The warm smoky scent of the turf filled the room. At some point, later that morning, she would need to open a window to let some air in, but she wanted to keep the heat in for a while longer. Besides, she was well used to breathing in peaty air.

She spent some of the morning reading past editions of the newspaper, covering the year she had spent in New South Wales. The workhouse situation in Galway had deteriorated. It had filled up quickly last winter when 1846 turned to 1847. Then they had suffered another bout of the typhus fever that had killed Aoife in April '46. The archive was full of grim news.

After a while, she put the old newspapers back in the cupboard. They made for depressing reading and she had seen nothing to make her think that times were improving, either.

However, Thursday was her favourite day of the week, when she worked at the typesetting table in the print room. She liked to test herself by reading the mirror-set type. That morning, however, she read about an eviction that took place on Christmas Eve. She shook her head, because it resembled that of her cousin, Brendan, two years previously.

This eviction differed only because it wasn't just the one family, it was a whole village to the north of the town. The tenants were told to take themselves off to the Union workhouse in Galway. There was no mention of the name of the people who carried out the eviction, but she read that the leader was a police constable who had help from army troops to do the deed. If it was Smullen, then he was still at his dirty work. But he had told Jane at that meeting in October that he had left the police. It couldn't have been him, unless he had been lying to them.

She shivered at the thought of cold nights on the road with no shelter.

'Paddy, do you know any more about these evictions?' she asked the pressman.

He nodded. 'They all came into town on Christmas Day, from a village up near Lough Corrib.'

'That's a fair walk in this weather.'

'It is to be sure. There were over a hundred of them turned up at the workhouse gates. And they sat there for three days until the authorities found somewhere for them to get in out of the weather. The workhouse is not accepting any more homeless people, for some reason.' Paddy shook his head. 'The poor *crathurs*.'

'There's no end to this, is there?'

'Not as far as I can see,' Paddy replied. 'The government have washed their hands of it all. They want the landlords and businesses to pay for this disaster. Sure, some of the landlords, only a few mind you, are doing their best by their own tenants, but they can't take on any more tenants or they'll all go down.'

'Mr Lynch, the farmer I bought the ass and cart from, the one who left for America, quoted something from the Bible. "To everything there is a season. And a time to every purpose under heaven." Is there a purpose to all this, Paddy?'

'There may be, but I don't think the good Lord has much to do with it, as much as their Lordships in government like to say it is Divine Providence.'

'No, you're right, and I think Mr Lynch meant it was his time to go.'

'True enough.' Paddy studied Jane. 'You were away for a good while. Where did you get to?'

'I worked in Dublin, at The Nation. You know that.' She made no mention of Melbourne.

'Then what brought you back here? And why do you stay?'

'I wanted to find my family.' Jane turned away. It was a reasonable question. She had found her cousins, and now there was truly nothing to keep her here. So why did she stay? She sighed, and a weight seemed to lift off her shoulders. If she left, she could maybe bring the two children with her. However, she really had no answer to Paddy's last question; why did she stay?

'I'd better finish this, Paddy.'

His questions had opened a gap in her thinking. In a way, she was free now, and maybe would soon be free of the past, too. But then where would she go?

132

* * *

Later, when the work was finished and she was getting ready to leave, she asked Paddy.

'Have you heard of the Irish Confederation?'

'I have indeed. Them young fellas want to raise the country and fight for independence, or some such nonsense.'

'Would you join them?'

'I'll do anything that doesn't get me arrested, Jane, but that sounds a bit political to me. And that Constable Smullen will be all over anyone who joins.' Again, the mention of Smullen. His name gave her pause to think. He was still out there. She pulled on her cloak against the chilly air outside and walked up the town to the National School. She was early and waited at the gate for the children to be let out. Fahy would be along shortly and they'd go off home together.

Mothers and fathers waited alongside her. What was their situation, she wondered. They had managed to keep their children in school through these last hard years. Yet they all had a look of aged poverty about them. They were mothers of indeterminate age, and covered in their shawls against the sharp breeze; many of them went barefoot. How long could people go on like this, living lives of deprivation? She swallowed hard, for in the case of her own family, she had the answer. Not long at all. They had all died prematurely from hunger or violence or disease.

She turned and glanced along the road. There came Fahy, urging the ass along, to be at the school on time to meet the children out. She waved to him and tried to push thoughts of death out of her mind.

At the same moment, the door to the schoolhouse opened

and a stream of children flowed out towards the gate.

Jamie raced over to Fahy and jumped up on the driver's seat next to him. He dropped his schoolbag in the well of the cart and reached down to give Sorcha a hand up. They both looked across at Jane and waved. Lucy, Grace and Maria hopped up into the cart, followed by the three older boys. They were ready to get off home.

Jane looked at the eight orphans in the back of the cart. Today had given her something to think about. Her future. Where would she live and, more importantly, how did she want to live? But what of all these children, what would become of them? They have Father and Mrs Flynn to look after them, and Fahy. She consoled herself with that thought.

14

Meets up with Owen, January 1848

Later that same week, Jane collected a letter from the post office.

'It's from Owen. He's back in Ireland.' She read the letter aloud to the priest and Nan.

Dearest Jane, I have come home at long last. I got
your address from Mr Duffy at The Nation earlier
today and I hope this letter arrives safely.
I'm on leave for five days. I'm on my way to Wicklow
to see my family, then I'll come to you in Galway. I
can only stay a day or two before I join my regiment
in Clonmel.
I expect to be in Galway on the 8th or the 9th of
January and I'll call straight out to Saint
Vincent's church. I hope you are well and I look
forward to the day we can meet up again.
Your loving friend, Owen Doran.

Jane didn't read out the last line but she saw Mrs Flynn squinting at the letter.

'Sure, that's great news,' Mrs Flynn said. 'And is Owen your intended?'

'He was a good friend to me when I needed one. But he's not my intended, no.' She was fairly sure that he might be, one day, and she smiled to herself.

* * *

The next day, Jane waited for Owen to come. She paced up and down the path outside the church. It was almost nine months since she had last seen him at the dock on Phillip Island, in New South Wales. He'd held her hand as she stepped down into the small fishing boat and headed for the whaling ship that would take her to freedom. Meanwhile, Owen had stayed on the quayside and watched her leave. A serving soldier, he had no option but to stay. If he deserted from the army, he'd be caught and executed by a firing squad. The letter was the first time she had heard from him since that day.

* * *

Then, in the evening, he was there, standing in front of her. He was thinner, darker in the face and his sideburns curled down to his jawline, making him appear older than his twenty-three years. He took his army cap off.

'Can I kiss you, Jane?'

She held her arms out to him. 'Yes!'

Their kiss was sweeter than she remembered, his lips softer.

Both looked into the other's eyes. Jane blinked and kissed him again. She gazed at him for a few more moments.

'You're beautiful, Jane,' he said.

'Not with this nose!' She laughed, and pinched the bend in her nose. She was almost as tall as Owen, her eyes framed by dark, straight brows and long lashes. She had put her hair up in a bun and knew she looked her best in her straight skirt and fitted jacket.

'Come with me and meet everyone. Father Hanrahan, and Mrs Flynn, his housekeeper, and Fahy, my old neighbour. Oh, and the children.'

'What children?'

They heard voices from inside the chapel and walked in together. Jane saw Father Hanrahan waiting for them on the altar. One day, maybe, she smiled.

The children took to Owen straight away. He had a sense of humour and they liked that, even though he didn't speak much Irish. It gave them an opportunity to practice their English.

Owen and Jane sat together while the children ate their supper, then they all knelt with the priest to say the rosary. Owen just managed to keep up with the Galway-Irish prayer. Afterwards, Mrs Flynn and Jane took the children to the sacristy to get ready for bed.

When they were settled, it was time for the adults to eat. The women dished up a vegetable soup and a plate of bread and butter for the five of them. Father Hanrahan said Grace, and they began to eat.

'Tell us how you ended up in New South Wales, Owen,' the priest said.

Owen looked at Jane. 'Do they know?'

She nodded. 'Yes,' then paused. 'About the transportation.' She held her breath pressed her lips together until she saw understanding in his eyes. He wouldn't mention her attacker or Margaret.

137

'I was serving in Dublin and assigned to accompany a group of women convicts to New South Wales. I met Jane on board the ship. When the ship was damaged in a storm off the Cape of Good Hope we all transferred to The Maitland and ended up in Melbourne. And nearly a year later, for my sins, I helped Jane escape!' He laughed. 'They didn't know we were friends, so no-one came near me.'

'And are you glad to be home?'

'Well, I think so,' Owen put his spoon down and sighed. 'It's good to see my family and they are all well, thank God. My mother and father and brothers and sisters live just outside Wicklow town. But I see a lot of hunger everywhere. People on the roads, displaced. I read about it in the newspapers in Melbourne, but until you see it, all these poor people.'

Jane sat opposite Owen and studied his face. He glanced at her and half-smiled. He leaned forward to dip a piece of bread in the soup. She remembered how he had lain back in her arms when she taught him to swim in Port Phillip Bay. He was strong and wiry in build. She soon found out he swam very well; he just wanted an excuse for her to hold him. The thought made her smile and she felt a hot blush reach up her neck into her face.

At the end of the meal, Owen stood up. 'I'd better be getting back. If I'm late, I'll be locked out of the inn. Mrs Flynn and Father, thank you for your hospitality. Fahy, I hope we meet again.' They shook hands.

'I'll walk with you in the road a way,' Jane said, and pulled her cloak around her.

They left Fahy helping Mrs Flynn to clear away the plates while Father went off to say his breviary.

* * *

Jane and Owen linked arms and walked along the lane towards the road. Across the fields she saw the outline of Barna Woods in the distance, lit up by the moonlight. The sky was filled with a sweep of glittering stars. To Jane, it felt as if they had never been parted, and they walked in step with each other.

'Do you remember when we were anchored off Cape Town?' Jane asked him.

'When you tried to jump off the ship and swim away?'

'No, not that,' she laughed. 'The sky, the diamonds.'

'Ah, I do. I said the British were there because of the African diamond mines. Is that what you're thinking?'

'Mm. I think that's when I knew.'

'Knew what, Jane?'

She heard the smile in his voice. 'That you're a good man. And that one day I'd love you.'

He stopped and turned to her in the glimmering night air. 'And has that day come?'

'Yes. It has, Owen.' She leaned forward and kissed him. 'I've missed you.'

They kissed again and she knew for sure. She'd found her love. He knew all of her secrets, was the only one in the world who knew everything about her. They sat together under an oak tree. It was cold on the ground, but her cloak kept them warm. He was careful with her for he knew she had suffered and that she must still suffer, from the rape and the loss of her baby.

Jane entrusted her body and soul to him. He was as gentle with her as she remembered he had been in Melbourne. She called out his name, and he kissed her tears. His own tears fell on her face. It seemed to Jane that they slept together for a while, wrapped in her cloak, in the shelter of the oak tree.

* * *

The cold night air on her face woke her. '*A ghrá, love,*' she whispered. He was still asleep and she kissed his eyelids. 'Wake up. It's late. You'll be locked out!'

He woke and stood up. 'Then I'll come back for you. We can do this all over again.'

'Go. Come back tomorrow. I have something to tell you.'

Owen held his hand out to her, then he pulled her into his embrace. He picked his hat up and put it on. 'You go home. I'll go on from here.'

'Kiss me again,' she said.

He knelt before her and kissed her hands and pressed his face into her belly. Then he stood and kissed her mouth. 'Tomorrow.'

She watched as he walked off to the end of the lane and turned onto the road towards the town. That night, in her dreams, the two of them walked down the aisle of Saint Vincent's church together, and Father Hanrahan married them. It would be a time to rejoice.

* * *

The next day, she met Owen in Galway and walked with him to the coach station to say goodbye. They were early and waited while the horses were hitched to the heavy post coach.

'I told Mr Duffy and Tom Meagher that I'd try to speak to the Old Irelanders, at the Repeal Association here in town.

Fahy came with me, but they weren't interested. They all want to stay on the right side of the government.'

'You might be talking to the wrong person here, Jane. Look at my uniform. I'm just one of thousands of soldiers who've been brought back to Ireland in the event of a rebellion.'

She studied his red coat and black trousers. The feather trembled in the shako he wore.

'If there is a rebellion, whose side will you be on?'

'I've not thought about it much. But I've seen some sights since I got home, I can tell you.' Owen shook his head. 'Maybe it's time I did think about it, *mo ghrá,* my love.'

The coach driver hoisted himself onto the driver's seat. It was time to go. Owen threw his pack up onto the roof of the coach and climbed into the carriage. He reached down to catch her hand. 'I'll be on leave again in March. I'll come to Galway. Will you write to me?'

'With all my heart,' she said.

15

Money from America and Soup Kitchen, February 1848

I t was early February, and Jane had to work late at the newspaper. Fahy would pick the children up from school and take them out to the church. She would meet them there.

When she had finished her typesetting, she had just enough time to call into the Post Office and check for mail from America. It had been months since she had written to Finn Power in New York. She had almost given up hope of a reply. Still nothing. Maybe the letter had gone astray.

She walked out the road to the church. She'd write just once more. She needed some help if her plan was to work. No use heading out with empty pockets. She had some money left in the bank. That would get her started, but if Finn sent money she could use that, too. Her boots crunched on the stony road. The winter evening was beginning to stretch and the moon overhead cast an icy, silver gloss on the bare branches above her head.

She'd have to speak to Sorcha and Jamie about her plan.

There was no possibility she could bring the children with her to the northwest of Ireland. She planned to head off up around the west coast and maybe get out to some of the islands, to see how they were faring. She'd go to Westport and Sligo, and further north into Donegal, until the money ran out. She knew she couldn't feed everyone she met, but now was the time to do what she could. It was bad here in Galway, and she knew it could only be worse in the more remote areas of the country. Her friend, Annie Power, had set up a refuge for young women immigrants in New York. Recently, she'd read about an American woman, Mrs Asenath Nicholson, who had toured the country giving help wherever she went. If Annie Power and Mrs Nicholson could do good works, then so could Jane Keating. She sighed and shook her head. Jamie and Sorcha might not want her to go. What then?

At times, while walking along the road towards her old home, she felt as if she were a child again, going home to her mother and father. Then, for a few moments, her heart was light, until she remembered. The chilly air filled her lungs and she stretched her legs and strode on. It was getting late. A blackbird sang and its feathers gleamed against the glittering white frost on the hedgerow. It was a fine evening, but it would freeze hard again later.

The chapel was in darkness when she reached it, so she went straight to the presbytery. She was hungry after working all day, and hoped there'd be a bowl of something in the pot, keeping warm.

The kitchen was at the back of the priest's house, and the front door unlocked, so she walked straight through. Her heart lightened at the sound of voices. These people, the priest and his housekeeper, had stepped into the role of her beloved parents. Two years ago, Mrs Flynn had trimmed fourteen-year-old Jane's hair so she could travel safely as a boy on the road to Waterford, and had packed her up a bag of food. The priest had shown Jane the way on his ancient book of maps, then blessed her for the journey.

She gave a light knock on the kitchen door. Mrs Flynn, Father Hanrahan and Fahy were sitting by the fire, as if waiting for her to come home.

'We'd almost given up on you, girl. The children are all in bed. Come in and get a heat by the fire.' Mrs Flynn stood and indicated to her chair, at the same time she picked up the teapot and began to pour a cup for Jane. Fahy pulled up another chair for the housekeeper.

Jane took off her cloak and hung it on the back of the door, and went to sit down. She saw an unopened letter on the table. Was it the one she had been waiting for?

'Is that for me?'

'It is,' Father Hanrahan said. 'I was in town earlier and thought I'd save you the trouble.'

'Well, had you better open it?' Fahy asked.

Jane laughed and read the post mark. 'It's from New York. Please God, there's money in it!'

There was a letter, two sheets of paper folded tightly into the envelope. No dollars, though. Jane sighed and took out the pages and began to read.

'Yes, it's from Finn!'

```
Dear Jane,
We were so pleased to get your letter and to know
```

144

that you are well and have found your cousins. We
are well here, too. Kattie is grand. She sends her
love. She is working hard at school. The girl is a
scholar, like Annie was, God rest her.
Bridie sends her best regards, and she put ten
dollars into the pot of money I collected. I spent
two weeks after your letter arrived going around
churches in Manhattan with my begging cap out. And I
collected fifty-four dollars.

Jane paused and looked at her friends. Mrs Flynn clapped her
hands. 'Well, that's some job for a young fella to have done.
Good man!'

The priest nodded. 'I'll second that! What do you say, Jane?'

'My prayers have been answered.' She swallowed back tears.
'I think I need a sip of that tea.' She took a big swallow of the
tea. 'That's better.'

She smoothed her hair back and began to read again.

'I've enclosed a banker's draft in the envelope. You
can change it in any bank. One thing I would ask is
that you write to me saying what you spent the money
on. Then I can go back to the churches and tell
them. That way I might get more donations.
I'm only sorry I can't make the journey to Ireland.
I think when I'm older, I'll come back for a visit,
but for now, I need to look after Kattie. You know
we've both taken Annie's death very hard, although
aunt Bridie is very kind to us.
My food stall is doing well. I sell bread and cheese
or cooked ham, and tea or milk for a drink. Colleen,
from Annie's Refuge, helps me when it gets really
busy.

```
That's all my news.There's still no end to the
crowds of people coming into New York from Ireland.
They're better off here, even if life is hard.
Write and tell me you got the money, dear Jane.
Love to you from me and Kattie and aunt Bridie.
Your friend
Finn Power
```

She unfolded the second page of the letter. It was a bank draft. 'Sixty-four dollars. I'll change it tomorrow in the bank. There's generosity, and from strangers!' Maybe now she could put her plan into action. She looked down at the piece of paper, then glanced at Fahy.

The priest stood to take his leave of them. 'They are our brothers and sisters in Christ and our prayers have been answered. The children will see you in the morning, Jane. I'll say goodnight to you all.' He sketched a blessing. 'God bless. I'll say a mass for Finn and his family tomorrow.'

Mrs Flynn started to bank the fire down for the night. 'I'll get away to bed, too. Good night, Father. Good night, Jane and Fahy.'

* * *

The two of them, Jane and her old friend, sat up late beside the still warm fire.

'I've been thinking about a plan, Fahy.' She twisted her fingers together and looked away from her friend. 'I read about an American woman in the newspaper,' she said. 'Her name is Mrs Nicholson. She has spent the last year travelling around Ireland, giving away alms and money wherever she goes.' Jane took a deep breath and said it. 'I want to do the same. I want to travel up around the coast to see what end of them up there in the north-west counties. I've got this money from Finn I want to use it to help.'

Fahy frowned and stood up. He walked away from the fire then came and sat down again. 'I'd say you know what end of them up there, Jane. There's famine and there's fever, dysentery being one of them and typhus another. Then there's death, and it's everywhere. Sure we have it all here in Galway, is that not so?'

Jane nodded. She saw that he was not happy about her plan.

'And this Mrs Nicholson. Is she an older woman?'

'Yes. Why do you ask?'

'She's a stranger, you said she's an American and an older woman. Sure, no-one would rob her. Now you, on the other hand, you're still a slip of a girl, going off with a bag of money. Anyone would rob you, Jane. Why put yourself at risk on the road in these times? In fact, why not spend the money closer to home?'

She looked at her friend. 'Nothing is changing. I want to help people.' Surely he must understand that.

'I know you do, girl. And you can, but think about what I've said, before you pack up and head out. And what'll you tell Jamie and Sorcha?'

That was the real problem, she saw that. Fahy reached across the table and tapped the back of her hand. 'The younger Mrs Smith runs the soup kitchen with her mother-in-law. Well, by the looks of her she will be due a baby soon. Not that I'm an expert, mind you.' He sat back and smiled. 'Here's a suggestion. Why don't you offer to take over the soup kitchen? Them two women are at the end of their tether with it.' He stood again and stretched. 'You must be tired. Get yourself off to bed. But think on what I've said. Good night, Jane.'

'Good night, Fahy.'

She didn't sleep much that night for thinking about what to do with the money. Fahy's wise counsel made her think twice about going on the road. There were hungry people in Galway town and in the surrounding small villages and townlands. Not just hungry, but starving people everywhere. If she spent the money on her travels, then she would have none left for her own neighbours. It was the early hours before she made her decision. Then she was able to sleep.

* * *

The next morning, she went into town with Fahy and the children. They were all well wrapped up against the sharp breeze coming in from the bay. After they dropped the children to school, Fahy drove the cart back to the bridge.

'I'll not come with you,' he said. 'I don't want Mrs Smith to think I've been talking out of turn. Just make the offer and see what she says. She lives with her son and daughter-in-law on O'Connell Street.'

'Thank you, Fahy. I'll call round there now.'

It took just a few minutes to find the house. It was a fine two storey building with a small front garden enclosed by decorative iron railings and a gate. A housemaid answered Jane's knock on the door. She told the maid what her business was and was invited to join Mrs Smith in the parlour.

She saw a smallish, older woman, about fifty, dressed in black, with her grey hair tidied away in a white, lace-edged

148

cap.

'My name is Jane Keating. I heard from a friend of mine, Mr Fahy, that you run a soup kitchen here in the town.'

'Yes, Michael. He's such a great help. Take a seat, Jane, and have a cup of tea with me.'

Jane smiled. Now she knew Fahy's first name. 'Well, a friend in America sent me some money to help with the hardship and hunger. I want to use it to feed some of the hungry people in Galway. I see them everywhere, but I'm not sure how to start. Mr Fahy said you might be able to advise me.' She watched Mrs Smith's lined face brighten and the older woman breathed a sigh of relief. 'Ah, the Lord has provided. I have prayed and prayed for someone to come and take up this burden.'

Jane sipped her tea while the woman wiped her eyes with a tiny handkerchief and composed herself. The small front parlour was cosy and warm. Jane unbuttoned her cloak and caught a glimpse of her reflection in the silver tea urn displayed on the dark wood sideboard.

'Forgive me, Jane. I have spent the last year and a half out in all weather with these poor people. It breaks my heart to have to stop. But my daughter-in-law is having her baby soon, and we just can't keep going.'

'Is she the one who helps you?'

'Yes. We feed eighty or more people every day, but poor Maria is exhausted and, in truth, I am, too. My son is really not happy about us doing this for much longer. You have come at just the right time. The Lord be thanked.' The woman sighed. 'Are you sure about this?'

'Yes. I am sure. What do I need to do?' Jane asked.

'You can use our soup boiler, it's in the stables at the back of the house. Do you have something to transport it?'

'I have an ass and cart. I'm staying at Saint Vincent's Church, out past Barna. Do you know it?'

'I do. But you'd be better off if you lived in the town. If you're going to take over the soup kitchen, then you'll need somewhere to cook up the soup. It takes a bit of organising. And it must be done every day. If you start, then you can't decide to have a day off. These people have nothing.'

Jane frowned. 'I'm sorry, I hadn't thought about all this.'

'The Lord will help you. The boiler will be here when you need it. I am planning to finish this work at the end of the month, but if you can take it over sooner, I will be grateful.'

They finished their tea and Jane said goodbye and promised she'd be back soon.

She'd have to think about her next steps with this task she had set herself. And she'd need to think fast, if she was going to be ready to feed starving people. But she had a task and it would help settle her mind.

* * *

After she left Mrs Smith's house, she walked over to the river. The workhouse was nearby and each side of the bridge was full of people begging or just sitting and waiting in the chilly air. Poor old grandfathers and grannies, who seemed to have been abandoned to the road.

She stopped to look down at the river water as it rushed past the stone columns that supported the bridge.

She put her elbow on the stone wall and leaned her chin on her hand. How do we get back from this devastation? All these people, homeless and hungry. Must we wait until they are all dead, or have emigrated? She turned and looked at the crowds gathered at the end of the bridge. Will Ireland ever recover from this? Some, the fortunate ones who had the means to hunker down, might make it through. There'll be years more of this, she reckoned as she began to walk out the road to the chapel.

And what of you, Jane Keating? she asked herself. And Sorcha and Jamie? What kind of a life will the children have? Right then, at that moment, she had no answers to her questions. One thing was clear to her. At some point, she'd need to find the answers, before she had spent all her money and ended up in that crowd of paupers on the bridge.

* * *

In the meantime, she accepted that she'd need to be living in the town if she were to boil up soup and serve it out every day to almost a hundred people. She had forgotten to ask Mrs Smith how exactly she made the soup. She'd see her again soon and ask some questions.

It was Friday and Jane made her mind up. By Monday morning she'd be ready to serve up the soup. She planned as she walked. Tell Father and Mrs Flynn and Fahy. And the children?

And where would they live? She began to understand why the Quaker woman had said "The Lord will provide." It was much easier to trust in the Lord when a problem was too big. Maybe she'd need a bit more time than three days.

She got back to the presbytery and found Mrs Flynn in the kitchen, putting the finishing touches to a pie for the supper. Heat rushed out of the oven when the housekeeper put the pie in to bake.

'Mrs Flynn, I want to talk to you. I'm going to take over a soup kitchen in Galway. The one that Fahy helps with. The two Quaker women are having to give it up. Mrs Smith said I can have the boiler. But I'll need to move into town if I'm to be able to do this.'

The older woman stared at Jane. 'What did you say? The soup kitchen. But what about Sorcha and Jamie?'

'They'll come with me. You have enough to be going on with here, without my family.'

'And where will you live? And how will you pay for a house, more's to the point?' The housekeeper gathered up the rolling pin and the baking bowl. She sighed. 'I don't know, I'm sure.'

Jane picked up a cloth to help wipe off the table. 'I have money. Some left from the money I brought home with me, that will pay for the rent for a while. And the money we got from America will pay for the soup. I'll write to Finn and asked him to send more, if he can.'

'Then, how can I help, girl?'

'Where will I live?' Jane laughed. Mrs Flynn reached over and patted Jane's hand.

'You'll need a man to sign the contract, that's one thing I know.'

'Ah.'

'How about that fine young man of yours, Owen?'

'What about him?'

'Could he rent the house for you?'

That might be asking too much of him, she thought. 'I need to find a house first.'

'The town is full of empty buildings. You'll find one easy enough, but do you need a whole house?' Mrs Flynn thought for a minute. 'Get Fahy to go with you. The two of you will find a place. He's going to pick the children up from school soon. Go and talk to him.'

*　*　*

Jane said goodbye to Mrs Flynn and went off to see if Fahy was ready to leave for town.

On the way to the school, she spoke to him about the soup kitchen.

'I thought it would be easy. I have the money and I want to help. But now I have to move into town, rent a house, cook soup and look after two children and an ass!'

Fahy smiled. 'No, it won't be easy, but I'll help you. Just remember, those Quaker women had an organisation behind them. They have soup kitchens all over.'

'Fahy, you suggested it!'

'I did, and I'll help you. At least I know how to dish up the soup. That's one thing.' Fahy sighed and muttered under his breath. 'I don't know! I can never seem to get free of women and children!'

'Thank you, Fahy,' Jane sat quietly while the cart took them along the road to town. 'Will you help me find a house to rent?'

When Fahy looked at her, his craggy face broke into a smile and he held his thumb out. 'Right there. That's where you have me, under your thumb.'

16

Finds a cottage in town. Early February 1848

It was another wet and windy day, and when the children were all safely inside the school gate, Jane and Fahy drove to the Long Walk. They tied up the ass and cart on the quayside and went for a stroll around the town. Mrs Flynn was right, there were lots of empty houses, but many were in disrepair. It seemed as if some families had just closed the door behind them and left.

The houses were two and three stories high in the centre of the town. Many were vacant and some had slate roofs with stringy green weeds growing through from the attic, letting the rain in. Jane pulled her cloak up around her head. These shabby, abandoned places were bereft of life and energy. Perhaps their inhabitants had left for better opportunities elsewhere. At least, that's what she hoped, and not just to move into the workhouse.

A sign caught Jane's eye. 'Rooms to let.' It was a three-story house, off Eyre Square.

'Let's look there,' she said. 'Maybe a room will do.' They

knocked on the front door and heard the brass knocker echo inside.

A girl of about Jane's age opened the door. 'Yes?' She had a hard-faced, impatient look about her.

'We're here about the rooms to let.'

'Come in. I'll call my mother.' The girls stood back to let them in, then closed the door and led them along a narrow, dark hall to the back of the house and into a small sitting room. 'Take a seat.' She didn't stop but continued on through the room and they heard her speaking. The smell of old boiled cabbage filled the room. The windows were glazed but cloudy with layer of oily grime that kept most of the daylight out. A moment later, a large, older woman came in.

'You're looking for a room?' The woman's round, red face and small, puffy eyes betrayed her liking for porter.

'Yes. For me and two children.' The woman looked at Jane and Fahy, as if trying to work out their relationship. She shook her head. 'I only take single people here. I have the one small room and it wouldn't be suitable.'

No more was said and they followed her back to the front door. As soon as the door was shut, Jane caught Fahy by the arm and they both laughed and hurried off around the corner.

'Did she really think we're up to no good?' Jane asked. 'We'd better say you're my uncle, or we'll get nowhere. Let's look further out. We have to find somewhere with more than one small room. Let's look around the docks, and if I smell cabbage again, we're off!'

Fahy, obliging as ever, followed Jane to the port area.

They tried several lodging houses and some already had children living there. Many of these seemed to live on the stairs or in the hallways.

'I'll not be able to cook up soup anywhere, if they are all like these,' Jane said. 'And Sorcha and Jamie won't like playing in a stairwell!'

They turned off Dock Road into another side street. There, at the end of a row of houses, they came across an empty thatched cottage. It looked as if it had been attached to the row as an afterthought. There was a sign in the window. 'To rent. Enquire next door.' Jane knocked on the door of the adjacent house.

'I'm interested in looking at the cottage. How much is the rent?'

'Who wants to know?' The old fellow who answered the door asked.

Jane was running out of patience by this time. She had spent the entire morning walking around the town trying to find a place to live.

'We do. My name is Jane Keating, and this is my uncle, Michael Fahy.'

The man reached behind him and took a key from a hook on the wall. 'Right, come with me. I'll show it to you.'

He led the way to the front door of the cottage, opened the door and they followed him inside.

The cottage had just two rooms. The small sitting room was the right size for her and two children. Instead of an open fireplace there was a small cast-iron range for cooking and heating. A table and chairs stood in front of the range. The bedroom in the back room of the cottage had a metal bed frame, but the mattress was torn and filthy. Outside in the yard, a small square of scrubby ground had a privy and a gate led onto a narrow lane.

'How much is it?' she asked.

'Two shillings a week,' the man replied. 'Three months in advance.'

Jane looked at Fahy. 'What do you say, uncle?' She smiled.

'There's not enough room for the soup boiler in that kitchen, but I've got an idea.' Fahy turned to the owner. 'We plan on boiling up soup for a charitable work. There's enough room out the back there to put up a shed and a small stove to make the soup. Would that be alright?'

'As long as you don't burn the place down. Keep it clean. There's a water pump out in the back lane, and a night soil collection once a week.'

'We have the deposit. When can I move in?' Jane asked.

'Well now, let's see the colour of your money. Come next door and we'll get you signed up.'

And it was that easy. After scouring the town, Jane had found an almost exact replica of her old home. Fahy signed as guarantor and the owner agreed to replace the old mattress. She'd move in soon.

'Thank you, Fahy. I couldn't have done it without you.' She laughed. 'To think we nearly ended up in that horrible boarding house!'

'You're welcome, girl,' Fahy said. 'I do wonder how you'll be able to pay the rent, in the longer term, though.'

'Don't worry about me. I've written to Finn Power already and if the money runs out I'll get another job, or more hours at The Star.' She still had her last gold nugget to fall back on.

'We'll do it together then,' Fahy said. Jane thought he was seemed relieved that the soup kitchen wasn't closing. It was his lifeline, too.

* * *

Fahy spent the next few weeks, through February, building a shed in the yard, then he installed a small stove It was a squeeze, but there was space to prepare and cook the soup and transfer the boiler onto the cart.

It was almost the end of February and Jane spent a couple of mornings working with Mrs Smith to learn how to cook the soup. Then the Quaker lady introduced her to the grocer and the baker who supplied the vegetables and grain.

Jamie and Sorcha were reluctant to move again, but with the promise of seeing their friends every day at school and at the weekends, they agreed to it. They brought Jamie and Sorcha's bed from the presbytery. Their landlord replaced the mattress and Jane was ready to move in, until a letter arrived from Thomas Francis Meagher with an invitation she couldn't turn down.

17

The Tricolour , Waterford, 7th March, 1848

Fahy unhitched the ass from the cart and left the animal to graze at the side of the path and they headed into the presbytery.

The children raced in ahead of them and squeezed onto benches around the kitchen table. Mrs Flynn began to pour out mugs of milk and smiled as they devoured a plate of oatmeal biscuits.

Jane had brought the letter with her. She had written to Owen in Clonmel, to tell him about her journey to Waterford, and now wanted to show it to Mrs Flynn when she asked the favour.

```
25th February,1848.
Dear Jane
This is a quick letter with some news for you.
William Smith O'Brien and myself went to Paris to
bring the congratulations of the Irish people to
Lamartine, the new President of France, after their
```

```
rebellion. We hoped to get some support for our
fight for Irish freedom.
I'm sorry to say that the meeting was a major
disappointment. President Lamartine says France
can't get involved in Britain's internal affairs.
The British government got to him first, I think.
Instead, he gave us a gift.
I'm in Dublin now and I'll be going home in a couple
of weeks to show off the gift to the people of
Waterford.
Speranza is coming, too, and we would both love you
to come and meet us on Tuesday,7th March. She will
write to you, too.

All good wishes until we meet again.
Your friend, Thomas Francis Meagher.
```

Jane folded the letter. 'What do you make of that? He's been arrested and then went over to France. Isn't that dangerous? He is so brave.'

'I'd say you're well out of it, Jane. You won't go to Waterford now will you?' Mrs Flynn put her hand out to Jane who caught it and held it.

'I want to see what he has brought back, Nan. I'd have to travel on Monday. I'll be back on Wednesday night.'

Jane saw a look pass between her old friend and Mrs Flynn.

'Mrs Smith has agreed to keep the soup kitchen going with me until you get back,' Fahy said.

'Jamie will stay here with you, Nan. I'll take Sorcha with me, we'll get the post carriage through to Waterford. It'll be there in a day. Say yes, Nan.' Jane hugged the older woman.

'I suppose, if it's only for a few days. And, sure, Jamie won't miss you. Don't you go getting yourself and Sorcha arrested now, will you?'

Jane laughed. 'No, I promise. Thank you, both. I won't be away long. I'm curious to know what Tom has to show me. A gift from the revolutionaries in Paris. What could that be?'

* * *

Jane bought a ticket for inside seats for herself and Sorcha on the post carriage, with return travel on the Wednesday. Jamie was happy to stay at home, he didn't want to miss school with his friends.

She wore her black skirt and the grey wool jacket, with a lace-trimmed blouse. Then she put on her Galway cloak to travel in, for it was still chilly out in the air. She smiled grimly; she was one of the lucky few to be warmly wrapped up against the cold.

She had bought a ready-made woollen dress for Sorcha. It was expensive, but she wanted her cousin to look her best when she met Tom and Speranza.

For a change, she slept well the night before they left; a whole week of nights with no nightmares of the attack and rape, or the sleeping face of her tiny baby. Please God, those dreams that left her trembling and sweating were fading. Jane tried to forget the face of her rapist, but vowed that she would remember to her dying day holding the body of her still-born daughter.

Early on the Monday morning, Jane and Sorcha waited outside the Post Office until the post bags and passengers' luggage were loaded onto the roof of the carriage.

They took their seats next to another woman and opposite

three men. The carriage itself had enough room to fit up to ten passengers inside, and there was room outside at the back of the coach for more, but those hardy passengers were exposed to the weather for the whole journey.

The driver cracked his whip and the horses set off along the road across the country to Waterford. It was a bright morning and Jane cuddled Sorcha close to her. The windows were draughty, but with the men smoking pipes and cigars, it was as well to have some cold air running through.

Leaving Galway, the carriage headed south and retraced Jane's steps on her first journey away from home. That was more than two years ago, after the death of her entire family, she had left Galway in a futile quest to find her mother's relatives in Waterford. Then, as now, the fields were empty. There were still no potato crops.

The coach passed through deserted villages filled with torn-down cabins and cottages. The result of the landlords' fever for evictions. She shook her head as they rolled past the ruins of a big farmhouse. 'There'll soon be no-one left in this place,' she whispered to herself.

The woman next to her in the carriage turned to look out of the window and nodded. 'I knew that farmer and his wife. They had a grand family, so they did.'

'What happened to them?'

'Even the bigger tenant farmers are being turned off their land. They have no rights, you see. The landlord can just evict them at will.'

'And where are they now?'

'They took off for America last summer. Good luck to them, I say.' The woman looked at Sorcha. 'Is she yours?'

'No. She's my cousin's child.'

'She's lovely, God bless her. Her parents?'

'They died,' Jane whispered and put her arm around Sorcha.

'She's fortunate to have you then.' The woman turned to look out of the window again, and said no more.

Sorcha played with her dolly. She seemed to find everything an adventure. She had the Keating family look about her, with her dark hair and eyes, and her smile reminded Jane of her own younger brother, Seamus. Strangely, Jane was comforted to see the family likeness. It felt as if part of her brother lived on.

They travelled for a few hours then the carriage stopped to change horses in Limerick. This allowed the passengers to stretch their legs, use the privy, and buy some food at the inn, before heading off again. The roads were rutted, but passable. The day itself had started out clear and bright but as they headed east a thin drizzle fell over the countryside. The hills in the far distance melded into a grey-blue haze.

The hours passed on their journey and the daylight dimmed. Sorcha slept for part of the time, cuddled in Jane's arms, while Jane dozed in the comfort of her cloak.

The woman beside Jane nudged her awake. 'Look, there!'

The coach was trundling through a small village alongside the road. There wasn't a house or cabin left standing. The moon illuminated broken walls and roof beams and cast shadows on moving figures beside a turf fire. The coach didn't stop, but there must have been several families sheltering in the ruins of their former homes. One of the other passengers coughed into his handkerchief. Jane felt his attention on her and glanced sideways. He looked out of the window.

'It's everywhere,' Jane murmured. 'It's never-ending. I thought it would be over by now. But it seems to be getting worse.' She looked at her neighbour. 'Are you alright?'

'I am, thank God. I have a business, an inn, in Clonmel. It keeps us going. I've just been back to Galway to visit my parents. I want them to come and stay with me, but they won't leave. Until they get evicted. Then they'll come to me.'

The women sat together in grim silence and watched the countryside pass. The male passenger relaxed back into reading his newspaper.

* * *

It was early evening by the time they stopped at Clonmel and the woman disembarked. Jane and the woman touched hands, 'God go with you.' The coach headed off straight away for the last stop - Waterford. It was after nine o'clock when it pulled up outside the Post Office on the Quay beside the River Suir. The city was quiet and dark. The only light came from lamps on the rigging of berthed ships alongside the quays. The clang of a bell echoed across the water, signalling a change of watch on one of the ships.

Jane opened the carriage door and breathed in the fresh, salty air from the river, then she woke Sorcha and they stepped down onto the path. The driver threw the bags down from the roof of the carriage. Jane picked her bag up and held Sorcha's hand and they walked to the nearest inn to check in for the night.

They had a clean bed in a room to themselves. Jane ordered hot chocolate for a nightcap and helped Sorcha get into her nightshift, then washed and got ready for bed herself. Both of them slept soundly.

* * *

They rose early the next day and got ready to meet Speranza and Thomas Francis Meagher. They had a quick breakfast and walked along the quay to Tom's family home. The clerk at the inn had told Jane that when in Waterford, Thomas Meagher stayed with his father, the Lord Mayor of Waterford, in a Georgian mansion that spread across a whole block of the quay. It overlooked the River Suir and the merchant ships at anchor.

The tide was full in, and the ships rode high against the quay walls. Sea birds squawked and perched on the yardarms. Most of the ships had their sails furled, but some were ready to cast off and had a full spread of canvas. The air was full of movement; masts swayed, sails flapped and banged in the breeze. Behind them, the pale blue sky was a backdrop for light white clouds that scudded past high above.

'Are the ships going to America, auntie Jane?' Sorcha asked.

'I don't know, *acushla*. My friend Annie sailed from Dungarvan, not far from here, so there might be some ships that go to America. We can ask Tom when we meet him. That's his house, I think.'

The other buildings were mostly businesses: ships' chandlers, inns and banks, as well as the Post Office. This looked to be the only family residence.

They stopped at the grand entrance to the mansion which stretched to four storeys in height. Jane had not realised that Thomas Meagher came from such a wealthy family. In Dublin, he made friends with everyone he met, including Jane herself, when she passed as the young typesetter, Jack. Speranza said he had laughed in disbelief when she told him that young Jack was in fact, Jane, and on her way to Melbourne, transported in place of Annie Power, back in 1846.

Jane lifted the heavy brass knocker and let it drop, and was relieved to see that Speranza answered the door.

'Good, you're here. I'm ready to go. Tom left earlier to prepare. He'll be making his speech soon, so we need to hurry. It's only five minutes' walk from here.'

Speranza turned heads everywhere she went, and that morning, her choice of a white satin dress matched her flamboyant personality. Her dark hair was studded with her favourite pearls, her lips glistened and dark eyelashes and brows set off pale ivory skin. She was lovely as well as beautiful, and she had always been supportive of both Jane and Annie. Jane knew that she and Annie were just two of a number of Irish country girls that she helped to get work or published their poems. Jane was grateful for her support and for the help she had given so freely to Annie, for without it, Annie's escape to New York would have been almost impossible.

They walked together along the quay, which had started to fill up with people.

Speranza was quite taken with Sorcha. 'Ah, the darling child is so fortunate to have a kind soul like you, Jane.'

'Not at all, I am the fortunate one. She and her brother are the last of my family. I am forever grateful to have them.' Sorcha's fingers tighten in her hand and Jane glanced down at her cousin. Blessed, indeed.

'Did Tom tell you what he was bringing back with him?'

'No. Nor you?'

Speranza shook her head. 'No. However, we won't have long to wait now.'

The Wolfe Tone Confederate Club stood around the corner

on a road running east to west, away from the river.

The three of them turned the corner and walked into a crowd of excited people. They were not queuing for food or soup. These people, and there must have been a couple of hundred or more, were gathered outside Number 33, The Mall.

'Is this the place? They are all waiting to see Tom, too?' Jane asked.

They had stopped beside an old stone monument on the corner, and couldn't go any further. Jane lifted Sorcha up so the child could see over the crowds in front of them.

'Let's try to get in,' Speranza said. 'They'll let us in.'

Before they could move, the full length bay windows on the upper floor opened inwards and Tom Meagher stepped from inside the room onto a balcony to look out over the crowd. He spotted Speranza and waved to her and Jane. He had just gotten back from a long journey to Paris, France and seemed almost triumphant. His hair ruffled in the breeze and his white teeth flashed in a smile as he held his hand up to quieten the cheering crowd.

'Friends, welcome on this historic day. Most of you know me. My name is Thomas Francis Meagher.

'This building is named after Wolfe Tone, an Irish freedom fighter. I'm here today to tell you that I, too, am a freedom fighter.' He stopped to let the crowds cheer again. 'I travelled to Paris, in France, with William Smith-O'Brien to congratulate the leaders of the French Revolution. I tell you, the French know how to fight against tyranny! The President of France, Mr Lamartine, gave us a gift to bring back to the people of Ireland, and I want you to be the first to see it.'

He turned to someone behind him and brought out a flag pole. He leaned out over the balcony and let a huge flag unfurl.

167

The crowd roared in delight as the fabric began to catch the breeze. It was made of three vertical stripes of green, white and gold silk that seemed to float in the light airs from the river.

'The Irish tricolour, the flag of Ireland. From now on, this will be our flag.'

Sorcha put her hands over her ears to quieten the noise from the crowd, but she seemed to be more curious than frightened and she stared up at the handsome young man on the balcony.

'The London government don't want to lose us, their sister island. If they let Ireland go, then they will have to free others in their empire.'

Tom raised the flag-pole and waved it again, to the delight of the crowd. 'No, my friends,' he shouted and his voice cracked with emotion. 'They won't let us go. Neither will they comfort us in these years of great need. Our brothers and sisters, our neighbours, many of you, are starving, and more are sick from disease. Thousands are leaving Ireland every day. Driven out! And what has the government done? They declared the famine over and shut down the soup kitchens. They have abandoned us!'

Tom hoisted the flag again, out over the heads of the crowd and it caught the wind and fluttered its bright colours over the people below.

'Remember this day. The seventh of March, 1848. This is the beginning of the end for the British rulers of our ancient island.' He paused. 'Who is with me?'

Jane was almost deafened by the roars and cheers that echoed across the street and bounced off the buildings on either side of The Mall. At her side, Speranza was silent, her mouth was open as if to ask a question, then she swallowed and shook her head.

Sorcha hid her face against Jane's shoulder. Jane hugged her cousin. 'We'll remember this day, won't we, *acushla*, my darling?'

Jane's heart was too full to say any more. The dream of a free Ireland seemed such a wonderful thing. She imagined men like Thomas Francis Meagher and the barrister, Charles Gavan Duffy, in charge of an Irish government. They would surely put an end to the relentless misery and starvation in this jewel of an island. To be free, to be a nation!

Tears ran down her face, but when she turned to look at Speranza, she saw that her friend was dry-eyed.

'Do you believe this can happen, Speranza? Can we really be free?'

Speranza took out a lace handkerchief and leaned over to wipe Jane's tears. 'I truly hope so, Jane. I, too, want to believe that Ireland can be free one day. But it will take more than mere rhetoric.'

'What do you mean?'

'Fine words, no more than that. A dream.' Speranza put her hand on Sorcha's curls. 'Maybe in time, when you are grown, *acushla*, we'll taste freedom in our small island. The British Empire is a mighty construct and the Americans fought for years to gain their independence. It will take more than waving a flag to win our freedom.'

The excited chatter of the crowd around them began to dissipate. Speranza spoke quietly.

'Did Tom tell you they have been arrested for sedition?'

'No!' Jane whispered.

'Three of them. Tom, William Smith O'Brien and John Mitchel are to go on trial in May. The government is expecting trouble. They have brought in thousands more soldiers. The Dublin garrison is full and there are two ships of war anchored at Kingstown. I don't think it will go well for the men.'

Jane touched hands with Speranza. 'Will you go to the trials?'

'Yes, I can't miss it. I'll be there for Tom and Charles.'

'I'll come, too, if I can get away. They'll not send him to prison, surely?'

'Dublin is different. He's not a hero there, and the government needs to make an example. The whole of Europe is rebelling, and they don't want a rebellion to start here.' Speranza paused and pursed her lips as if to stop her next sentence, but said it, nevertheless. 'If they're convicted, they can be hanged, drawn and quartered for sedition.'

Jane had her hand on Sorcha's shoulder and felt a shiver run through the child. It was cold and the wind whipped around the ancient tower, but she guessed that Sorcha had understood some of what was being said; the shiver was of fear as well as cold.

Tom had gathered the flag back inside and the balcony doors closed. The two women waited with Sorcha until a space had cleared in front of them, then they rushed across the street towards the house.

Jane caught Speranza's arm before she knocked on the door. 'I won't come in, I have something to do and I think Sorcha has seen enough for today.'

'He'll be sorry to miss you.'

'He'll have plenty of people to talk to. But, I truly think we will be free, one day. It is the only way to put an end to this hunger and poverty. Tell Tom I think he is wonderful.'

Speranza avoided looking into Jane's eyes but dipped her head in assent. 'I'll tell him you said that.'

Jane reached out to embrace her friend. 'I'll come to Dublin! Write to me!' Speranza went inside.

On the walk back along the quay, the crowds and the excitement seemed to have vanished like the mist on the river. People went about their business as if nothing had happened. There were a few small groups of hungry paupers congregated on the corners, but these were not in the numbers she saw every day in Galway.

She had some silver thruppences and sixpences in her pocket and gave them out. The coins might buy some bread, at least.

Sorcha tugged at Jane's hand. 'Is that nice man with the flag going to be hanged?'

'No, he's not, *acushla*. Miss Speranza was wrong to say that.'

* * *

Just before they reached the hotel, Jane saw an advertisement in a shop window. She glanced at it once, then looked again and smiled in disbelief. She kept on getting reminders of her time in Melbourne. It was strange. The advertisement was for an auction. The Waterford Odyssey, a local newspaper, had gone bankrupt. The printing press and all the equipment and the business premises were going up for sale or rent on the 20th of April. Sad, she thought, and pushed open the door to the hotel. The act of opening the door and catching Sorcha's hand didn't stop the next thought from flitting through her head. She smiled. Jane Keating, Owner and Editor.

She settled up the bill for their stay at the hotel.The manager, Jane noted his Wicklow accent, tallied up her account and she handed over the cash. 'Did you enjoy your stay here, Miss Keating?'

171

'We did indeed, thank you. Were you at the Mall? To hear Thomas Francis Meagher speak?'

'No, unfortunately I was on duty. I hear he's the great man, like his father.'

Jane caught the acid edge to his voice. 'He is a true Irishman. We are fortunate to have such a man go all the way to France and bring back our flag.'

The manager nodded. 'You may be in the right of it, Miss. I hope you are.' He smiled at Sorcha. 'What's your name, little girl?'

'I'm Sorcha Keating.'

'And she's the best girl, aren't you, darling?' Jane said to Sorcha who peeped over the counter to look at the manager.

'Before I go,' Jane added. 'You might be able to tell me. I saw a notice in the window next door. A newspaper is for auction next month. Do you know anything about it?'

'Ah, sure, that was a sad story. The Odyssey has been a Waterford newspaper for fifty years or more. It's been going downhill for the last few years, what with the troubles we've had. The owner tried to sell it, but in these times . . . '

'And what did he do then?'

'Why, the poor unfortunate man died of the fever. The business folded and it is up for sale or rent to the highest bidder, as you saw for yourself.'

The manager looked past Jane to the door as another customer came in. 'Excuse me, Miss Keating. I'll have to get on. Have a safe journey home.'

She packed her bag and they headed for the coach station along the quay. Owen was waiting for her in Clonmel. She'd catch a 'Biam', a fast coach, and be there in a couple of hours.

18

Owen in Clonmel

Owen met her off the coach in Clonmel that evening. She spotted him through the window as the coach drew up to the stop. He was in uniform, and had written to tell her that he'd got a couple of hours off. He kissed Sorcha and admired her dolly. 'Her name is Lizzie,' Sorcha explained.

Owen put his arm around Jane. 'Come here to me.' They kissed.

It was a bright spring day and Owen led the way to an inn where they sat in the dining room and ordered an early supper.

The menu had only one thing ready to eat, so they ordered bacon and cabbage. 'Still no potatoes?' Owen asked the waiter.

'Not at this time of year, sir,' the young waiter said. 'Hopefully there'll be a few later in the autumn.'

They sat at a table in the corner of the room, beside a window that let in the sunlight. Sorcha sat on Jane's lap and snoozed.

To an observer, they would have looked like a handsome young couple with a child. Closer observation would have shown that Jane was young to have a five-year-old child.

From the window, Jane saw lots of armed police and soldiers as they moved through the small town. The only difference between them was the colour of their uniforms. She nodded at Owen's red jacket. 'How many of you are here?'

'Upwards of five thousand. And hundreds of armed soldiers. They're getting ready for the rebellion.' Owen said. He smiled as Sorcha gave a little snore. Jane stroked the child's hair and tucked Lizzie, the dolly, in close to the sleeping child.

'I've heard a rumour. I wasn't going to say anything about it, but now you're here. . .' He leaned across the table as if to impart a secret. 'There's to be a new contract for the British Army.'

Jane's nose almost touched Owen's. 'What does that mean?' she whispered. She blinked when his breath touched her face.

'It'll be seven years. Not twenty.' He sat back and let her think about it.

She saw it straight away. 'Oh, my God! How long have you served?'

'Seven. Since last January.' He chuckled. 'I joined at sixteen. If they bring it in, I can leave straight away.'

'But that's wonderful news.'

He sighed and reached across the table to caress her face. 'I've had enough, Jane. I've travelled the world with the army and I can see how the British Empire works. It's all about power. And there's no humanity in it. You saw it, too, in Melbourne. The way they treated them poor Aborigines - in their own land, for God's sake! As soon as I came back to Ireland I saw exactly the same thing here. The English newspapers print horrible things about us. As if we're not even human, like apes in a jungle.'

His voice raised from a whisper and made Sorcha stir. Jane

held her breath as the child turned over on her lap and settled again.

Owen sighed. 'I'm sorry, sweetheart.' A muscle in the side of Owen's face twitched. 'Forgive me, she doesn't need to hear this.

'Anyway, as soon as they bring in the new contract, I'm done. I've got savings.' His eyes brightened and he lifted her hand in his. 'We'll talk again when that happens, my darling.' He smiled as he let go of her hand and she saw a glimpse white teeth. Then he pursed his lips together.

'I want you to take care of yourself, girl. And the little one,' he nodded to the sleeping child. 'And Jamie. Promise me?'

'I promise.'

Owen looked at the clock. 'I've got to get back. I swapped my duty to meet you and I'm on at eight.'

'When will you come and visit?'

'As soon as I can. There's something going on at home in Wicklow that I can't get to the bottom of. I've got to get up there first. But I'll come, my darling.'

He stood and put his shako on his head. 'Will I carry Sorcha up to the room?'

Jane laughed. 'I don't think you'll be allowed upstairs!'

'I'm in uniform. Soldiers can do anything they please,' he said grimly.

After he left she lay down on the bed with Sorcha and dreamed of a life with Owen and the two children.

19

Home, March 1848

They got back late on the Wednesday night, two weary travellers, but it was only a short walk to the little cottage near the Spanish Parade. Sorcha fell asleep as soon as she lay down on the bed. Jane locked up, got herself undressed, and slept soundly.

The next morning she was ready. She and Fahy would start to cook their own soup and take over from Mrs Smith. At last, Jane was satisfied that she was doing something to help keep people alive, and she'd made a little home for herself and the two children. She prayed that one day, Owen would join them.

Sorcha was up early to go to school, so they had a quick breakfast of porridge and walked off up the town. Before she left, Jane checked the outhouse and saw that Fahy must have cooked the soup yesterday. The boiler would only need reheating, so she lit the fire in the stove.

At the school, Jamie and the other children were in the playground and Sorcha ran to join them. Jane waved to them as they lined up to start their day. Fahy had left already, but she would catch up with him later that morning. On the way home, she shopped for some fresh food for herself and the two children. Back at the cottage, she had missed Fahy again; he must have collected the soup while she was out. She unpacked and washed their clothes, dusty from travelling.

Then it was time to catch up with her friend and Mrs Smith at the soup kitchen. She wanted to tell Fahy all about the flag.

She slowed as she got to the bridge. Fahy was across the other side of the river and a man was talking him. Where was Mrs Smith? She stopped, unable to believe what she saw. It was Constable Smullen. He wasn't in uniform and he looked thinner, not such a bull-dog, more a scrawny stray. But it was him, no mistake. She didn't know whether to go forward or backwards, and made a decision after a few frozen moments.

She turned and walked away. What was he doing there? She had dreamed that one day he would be arrested and charged with the murder of her cousin, Brendan. Why would Fahy even speak to him? Her friend and neighbour, Fahy, as soon as she went away, he had . . . Just what did he think he was he doing?

She turned the key in her door and went inside, still in a daze. It was not possible, the two of them looked so friendly, laughing with the people in the soup queue. Her mind was blank, she stared into the embers of the fire and glanced at the stove, reached over and picked up the smoothing iron and felt the heft of it. The handle was still warm, although the fire was nearly out. She banged the iron on the edge of the stove, and then did it again, and again.

At that moment she was back in the kitchen of the servants' house in Melbourne. Her arm flexed and she heard the hard blow as the iron connected with Colonel Johns' head, saw him collapse onto the floor.

She panted, and tried to catch her breath. She could have killed him that day, for what he had done to her. She dropped the iron on the floor and slumped into a chair. She blew out a breath, tried to clear the thoughts away and still her hands. And now here was her cousin's killer. At her soup kitchen, with her friend. What could she do? She closed her eyes and let out the pain of betrayal, in retching sobs, until she was drained and exhausted.

She had to speak to both men. Find out what had happened to bring him back.

She had seen Smullen shoot Brendan, right in front of her. The children, Sorcha and Jamie, had stood in the shelter of the cottage doorway, their faces hidden in their mother's cloak, as the rain lashed from the heavens.

She relived the murder in her dreams, smelt and tasted Brendan's blood. It happened over two years ago, and Fahy had been there, yet he was still unsure of what he had seen. She was the only one, the only witness to this murder.

She stood up and smoothed her hair back. Took a sip of water and wrapped her cloak around her. The shutters were still across the window and the room was dim and quiet without the children. They'd finish school soon, but first she'd go and talk to the two men and find out what the hell was going on.

* * *

Smullen was still there, helping Fahy to pack up the cart. The soup had been dished out and they were just about ready to bring the boiler back to the cottage.

She paused. Could she bring herself to speak to that man? She remembered his angry face when she had accused him of killing Brendan. What if Fahy sided with him? What would she do then? There was no turning back, and she walked over to the cart.

'Fahy.' She looked at Smullen. 'What are you doing here?'

'I came to find you, Jane. Fahy said you were in Waterford.' Smullen looked across at Fahy who stared at him. 'We need to talk about Brendan.'

'I don't want to hear anything you've got to say. You've no business here. And don't call me by my name!'

She looked at her friend. 'What have you done?' Bright tears fell as she blinked at his betrayal.

Fahy's face contorted and he took a step towards her. 'Jane, we can't talk here. Let's go back to the cottage. There's things you need to know, girl.'

'If you think I'll bring him into my home, then you're mad!' She almost screamed the last word. Her whole body trembled. Strangely, she saw her dead cousin Brendan smile at her and felt the weight of the smoothing iron in her hand. Her memories had all jumbled up in her head, then her knees gave way and she staggered against the cart, and caught hold of the top of the wheel to stop herself from falling.

Both men moved towards her. 'Don't let him touch me!'

Fahy put his arms around her. 'You're safe. I have you. Rest your head on my shoulder and take some breaths. Here, let me wipe your eyes.'

She heard him speak to Smullen. 'Go. I'll come and find you later.'

Fahy helped her onto the cart. He sat up beside her and put his arm around her shoulders and clicked for the ass to move

179

on.

They were home in only a few minutes and Fahy helped her into the house. She sat in the chair while he blew a flame from the smouldering heart of the fire.

'Stay there while I bring the soup boiler round the back.'

Still in a daze, her mind was frozen, as if in shock, then a jumble of thoughts raced through. She stared into the fire and her breathing slowed, her glance snagged on the iron that had set it all off. She wept, for herself, for her cousin, his orphaned children, her stillborn child, and for the poor, desperate people she had met every day since coming back to this blighted land.

Fahy came in and sat beside her at the table. He handed her a cloth to wipe her face, but didn't speak until she had finished.

'It's all too much, girl. Isn't it?'

She nodded and blew her nose. 'I didn't tell you about what happened to me in New South Wales. It keeps coming back to me.'

'Will you tell me now?'

She shook her head, but the words rushed out anyway. 'My employer in Melbourne, he raped me. And I see it in my mind's eye, all the time. The rape and my . . .' She stopped. No, not the baby.

'Then I see poor Brendan's face. His blood went all over me. You were there! Sometimes I can taste it, or smell it. I think it will never leave me.'

'Shh, shh, there now.' Fahy got down on one knee and put his arm around her. They stayed there for a while until her friend stood and stretched. 'I'm getting too old for kneeling. Listen, there's a spot of soup left over. I'm going to heat it up for you. You need something to eat.'

'I have to fetch Sorcha and Jamie.'

'They're not out for a while yet. Have something to eat first, then we'll go to collect the children. You've had enough for today. Why don't you come out to the chapel and visit with Mrs Flynn and Father? You can tell us about Waterford. It'll help take your mind off all this.'

Jane ate the soup with a piece of bread. Afterwards, she washed her face and hands; her eyes were swollen, but the cool water eased the ache in her head.

Fahy held the door for her to walk out to the cart. 'I have to tell you about Smullen. It's not all what you think, Jane. But it'll keep until tomorrow.'

She shook her head at the mention of his name.

* * *

They collected the children from school and headed out the road to Saint Vincent's chapel. The cart was full with the children and two adults, and the poor old ass struggled up the hills, for no-one was of a mind to walk. After a couple of miles, Fahy told the boys to jump down and run on ahead of the cart to tell Mrs Flynn they were on their way. That lightened the load considerably and they made better time.

Jane sat like a dull lump and stared out at the road and the fields while Fahy called out the odd greeting to other cart drivers. The air blew through her hair and against her face, and ruffled her cloak. Blackbirds in the trees beside the road flitted across the track and sang to each other, and gradually she came back to herself. Her head was still heavy, but the ache across her forehead had lessened by the time they arrived at the chapel. The ass was rewarded with a bucket of water to drink and some sweet grass at the side of the path.

In the kitchen, Jane saw Mrs Flynn narrow her eyes as she took in Jane's appearance.

'Ah, you're back. Will you have a cup of tea? And Fahy?'

'Thank you, I will,' Jane said.

Fahy put his cap on the table. 'I'll join you if there is a drop left on the pot, thank you kindly, Nan.'

Mrs Flynn put out two extra cups and poured the tea. 'Sit down there and tell us how your visit to Waterford went. You look a bit weary after it, I'd say.'

'It was a lot of travelling. But I'm glad I went.' Jane sipped the tea.

She felt Jamie's arm around her waist. 'And I'm glad you're back, auntie Jane,' he said.

'Oh, so I'm auntie now?'

'Well, Nan says we can call her, Nan. So I'll call you auntie, if that is alright?'

'Ah sure, do, *acushla*.' Jane said in a soft voice, and hugged him back. To hear those words from her young cousin. He loved her, it was that simple.

The older woman smiled. 'I think it's about time you called me, Nan, too, don't you? Everyone else here does. Even Fahy!'

Mrs Flynn and Father Hanrahan had both helped when she had nowhere else to turn. They knew her. Jane put her hand out and squeezed Mrs Flynn's hand. 'Thank you, Nan.'

She told them about the flag and Thomas Meagher's speech about Ireland and her meeting with Owen. 'He promised to visit soon.'

She recalled, but didn't mention, the advertisement for the newspaper. Was it possible? It would mean that she would leave behind her friends and the children's Nan. Could she move again? She brushed a hand through her hair, and shook her head slowly.

* * *

Later, they went back out to the cart and started the return journey to town. Sorcha and Jamie chatted all the way, and Jane was forced to concentrate and respond to the children.

Fahy left, promising to call back early the next morning, to start the soup. He didn't mention Smullen, but Jane knew she'd have to listen to whatever it was he wanted to tell her. In her heart and soul nothing, absolutely nothing, would change her mind. She saw what she saw, heard that shot, and had tasted Brendan's blood.

* * *

When the children were in school, the next morning, Jane and Fahy began to chop vegetables for the soup pot. The soup itself wasn't an expensive item, with carrots, onions, swedes, peas, barley and oats. Some days Fahy would turn up with a rabbit hanging by its legs and he would skin it and joint it, then add it to the mix. That morning, they just had the vegetables and grains.

They chopped and Fahy spoke, finally. 'I have to tell you how Smullen came to be at the soup kitchen. Hear me out, please. I don't want you getting upset again, Jane.' He placed the knife on the the surface of the chopping board and pressed his hands on the table.

She peeled another onion in silence, sure that it was the onions that made her eyes water. 'Just say it, then. Whatever it is.' She focused on the onion, and sliced it into tiny pieces.

183

'I spotted him in the queue for soup, last Friday. He looked terrible, much like all the rest of them for that matter. He told me he hadn't eaten for days, and I think, when he saw you weren't there, he came over for a bowl of soup.

'Afterwards, we spoke. He told me his story. Well, most of it you already know. He's not been right since the eviction. He left his job in the Irish Constabulary, and he helps his wife run a haberdasher's shop off Eyre Square. But business is poor.'

'And now you feel sorry for him,' Jane whispered.

'Not at all. He told me about that day, at Brendan's. He said he was terrified of the bailiff, that he was like a madman. The bailiff told him that Brendan was armed and had made threats to kill them. Smullen swore to me, his gun went off accidentally, but it was the bailiff's gun that killed Brendan. He said he was in shock when you went back to accuse him of murder. He's a haunted man, Jane.'

'And so he should be. And he's a liar! Brendan had his shovel, that's all.'

'You're right. He is a liar. I don't know if any of that story is really true. But I tell you one thing, I wasn't going to turn him away from the soup. He hadn't eaten for a week. I was sure of that.' Her friend picked the knife up and began to peel and chop parsnips. Jane felt his eyes on her and glanced at him. His greying eyebrows were drawn together in a frown.

'So anyway, the next day, he came back and offered to help. And he came on Tuesday and yesterday. He helped me give out the soup. He's looking a bit better, not so desperate.' He stopped work and came around the table and stopped her hand from chopping the onions. 'Mrs Smith wasn't able to help me. Her daughter had her baby last week.'

'Well, I'm back now. He can go somewhere else.' She shook

off his hand and forced the tip of the knife into a pale swede and sawed it back and forth to cut it in two. Then began to peel the thick outer skin from it.

'I'll tell him.' Fahy said and went back to his side of the table.

They soon finished preparing the vegetables and piled them into the boiler. Fahy made a few trips to the water pump in the back lane for buckets of water. He poured the water into the boiler and added the oats, put the lid on, then stacked more turf on the fire. 'There now, that's done. Let's get out for some air.'

They left the soup to cook and walked towards the River Corrib.

* * *

The dark grey-green river water, on its way from the great Lough Corrib, a few miles to the north, leapt and sparkled under the bridge, where the river banks widened into the estuary .

Fahy picked up a handful of stones, selected one to throw and watched it bounce across the waves. He handed one to Jane and she did the same; her stone bounced three times, then vanished. They spent a few minutes throwing stones and stood and watched the river flow into the bay.

There were only a couple of small fishing boats out on the water. Most of the bigger ships didn't bother to call to this port lately. The only goods to buy, or sell, were the sacks of grains for workhouses and soup kitchen food.

'Do you want to get rid of me?' Jane asked. She dreaded hearing his answer. He had to be her friend and ally.

'Jesus, Jane! Not at all.' He swung his arm back over his

head and let a large stone fly across the water. 'But things have changed. You have those two orphans and they're your responsibility now. Do you want them? Or have they been foisted on you? Be honest.'

Jane sighed. 'I suppose I do. They're my only family, but I don't think I'm any good for them, Fahy. I don't sleep most nights. I'm haunted by ghosts. They need someone who can love them.' She looked at her father's friend who had helped her since she came back from her exile, and shook her head. 'I don't think I have much love left in me, since we're being honest with each other. I'm no good for them, or anybody.'

'God bless you, Jane,' Fahy said. 'I'm not going to tell you what to do, girl. But I will advise you. You're all the family those two children have. Focus on them. From what I see they love you and you love them.' He bent and picked up another stone and handed it to Jane.

'Let's keep the soup kitchen going between us for the spring and summer months. We still have the money from Finn. And, you never know, times might pick up.'

Jane smiled and shook her head. 'I'll tell you something, Fahy. When I was in Waterford, I saw a newspaper advertised, for sale or rent. The whole business is bankrupt. I thought I might use the last gold nugget to make an offer for it and live near where my friend, Annie, lived. They're not so hard hit there in that town. Not like here.' She rubbed the stone between her fingers, but didn't throw it. 'Well, you don't see dead people by the side of the road, so much.'

Fahy put his arm around her. 'It sounds like a good plan to think on. Make a change for the better. Come on. Let's go back and see if that soup is ready. You're not quite done with it yet!' Neither spoke of Constable Smullen.

20

Saying Goodbye, May 1848

As Fahy had foretold, the next few months were full of hard work for the two of them. Jane worked at the newspaper on Tuesdays, Wednesdays and Thursdays. The other days, including Sunday, she worked with Fahy. Together they would prepare a large pot of soup and set it to boil on the range. When that was cooked, they loaded up the cart and headed off to their usual spot on the south side of the bridge, stopping on the way to collect a batch of fresh bread to give out with the soup.

Their regular families waited for them to arrive at around one o'clock. For the next hour, she and Fahy served up bowls and cups of the soup and gave out chunks of bread. She helped Fahy make the soup in the evenings on the days that she was working. That way he only had to reheat it the next day.

Once all the soup had been dished out, and the cups and tins returned, they'd load up the cart and head back to the cottage. By the time they had washed the pot and the mugs, it was time to collect the children from school.

One thing Jane knew for sure. She quickly became bored

with the drudgery of cooking and serving food to starving people. They were grateful, but they all seemed to be stuck in the same hole that Jane found herself in. Until something changed - perhaps the potato crop would grow again, or the unlikely revolution overturned the government - then Jane saw herself doing the same job for years to come.

The British government surely were not going to come to their rescue. They seemed intent on letting people die. She'd read a report in The Nation that the London government had not bothered to count the number of deaths that occurred. And the money she had gotten from Finn in America was running out. She had written to Finn and was waiting on a letter, with more money.

She thought of Sorcha and Jamie and the other orphans at Saint Vincent's. She might be bored and frustrated at her situation, but neither she nor they were starving, and she still had her last gold nugget.

* * *

Then, one Saturday morning, when they were serving the soup, Owen arrived. He was out of uniform, dressed in a dark suit, his hair had grown longer. She looked twice and saw it was him, then spoke quickly to Fahy.

She ran over to hug Owen. 'It's so good to see you. Come and talk to me.'

'So, this is it! You have a good set-up here.' Owen waved to Fahy and they walked a little way away from the queue of people. 'I've got news, and I didn't want to put it in a letter.'

'Good news?' When she saw his serious expression, Jane thought perhaps not.

'Yes, some good news. I've been discharged from the army. The army brought in the new contract last month. I'm a free man, Jane.' He didn't smile when he said it, instead he looked across at Fahy and the soup boiler.

'Owen, that's great news! You can come and help us with the soup kitchen.' Jane narrowed her eyes, she wanted to put her hand out to him, but held back, as if suddenly unsure of him.

He turned to face her, then looked away again. 'That's what I've come to see you about, my love. We need to talk. But not here. Can I come and see you tonight?'

'Yes, but why can't you tell me now?' She half smiled at a brief thought, does he want me to marry him? She dismissed the thought instantly. No, that's not it.

'I need to talk to you on your own, Jane. Look, I have to go and get sorted out at the inn. I'll call round later, when the children are asleep.' He bent and kissed her then he walked off quickly, with a soldier's brisk step.

* * *

Later that day when she had put the children to bed, she sat by the fire and waited for Owen. He didn't seem as if he was going to ask her to marry him. She didn't feel that from him. As if he was afraid of what she might say. What was he putting off telling her?

She didn't have much longer to wait. He knocked on the door and she opened it. He looked ill, pale and drawn; he walked into the kitchen.

'Come and sit next to me, Jane. I need to tell you right away.' He didn't kiss her or catch her hand. He took his hat off and

189

slumped into a chair beside the fire.

'What's wrong, Owen? You don't look like a man who's got his heart's desire. You're a free man.'

'I'm sorry, Janey. You're right. I am free. I had to get out of the army. I needed to choose a side and I won't shoot my neighbours. That's all they want us for. To protect the landlords and their estates. It's not for me. So I am glad to be out of it.' He glanced at her, then away, and stood up to pace the floor. 'But I have another problem.'

Jane heard his voice break and he cleared his throat and continued.

'My mother and father and the rest of them were evicted, last Friday. Right now they are in lodgings, in Wicklow town. I've got savings, and I paid for them to stay there or they'd have had to go into the workhouse.'

'Oh my God, Owen!' She put her hand to her chest as if a sudden pain stopped her breath, and she stared at him. 'I am sorry to hear that. I thought you sent money for the rent?'

'I did. It made no difference. They got no notice, just a letter telling them to get out. You know Tim and Sean are still overseas, with the army, but the younger ones are with my mother and father. And they can't stay there, Jane.'

'No, they can't. So, what will you do now?' She leaned forward towards the fire and wrapped her arms around herself and heard his words as if from a distance.

'The only thing I can do. We're emigrating. Going to Boston. I have enough saved to get us over there, and there's jobs I can do.'

She thought she had misheard, didn't understand what exactly he had said. 'Boston, in America?'

'We're away next week.' He stopped and looked at her and

took a deep breath. 'I don't want to leave you, Jane. I want you to come with us. Marry me, and we'll go together.'

Jane looked at Owen and half-smiled. '*A mhuirnin*, my darling.'

He stepped towards her, knelt in front of her and held her hands in his. 'You'll come with us?' he whispered.

For a moment her face lit up, but it was only a fleeting moment. She rested her head on his shoulder, then kissed his cheek. 'Sure, I didn't tell you, did I?' She brushed away tears. It wouldn't do to cry now, but the tears came nonetheless.

'Didn't tell me what?'

'Here, pull the stool up and sit down with me.' She held his hand. Her voice seemed to strain to speak. 'When I came back to Ireland, I made a promise to myself. Come what may, I'll not leave Ireland again. I'll live and die here, Owen. That was my promise then, and it still is now.'

Owen leaned forward and kissed her tears. His soft breath warmed her face. 'But everything has changed, Jane. You and Sorcha and Jamie can make a new life with me and my family. Come away from this place. It's dead! Can't you see?'

She nodded. 'Oh, I can see alright. I followed a corpse collector's wagon the other week. But there must be a change coming. We can't live like this forever.'

She reached over to the range and poured them out a cup of tea each and handed one to Owen. They sat without speaking or drinking, and the tea cooled

Somehow, she had thought this day might come. She knew then, that Owen, her wonderful love, couldn't be a soldier here. And now, well, he had to look after his family.

'Why is there nothing here for us, for your mother and father and brothers and sisters?' She stood and threw the cold tea in

191

the bucket by the door.

She hefted another piece of turf on the fire and watched it spark and flare up, breathed in the woody smell and turned back to Owen.

'Do you remember when I tried to jump off the ship in South Africa? And you stopped me? You said, I'd be caught, if I didn't drown first?'

Owen smiled. 'I remember the look on your face, Janey. You were terrified, standing there in your shift, one foot on the balustrade, ready to jump. I loved you at that moment and I still love you. Come with me!'

She shook her head. 'Later that night, in my bunk, I promised myself that I'd get back to Ireland and I'd never leave again. Here I am, and here I'll stay.'

'You didn't know you were coming back to this, did you?'

'No, and truthfully, I don't know if I can live here surrounded by soldiers and police and starving families. It breaks my heart every day. It reminds me of my mother and father and my brothers.'

She took a deep breath. 'But there's a revolution coming, Owen. What if it succeeds? It's happening in France and Italy. What if Tom Meagher and Mr Gavan Duffy and the rest of the Young Irelanders can do it? Then we'll have a free Ireland. One that will cherish its children. What if that happens this year?' She swung around in the small kitchen; her long dark hair gleamed in the firelight. 'I can't leave now. I won't leave now.'

'And if it fails?' he asked. His face softened, as if he hesitated to say the words, almost as if he pitied her delusion.

'If it fails? It won't fail. But if it does, then I'll decide.'

He put his arm around her shoulders and pulled her to him.

'You haven't lost your stubborn ways, Jane Keating.' He kissed her lips and it was a tender kiss, a farewell kiss.

'You must go,' she said. 'I can see that. You have a family to take care of. If my brothers were alive, I'd do the same.'

Owen shook his head, bright tears shone in his eyes. 'I'll not say good-bye, *astor*. We're not finished, you and me, Janey. I'll write to you with my address when we get a place. I'll wait for you, *mo mhuirnín*, my beloved.'

She sat by the fire and watched him leave. Until she met Owen, Jane had thought of herself as a child. Knowing him and loving him, she understood he was torn with love and duty to his family and his love for her. It would be so easy to follow him and call him back. They'd wake up Sorcha and Jamie and all go together.

But then, she'd never know for sure. If, by staying, she might do one thing to help those dreamers, those foolish heroes, as Speranza said, to achieve the dream of a free Ireland.

The slab of turf on the fire, cracked softly, sparks drifted upwards from the red-orange glow in the heart of the fire. Cooling grey ashes floated under the grate. The words of Father Hanrahan came into her mind and she leaned forward and whispered. "For everything there is a season and a time for every purpose under heaven. A time for war and a time for peace." Yes, the time for war is coming, then we'll have peace here in this beautiful island.

She banked down the fire, and before she pulled the shutters across the window to keep the night air out, she paused, and looked up at the sky, at the stars, a great swathe of glittering lights. She thought of her death, one day, here in this devastated land. She'd have Sorcha and Jamie by her side, of that much she was certain. Ireland was her home. She looked forward to her eighteenth birthday in October, and prayed that she'd live long enough to raise her two cousins. She was a mother to a stillborn daughter, and now must be a mother to Sorcha and Jamie. Maybe one day she'd be a wife and have more children. If not, then she accepted her situation. But perhaps she needed to do something more than dish out soup. She'd think on that.

'God bless you, Owen,' she whispered to the stars.

* * *

The next day, she started early on the soup. She left it to cook in the shed and sat in the kitchen, with Sorcha and Jamie. She told them a story about her time in Melbourne. About the boy, Jimmy, she had met and played with on the beach. The story turned into a game and when Fahy arrived the three of them were giggling and tickling each other. Somehow, Sorcha's dolly had gotten involved in the game, too.

The soup was ready and Fahy helped Jane load up the cart. Jane and the children sat up on the bench and clicked the ass to go on. The day was fine, and Jane's customers were waiting to be fed. On the way, she told Fahy about Owen.

21

Trials in Dublin, May, 1848

The trials of the Young Irelanders were due to start in Dublin. Jane went out to Saint Vincent's church.

'Father, I'm going to Dublin. You heard about Thomas Francis Meagher and two other Young Irelanders? Their trials start on Monday. Nan said she'd have Sorcha and Jamie for a couple of days. Is that alright?'

The priest nodded. 'She told me. They are welcome to stay, Jane. But you be careful over there in Dublin. These are dangerous times.'

'I'll take care. Besides, I know you'll say a prayer for me, Father.'

'Here, I'll bless you for the journey.'

She knelt and the old priest laid his hand on her head and sketched a sign of the cross over her. 'I didn't tell Mrs Flynn,' he murmured, 'but the Bishop has had word, from Rome of all places. The Holy Father has banned priests in Ireland from all political activities. The Pope's ban is to be said at all masses in the next few weeks.'

Jane sighed. 'The French President, Lamartine, told Tom,

when he was in Paris, that they couldn't help us either. Why will no-one help, Father?'

'Oh, I'm sure those politicians in London have a long reach, and that stretches as far as Paris and Rome.' Father Hanrahan caught her hand and repeated his warning. 'Be careful up there, won't you? Come back to us.'

'I promise.'

Jane took the ass and cart back to town. Fahy would make the soup for the next few days while she was away.

She pondered the priest's words on her journey to Dublin. The coach raced across the country and she looked out at the now familiar route.

* * *

She got to Dublin late to stay with Speranza in her hotel rooms on Wellington Quay. Speranza ordered hot chocolate for both of them and showed Jane to the second bedroom.

'The drinks will be here in a few minutes. I'd say you've got time to get changed out of your travelling clothes. We can relax and talk for a while,' Speranza said.

Jane's bedroom had its own bathroom with a jug of warm water waiting for her. She quickly washed and put on her night shift. She brushed her hair and checked herself in the bathroom mirror. She'd always been in awe of the famous Speranza, yet the woman had been nothing but kind to Jane. She saw a worried frown on her face in the mirror, and relaxed it into a smile, then went to join her friend.

Speranza had changed into a cream silk dressing gown. With her lovely dark hair down around her shoulders, Jane's friend seemed to glow in the lamplit sitting room.

'Come and sit with me. Now, taste that! Speranza said. They both sipped the sweet, creamy drink.

'Mm, it's lovely,' Jane said, and leaned back against the padded seat. 'I've been cramped in a coach all day. This is lovely. Thank you for your hospitality, Miss Speranza.'

'Enough of the Miss. Just call me Speranza. I'm not your mistress, I like to think of us as friends.'

'Then, tell me, how did you get involved with The Nation? Forgive me, but I don't think you're a Catholic, are you?' Jane asked.

'No, I'm a Protestant. My grandfather was an Archdeacon in the Anglican church. I never had any interest in politics up until I was eighteen. That was almost ten years ago, in fact.'

Speranza took another sip of her drink and dabbed her lips with a white napkin, then turned to Jane. 'I read an article by a Mr Charles Gavan Duffy and was immediately enthralled by the spirit of Ireland. I wrote a poem and sent it to Charles and he published it. Of course, I couldn't use my name, so I used a pen name, Speranza. It means 'Hope.' And I met some of the Young Irelanders, and then this terrible disaster happened.'

'You were really good to Annie. I know it meant a lot to her to have her poems published.'

Speranza nodded. 'I made it one of my missions to help young Irish women earn some money by their writing. I'm proud of that.' The poet turned to smile at Jane. ' And you. I think I guessed you were a girl when I first saw you as Jack Keating. You were too pretty. But the men didn't see it, so I said nothing.'

Jane felt heat rise in her face. 'I'm not pretty. Well, maybe pretty for a boy.' She smiled at the compliment.

Speranza put her cup on the silver tray and held her hand

out for Jane's empty cup. 'In a way I envy you, Jane. You've been to the other side of the world, and come back! But I think you have suffered, too. Am I correct?' Speranza stood and carried the tray over to a small table. The silver tray flickered and gleamed palely in the light of the crystal lamp.

Jane sighed and touched the bend in her nose. 'Yes, you must be a mind reader,' she whispered with a half-laugh.

'No, just observant and interested in other people's lives.' After a pause, her friend continued. 'I know you escaped from Melbourne. I want to know the rest of it.' Speranza sat down beside Jane and held her hand. 'Will you tell me?'

Jane closed her eyes and lay back against the cushions. 'I was working as a housemaid for a retired army officer and his family. One day, he raped me, I don't know why he would do such a thing. I really thought he was going to kill me, so I hit him with the smoothing iron and ran away. After that, I found I was pregnant.' She took in a deep breath and blew it out slowly. Yet, in the telling, she had felt the hard smoothing iron in her hand, and now it signified her own strength.

'And then?' Speranza asked softly.

'And then Owen helped me escape. Another friend was an Aboriginal woman. She gave me some gold. I'd helped save her son when he was attacked by bushrangers.' She had leaned forward to rest her head on her hands and her voice became muffled. 'That's it. That's my story.'

'What about the baby?' Speranza whispered.

It was as if another spoke for Jane.'She was stillborn, before I escaped, on the 16th of April, last year. I named her Margaret after my mother.' A shiver raced through Jane's chest and she felt Speranza's arm around her. Jane turned and rested her head on her friend's shoulder. She had almost fallen asleep with the telling of it, as if in a dream. Her breathing slowed and she saw the tiny body of her baby in her mind's eye. A cold tear trickled down her cheek and she woke to see her friend's face close to hers.

'Jane?'

'I'm tired.' She could hardly bring the words.

'Here, I'll walk with you to your room. You've done a lot today.'

Speranza helped Jane up and they walked together to the bedroom. Jane sat on the bed, lifted her feet up and lay back on the scented pillows.

'I hope I haven't upset you by asking about Melbourne?' Speranza pulled the covers up around Jane and blew out the lamp.

'I needed to tell it. Thank you.' Then Jane dropped into a deep, dark sleep; tears still wet on her face.

* * *

The next morning, Speranza hugged Jane, but neither mentioned the conversation the night before. After breakfast, they set out for the short walk to the Law Courts in Inns Quay. The streets and the quays along the Liffey were lined with soldiers. Everywhere she looked, armed soldiers stopped and checked people. She caught a glimpse of a tall young soldier who reminded her of Owen. He must be with his family in Boston, if they had left in March. He's well out of this, she decided.

'The government has sent ten thousand more soldiers to Dublin to keep the peace while the trials are on,' Speranza explained. They waited with crowds of supporters on the

Quay outside the courthouse for William Smith O'Brien to arrive from his lodgings. He was escorted by what appeared to be thousands of cheering Irish men, who waited outside when he went in to face trial.

Speranza and Jane joined a queue to get into the court. The poet talked her way into the Ladies' Gallery and they squeezed through the crowd of women. Speranza elbowed her way into a tiny space then gestured for Jane. 'There's room here, darling.' Jane avoided the black looks from the women she passed to get to her seat in the middle of the row.

The Ladies Gallery jutted out over the courtroom. Both Jane and Speranza looked down on the top of Mr Smith O'Brien's head and that of his Queen's Council, Mr Butt. Jane spotted Mr Gavan Duffy in the public gallery below her.

The court was called to order and the judge sat on his high throne-like seat. It was a short trial. At the end of it, William Smith O'Brien was acquitted by the jury even though it had been handpicked by the prosecution. One of the three Catholics on the jury had refused to convict. The court erupted into loud cheers and shouts. Outside on the quay, supporters of the Young Irelander applauded him. Smith O'Brien asked them to come back the next day to support Tom Meagher.

That evening the two women strolled with Tom, Gavan Duffy and William Smith O'Brien along the quay.

'You'll not to go prison, Tom,' Speranza said. 'They wouldn't dare after seeing all those men and women on the streets today.'

'Let's hope you're right, my friend,' Tom replied. 'But I have great faith in Mr Butt to defend me. We'll meet for supper tomorrow after I'm acquitted.' He laughed. 'Now I have to go and meet up with my father. He is beside himself with worry.'

'We'll go with you, Tom,' Gavan Duffy said. They said their farewells.

'Let's go back to my rooms, Jane. I think we need a glass of wine to calm our anxiety.'

* * *

The bubbles in the champagne tickled the inside of Jane's nose and she sneezed. 'This is lovely!'

'Well, we need to celebrate. And champagne is the perfect drink for it. But I had a feeling William would be acquitted.'

'Why? Is it because Mr Smith O'Brien is a Member of Parliament? I think he represents Limerick.'

'You're right. But that's not the best part of him. He's descended from Brian Boru, the *Ard Ri*, the High King of Ireland. And his father is a baronet, Sir Edward O'Brien, who owns Dromoland Castle in County Clare. I've visited there and it's absolutely huge.'

Jane laughed. 'No! But, sure, why would someone like that put his life and liberty at risk?' Her admiration for Smith O'Brien only grew. 'Why didn't they arrest Mr Gavan Duffy?'

'He wasn't at the meeting and he didn't print sedition. John Mitchel did, though.' Speranza raised her eyebrows.

'Do you think Tom will be acquitted?'

'I'm certain of it. You know Tom's father is the Lord Mayor of Waterford and the Member of Parliament for Waterford?'

Jane nodded.

'So the family can afford to get the best Queen's Council to represent him - the famous Mr Butt, who we saw today.'

'Ah, yes.'

'Tom will be freed tomorrow, and we'll drink more champagne. That's a promise!' The champagne seemed to have relaxed Speranza and she drank the last drops of her drink and shook the glass flute at Jane. 'But neither of them are soldiers, Jane. Do you remember the flag?'

'I do, it was a wonderful day.'

'I said then, that we'll need more than just a flag, if there's to be a rebellion. I guarantee your soldier, Owen Doran, has more knowledge of how to organise and fight a rebellion, than these two young, privileged men. The only one of the three of them I'm not sure about is John Mitchel. He set up his own newspaper, and has printed incitements to rebellion regularly. The government won't stand for that.'

'But they're so brave!'

'They surely are brave. Here, I'll pour us some more champagne. But we will need more than bravery to overturn the British Empire in Ireland. And I don't have to remind you that Irish Catholics have been starving for years now, and they're unarmed.'

Speranza poured the last of the champagne into their glasses, then pulled the cord to summon the hotel servant. 'I'll order us another bottle and you can tell me all about your life in Galway. How are your little cousins getting on?'

The next morning they hurried back to the Law Courts.

* * *

On Tuesday, May 16th, another Young Irelander was called to stand up before the judge.

'Thomas Francis Meagher, you are here on trial for inciting

hatred against Her Majesty Queen Victoria, and inciting people to rise in rebellion. How do you plead?'

Isaac Butt, Queen's Council, spoke for Tom. 'Your Honour, my client pleads not guilty to this charge. He would like the opportunity to address the court.'

Tom spotted Speranza and Jane and nodded to them, then turned his attention to his accusers. He looked confident. He was sure of being exonerated now that Smith O'Brien had been freed. They had both been arrested after speaking at a public meeting. Tom put his case that, as an Irishman, he was free to speak for the love of his country.

The judge threatened to clear the court if the observers continued to cheer Tom every time he stopped for a breath.

The jury took just half an hour to bring in their verdict. Thomas Francis Meagher was exonerated.

The trial of John Mitchel was postponed.

'They'll hand-pick a new jury for Mitchel. He published sedition in his newspaper, The United Irishman. They'll get rid of him one way or another,' Speranza predicted.

* * *

At supper that evening, Jane joined Speranza, Tom and Charles Gavan Duffy at the hotel. They talked about their plans for a rebellion in the autumn and agreed the leaders would go and set up groups of rebels around the country.

'I wish you success,' Jane said. They raised their glasses to drink to a free Ireland.

Jane told them of the newspaper business in Waterford that she had seen advertised for sale or rent.

'I was thinking, maybe I could rent it and get the newspaper running again.' She held her breath, and smoothed the sleeves of her dress.

Tom said. 'It's still there, it's not sold. Nobody wants it. You should put an offer in, Jane. There's only a few newspapers in the whole of Munster. It's a shame to lose another one. Have you still got some of that money left?'

'I have the gold nugget still. But I think I'd need a sponsor.' She smiled, then leaned across the table to address Charles Gavan Duffy. 'If you sponsored me, I could rent it, Mr Duffy. I have the money to get started.'

'It's a big undertaking, Jane.' Gavan Duffy pressed his lips together. 'I tell you what. Why don't you go and take a proper look at it? Tom, you go with Jane. Both of you, look at it and let me know the name of the auctioneer; I'll write to him and enquire about the background.'

Tom raised his glass of champagne. 'Let's drink to that. Jane Keating's new venture!'

Jane settled back in her chair and nodded to Tom.

That evening, they left behind talk of rebellion and spoke of their hopes for Ireland in the future.

22

Summer in Galway, June 1848.

The schools had closed for three months across the summer.

'Can we stay with the others at the church while we're on school holidays?' Jamie asked on the last day of term.

'Well, I'll have to ask Father Hanrahan what he thinks.'

'Nan thinks it's a good idea. We asked her last week. She said she'd say it to Father.'

Jane saw a look pass between the two siblings. 'You've cooked this up between you, haven't you?'

Sorcha giggled. 'What's cooked up, Jane?'

Jamie added. 'Besides, you're busy with the soup kitchen and work at the newspaper. Nan thinks it's better for us to be with the others. There's plenty to do there. Shay, and Liam and Billy have got work on Mr O'Brien's farm at Barna. They said I might be able to go, too, but I'll have to stay at the church if I'm to start work early. Nan says Sorcha can play with Lucy and Grace and Maria.'

'I don't believe you've arranged all this, Jamie Keating! I'll talk to Father and Nan. You know they have their hands full with six children already. I need to see if they are happy with this.'

'They'll be happy,' Jamie said, full of confidence. 'The four of us will be getting our dinners at the farm and Mr O'Brien said he'll pay us in vegetables and milk. Nan thinks it's a great idea!'

'Stop! You're addling me! Don't say another word until I've spoken to Father and Nan.'

'Fahy thinks it's a great idea, too.' Jamie added, and raced out of the door.

'What? Where are you . . ?' He was gone.

'I don't believe this. I've been worrying what to do with them for weeks now and they've gone and made their own arrangements. Just wait till that Fahy gets here.'

Jane grumbled away to herself and got dressed.

'Right, Sorcha, get your dolly and we'll go and set up the soup boiler. Fahy will be here in a few minutes and I've got to speak to him!'

* * *

Father Hanrahan and Nan confirmed that Jamie and Sorcha would be welcome to stay at the presbytery with the other children for the summer, until school opened again in September, when they'd move back into town with Jane.

'I'll come out and see you all every day as soon as the soup kitchen is finished. That way I can take Sorcha and the girls off your hands for a while.'

'Sure, you're a good woman. But your two are no trouble. And I think after the boys have worked all day on the farm, they'll be too tired to get up to mischief,' Father Hanrahan said.

It was agreed. Jane packed up the children's clothes and Sorcha's dolly and brought them out to the presbytery.

She stayed there overnight and the next day she walked to the farm with Jamie and the boys. Billy, who was now almost thirteen, and the brothers, Shay and Liam, reminded her of her younger self working with her father in their potato field. It seemed so long ago, but had only come to an end with the appearance of the blight three years earlier, in the autumn of 1845. Now Jamie was going on eight, and the older boys would look after him.

The farmer knew her, for he had known her father and her cousin, Brendan. 'So, this is poor Brendan's son. Well, he's a Keating alright.' The farmer put his hand out and shook hands with Jamie. 'I hope you're as good a worker as your father was, young man.'

He pointed to the table in the middle of the large airy kitchen. 'There's milk there and bread and butter, have some breakfast before you start, lads.'

He held the door for Jane. 'Step outside with me for a minute, and we'll talk.'

They stood on the path outside the farmhouse while the boys ate their breakfast. Jane looked out over his fields.

'Thank you for taking on these lads, Mr O'Brien, and especially Jamie. He's a bit young, but I'm sure he'll work hard.'

'I knew all their families. It's a shame what happened to them,' the farmer said. 'And if I can do a bit to help them, then I'll sleep better at night. Mary will give them a dinner every day and send them home with some vegetables and milk.'

'Thank you. Tell me, what's the situation with the potato

crop this year? Have you set any?'

'The blight is still in the ground, I'd say.' The farmer paused. 'I've heard there's been some potatoes set around here, but I don't hold out any hope for them. I'm sticking with the cattle and vegetables. Mary has hens and the dairy. Spuds are finished, for me, at any rate.

'Anyhow, I can't stand here gossiping, I'm going to put them boys to work. Jane, it's been good to meet you.' They shook hands and Jane walked back along the road to the church. There were some good people and she was thankful for that.

Back at the church, Sorcha was playing with Maria, Lucy and Grace, and didn't have time to say goodbye, as Jane headed back to town.

* * *

Jane was surprised to find that she missed the company of the two children, but she kept herself busy with making the soup and her job at The Star.

She had heard there was to be a Confederation meeting that week and asked Fahy if he'd go along with her. The meeting was well-attended, unlike the previous meeting where there were just a handful of local businessmen and farmers.

The chairman welcomed Jane and Fahy and business got under way.

Halfway through, the door opened and a late-comer walked in. 'Sorry, I'm late. I got held up at home.'

Jane looked at Fahy. 'I don't believe this,' she whispered. Fahy's expression showed that he felt the same way.

It was Niall Smullen and he slunk in and took his seat at the end of a row. He still had his hat on and only when he was sitting down did he take it off. He didn't look around.

'Niall, you're welcome. We're talking about the landlord's estate. You might not have heard but Lord Sinclair has been declared bankrupt and the Court of Chancery is managing the estate farms. That'll mean evictions, I'd say.'

Smullen nodded. 'You're right, they'll be on the case for rent-gathering.'

Jane stared over at Smullen. Oh, you'd know all about that, she thought.

'And what can be done about it?' Smullen asked.

'That's what this meeting is for. You may have heard of the Young Irelanders. They split away from our late leader, Daniel O'Connell's Repeal Movement. As a group, we were loyal to Daniel O'Connell, but since his death last year, there's been only infighting between the younger members and O'Connell's son, John.

'It's my understanding that the Young Irelanders have set up a separate group, the Irish Confederation. They want to work to get an independent parliament, but also land reform.

'I think it's time we supported the local farmers to get a fair land contract. It's no good just evicting them. We've talked about writing to the local Member of Parliament and getting him to raise it in the House of Commons in London.'

'I'll second that,' Smullen said.

It was agreed that the Chairman would write to the local MP, who lived in Dublin, and set out their wishes.

The chairman wasn't finished. 'I want us to think about renaming ourselves as an Irish Confederation group. We can invite one of the Young Irelanders to come and talk to us. What do you say to that?'

Jane looked around the room. There wasn't a lot of support

for it, but she raised her hand. 'I know some of them. I can get in touch and ask them to send someone to talk about land reform.'

'Thank you, Jane. I suggest we wait to hear from the Member of Parliament, first.'

Jane nodded, that sounded fair enough.

As the meeting drew to a close, Smullen raised his hand. 'I'd like to add a few words to the meeting if that is alright?'

He stood and looked around the room. 'Many of you know me. I grew up here and went to school with Jane Keating's cousin, Brendan.'

Jane caught her breath.

'I left to join the Irish Constabulary and worked for ten years in Sligo. When I got married, I transferred here, and I worked with the local bailiff, for a while, helping with evictions. The last eviction I was involved in was Brendan Keating's. I am sorry to this day about the outcome of that. You may remember Brendan died.'

Jane looked around at the men and women at the meeting. She saw a few nods in her direction.

'I want to say to you all, and especially you, Jane Keating, that was the worst day's work I ever did. That's why I have come along here. I want to try and make up in a small way, to help others who might be facing eviction.'

Jane shook her head. He sounded sincere, was almost crying as he spoke. He had told this tale to Fahy, who hadn't believed him, no more than Jane did now. Smullen was a liar and a coward in Jane's eyes. Nothing he said would change that.

The chairman stood up from his seat behind the table and came down where Smullen still stood.

'You're a brave man, to come and be so honest. I'm sure

that I speak for everyone here when I say that there are no objections.'

Jane kept silent. If Smullen was genuine, which she didn't believe for a minute, then she had to give him a second chance. If he was lying, then she'd make it her business to find out. And she'd find out soon, before he did any more damage.

* * *

Jane and Fahy stayed behind to let Smullen leave the meeting. He wore a countryman's knee breeches, woollen socks and hobnail boots. His dark jacket was buttoned up to the neck, and as he left, he pulled a wide-brimmed black felt hat down on his head.

'I'm going to follow him. See where he's off to,' Jane said.

'I'll come with you,' Fahy replied.

'No. He'll spot two of us. He won't see me, I promise.' She put her hand on her friend's arm. 'Meet me back at the cottage?' She took off down the street after Smullen.

There were only a couple of street lamps lit at this end of the town and all the shops were either closed or just shutting. Jane stepped over a pair of legs stretched out from a doorway. A thin bare arm and a hand stuck out. 'Spare a few pennies, Miss?'

She stopped and rooted in her skirt pocket for a coin. 'Here, God bless!'

A dog barked as she passed a gate and she ducked down, afraid he'd turn and see her. He was intent on wherever he was off to. He didn't stop, just continued on across the bridge over the Corrib.

'I know what you're up to,' she whispered, and stepped into

an empty doorway.

Smullen slowed and stopped halfway across the bridge. He leaned on the parapet and turned to look back at the way he had come, saw nothing, hacked a cough and spat out into the river.

She waited until she heard his footsteps start up again. The hobnails in his boots clattered against the stones on the bridge roadway.

'If you turn for the Constabulary building, then I have you.' She willed him to slow, but he kept on going right past the front door of the Irish Constabulary station.

She ran to the bridge and crossed it but he had disappeared into one of the lanes that ran off the main thoroughfare. He could have gone around to the back entrance of the police station. She hurried down the dark alley but the back gate was locked up. The only way in was through the front door.

'I'll catch you next time,' she promised.

She pulled her cloak around her head and retraced her steps to her cottage.

* * *

Fahy was leaning against her door. 'Well, did you see anything?'

'No. He went straight past the police station. Then I lost him.'

'I'll keep a look out for him when I'm up the town,' Fahy offered.

'Will you come in for a cup of tea?'

'No, thank you, girl. I have to get back to the presbytery. Make sure this door is locked now.'

'I will. Good night, Fahy.'

* * *

The next day at the newspaper, Paddy told her that the chairman of the committee had been arrested late last night and taken in for questioning.

'It's Smullen,' she said, convinced now that Smullen was an informer.

'Did you see him?'

'No, but it can only be him.'

Later that week the charges against the chairman were dropped, but at the next meeting there was no mention of an Irish Confederation club.

* * *

In early July, Jane read an announcement in the newspaper. Lord Sinclair, the bankrupt local landowner, had left Ireland for a tour around Europe on his yacht.

'Yacht?' she asked Paddy.

'Sure, they all belong to the Royal Dublin Yacht Club,' he informed her.

'Why do they do that?'

'Well, they can show off in front of their friends, and they can run and hide in France or Italy when the debt collectors come calling.'

Una added. 'The rumour is that his estate is going into the Court of Chancery.'

'What'll happen to the land?' Jane asked, but she got no answer.

Later that week, she called out to Mr O'Brien's farm to ask if he had heard the news about the landlord.

'I have. He's left us in the lurch. As soon as the courts decide to force a sale, the new owner will be able to clear the whole estate. Consolidation is the new word they are using.'

'What does that mean?'

'All the small farms like mine will be bundled together and rented out to the highest bidder. And I won't be one of them. It seems the government wants to change the use of the land from pastoral to arable, so that only crops like wheat are grown on big farms. All my work here will be gone for naught, the improvements to the land, this lovely house and the barn. I won't see a penny for any of it.'

'What will you do?' She dreaded hearing the only answer he could give.

The farmer shifted his cap on his head. 'There is only one thing to do. As soon as this harvest is in, I'll sell the crops and the cows and take the money and clear off to America.'

'No more work for the boys?'

'There'll be work for them till the end of July, then we're off. I'm trusting you not to tell them, Jane. I don't want word of my plans getting out.'

'I won't tell anyone. But I'm sorry you're leaving.'

'Until we get fair rents, fair recompense for improving the land, and protection from eviction, then there'll never be a way forward for Irish farmers.'

The boys were coming back from the fields, weary, but smiling and joking. Jamie waved to Jane.

'There's a bag of vegetables in the kitchen, don't forget to take it with you,' Farmer O'Brien reminded the boys.

That evening, the sun dipped late, the boys had worked a

twelve hour day, but they were proud of the work they had done and the food they were bringing home.

23

Waterford, 10th July 1848

She had waited weeks to hear back about her and Mr Duffy's offer to rent the newspaper in Waterford. Finally, Mr Duffy had written to tell her that his legal enquiries had been satisfactory and gave her his approval to go ahead with her offer. She had the letter and instructions to the auctioneer in her bag. The children were still at the presbytery, so she only had to let Fahy know she'd be gone for three days.

'You mind yourself with that gold nugget,' he'd warned her. It was to be the deposit on her newspaper. It was time to spend it.

* * *

She willed the coach to go faster to Waterford, but it still took the whole day, trundling along muddy roads and stopping and starting to change horses. She consoled herself with the thought that it had taken her four days of walking, the first time she did the journey, so this sitting in a coach for a day was an improvement. The time allowed her to dream of the new life in Waterford that she, Sorcha and Jamie would start very soon.

Of course, she'd still help Fahy to keep the soup kitchen going in Galway. But instead of handing out bowls of soup to starving paupers, she'd send him some money to help with the makings of the soup.

She was young and strong and, with help from Mr Duffy and Thomas Francis Meagher, she'd make a success of the Odyssey newspaper. She had dreamed of a better life when she was in Melbourne and she was almost there.

* * *

In Waterford, she went straight to Thomas Meagher's home on the quay to tell him her good news, and hoped that he'd go with her to meet the auctioneer.

Instead, she had to push through crowds of people on the quay outside the Lord Mayor's mansion. A black police van waited in front of the house. The horses stamped and rattled their bridles. Behind the van, twenty or more soldiers lined up on horse-back, and stretched out along the quay, waiting. She recognised the uniform of the Royal Dublin Fusiliers, and thanked God that Owen had got out of here.

'What's happening?' she asked an old chap in the crowd.

'They've come to arrest the Lord Mayor's son, young Thomas Francis,' he said. 'T'is a shame, so it is.'

'No,' she whispered. But it must be true. This was his second arrest this year.

The front door opened and Thomas was led out by two soldiers. His father came and stood by the door. Thomas

217

turned and embraced him, then he lifted his hand to the watching crowd.

A voice called. 'Will we save ye, Thomas?' At that moment, Jane would have stormed the police van, until she heard Tom's reply.

'No. Don't cause any trouble. I'll go with them. My barrister will speak for me in court.' The sun shone down on Thomas Francis Meagher as he bent his fair head and stepped into the back of the van. The door was locked and barred behind him. He hadn't seen Jane.

The soldiers readied their horses, and at a command from their captain, trotted behind the van along the quay towards a great ship anchored out in the middle of the River Suir.

Jane followed on foot. By the time she reached the landing wharf, Thomas had been transferred to a skiff and was on his way out to the huge warship. She stood and watched him climb the ladder up the side of the ship. She waved but he didn't look around; he followed his captors below deck.

Seamen raced up the rigging and let the sails out where they billowed against the pale blue sky and caught the wind. The anchor was raised and the enormous ship swung around in the river and headed out towards the estuary and Dublin.

'What will become of you, my friend?' She shook her head. He had been acquitted in April, why had they arrested him again? It reminded her of the night Owen had caught her about to jump overboard in the Cape of Good Hope. Owen was right, there was no escape. The British Government had a long reach.

She passed back by Thomas's house but didn't knock. She had no idea what she could say to his father. Instead she headed for the auctioneer's business premises.

* * *

The auctioneer remembered her from her previous visit with Thomas Meagher. She took out the letter from Mr Duffy, and placed it on the counter.

'I've come to put in our offer for the newspaper,' she said. 'Mr Gavan Duffy writes here that he will come to Waterford to sign the legal documents as soon as they are ready.'

Jane couldn't believe the next words she heard.

'I'm very sorry, Miss Keating, but the Odyssey is no longer for rent.' The auctioneer's face looked strained at having to impart this news.

'What do you mean?' To a stunned Jane, it was as if someone else had spoken; her voice was cracked and hoarse.

'The printing press has been sold to an English newspaper. The new owners shipped it out early this week.'

'But, I've got my offer right here. The bank has agreed that Mr Gavan Duffy will be my guarantor and partner.' She repeated all the information she knew he had received from Mr Gavan Duffy.

The auctioneer shook his head, his spectacles had slid down his nose and he looked over the tops of the lenses at her. 'I'm very sorry. I'm going to write to Mr Duffy today. This all happened very quickly. The bid came in last week and was accepted by the court immediately.'

There must be some mistake, Mr Duffy had been in constant touch with the auctioneer and the solicitors about renting the business. Jane stared at the man behind the desk.

He sighed. 'The Court of Chancery ran out of patience waiting for a sale. They accepted the offer for the printing press and ordered the premises and the machinery to be sold separately, to try to get some money in for the creditors.'

He picked up Mr Duffy's letter. 'I'd say you could put an offer on the building, if you're interested.'

She closed her eyes. 'It's no good to me without the printing press.' She held her hand out for the letter, turned and left.

Outside the office, Jane stood on the road, unable to think or move. Then, determined to see it one last time, her feet dragged on the walk along the broad quayside, past the bridge, to the edge of the town where the last business premises was the newspaper she had set her heart on. The door was bolted, as expected.

'Why did you think that you could own a business here? It's not for you, a poor cottier's daughter. That gold has turned your head.'

She sat on the doorstep in the summer sunshine and looked out over the river. She had imagined working here for the rest of her life, raising Sorcha and Jamie. What did her father call it? A pipe dream. A feral cat strolled past and glanced at Jane. Its lean body and alert eyes were on the look-out for easy prey.

Sounds from the river reached her, seagulls swooped and landed on the water, waders hopped along the shoreline, picking away at tiny worms deep in the sand. Across the other side of the river, a ridge of dark hills stood out against the blue sky and the sun was pale in the distance. Green fields were divided by low scrubby hedges. She searched along the landscape, looking for a stone wall, yet saw none.

At home, in Galway, the countryside was delineated with grey stone walls dividing up the fields into smaller sections of greens and golds, each framed in stone. She much preferred stone walls to hedges. The white or pale grey rocks were shaped and stacked one on top of the other, interleaved for strength and stability, yet fluid, rising up hillsides or curving along a lane or roadway.

She lifted her chin a fraction. Galway stone walls had lasted hundreds of years, perhaps even thousands, through every sort of wind, rain and snow. They were constructed for hardship, hammered and shaped by their makers. She half-smiled, like its people, too.

And she still lived and breathed; and her cousins lived, too. Jane was the last of her mother and father's children to survive, to get thus far through this desperate reckoning of hunger and disease. She'd been to the ends of the world, had been hammered and shaped by pain and grief. She would go on, and persist.

She looked back at the newspaper and raised her hand in farewell. It wasn't for her. 'So be it.'

She turned and walked back towards the centre of town and waited for the coach to take her home.

24

Goes to join Tom, July 1848

T wo weeks later, Jane read in the newspaper that Thomas Francis Meagher had been arrested again. This time, they charged him with both treason and sedition. Mr Butt, his barrister, had worked another miracle to get him released on bail. Jane guessed that Tom's father, the Lord Mayor of Waterford, would have been able to apply some pressure to get his son released until his trial. Charles Gavan Duffy had been arrested, too, but as the owner of The Nation, he was remanded in jail until the trial.

The Irish nationalist newspapers were full of the Confederation's plans for a rebellion.

A letter arrived that day.

```
Dear Jane, I'm keeping my promise to let you know.
I'll be stopping overnight in Nenagh, in the Coach
Inn on Thursday, 27th July.  My advice to you is to
stay at home.
Your friend TFM.
```

'It's started!' She would join them. It was time for war. She'd not tell her friends, she'd tell them when it was over. Owen should be here. We'd win, then. But I'll try for both of us, she vowed.

'I've got to make one more visit to Waterford, Father. I want to see Tom before his trial. I don't know when it will be, but I don't think he'll be acquitted the next time.'

'He's a brave young man, Jane,' the priest said. 'But you're right. I think the government is tired of all this talk of rebellion. They'll come down hard soon.'

'I won't be away long.' She paused. 'Father, if anything should happen to me, Fahy will look after Sorcha and Jamie. I'll speak to him about this.'

'But Jane, don't go near any trouble, girl, will you?' The old priest looked puzzled.

'If I'm called on, I'll help. Will you pray for me, Father?' She half-lied to the priest, but it was to save him from worrying about her.

'I will, to be sure. Come, and I'll bless you.'

She knelt in front of him and he rested his hand on her head. 'Lord, bless and keep your daughter, Jane, safe from all harm. Bring her home to her family, dear Lord and Father.'

* * *

Then she only had to say goodbye to the children. By now, they were used to her going on her journeys, so this was just another visit to Waterford. It was getting harder and harder to leave them, especially now that she knew she might be putting herself in danger. She hadn't said anything about the loss of the newspaper. At first, she didn't want to get their hopes up, and now they wouldn't be dashed. Only Fahy knew, and he sympathised with her disappointment. 'See it for what it is. For the best. You still have your gold.'

She smiled. 'I'll never get the chance to spend it, I think.'

'Are you taking it with you to Waterford?'

'No, I have it here.' She held the gold nugget out to Fahy. 'Look after it? It'll be for Sorcha and Jamie if anything happens to me. It'll keep them out of the workhouse till they grow up. I told Father that you'd take care of them if I don't get back. You'll do that, won't you?'

'What are you going into?' He took a deep breath. 'I want to tell you something before you go, Jane. You've been like the daughter I never had. Your father would be as proud of you as I am. Take care of yourself, won't you?'

'Thank you for saying that, Fahy, but they won't catch me. I'm a Galway girl, we're strong.' Like those walls up on the hillside, she almost said, and smiled at the thought, eager to start.

* * *

Jane bought a ticket for the coach to Waterford and walked out of the coach station to wait for her ride.

'Good morning, Miss Keating.'

She turned at the sound of his voice. 'Don't speak to me.'

Niall Smullen ignored her instruction. 'Off on another jaunt then? Where might you be going today?'

She took note of his use of the word, 'another', and breathed in the smell of sweat and unwashed clothes from him. He stood much too close to her. She moved away and put her ticket into her purse.

'It's none of your business. Let me pass.' The coach had drawn up to the stop and she moved to get past him.

He put his hand out to bar her way. 'It's an innocent question. I hear those Young Irelanders are out and about, trying to raise support. You wouldn't be going off to join them, now would you?'

She'd not tell him that she was on her way to find Tom Meagher. 'I'm going to Clonmel, if you must know, to see my intended. He's in the British army,' she lied, and hoped that Smullen hadn't heard differently.

Smullen narrowed his eyes as if trying to decide whether she was lying, then he nodded. 'Have a safe journey, then.' He turned away from her.

Jane waited until he had walked off before boarding the coach. 'Nenagh, please,' she said, and handed over her ticket.

25

The Rebellion, Thursday 27th July, 1848.

J ane caught up with Thomas Meagher early on the Thursday morning as he prepared to leave the Coach Inn.

'You got my letter, then. I told you to stay at home!' he said. But he smiled nonetheless. 'You're looking for trouble, Jane Keating!'

He was driving a sturdy pony and trap and she hopped up onto the seat beside him. They set off together in search of the 'Rebel Priest', Father Kenyon in Templederry a few miles away from Nenagh.

The priest had promised to raise twenty parishes for the rebellion. 'There's no point in waiting until they arrest all of us. We have to act now,' Thomas had told her.

It only took a few hours to get there and the seat in the trap was padded and had springs. The sun burnt her forehead and she squinted at the glare on the road ahead. It was all worth it to arrive in the village of Templederry. But it was also a surprise. The place was small and there weren't that many houses or cottages in it.

'They'll be in the parishes around and about,' Thomas explained. 'Let's find Father Kenyon. We'll gather our army.'

They found the presbytery next to the church and knocked on the door. Jane was stunned to hear the priest's first words, and thought Tom must have been, too. The priest didn't invite them in. He looked to be in his early thirties, dressed in a black cassock, and was clean shaven with short brown hair. He began to speak and stuttered over his first words.

'I c-c-can't ask people to join you. They're st-starving and they have no weapons. What are you going to fight with?'

'Father, you promised three months ago to organise twenty parishes with food and weapons. Have you not done that?' Thomas demanded.

'No.' The priest said no more, but his shamefaced glance at Jane told the tale.

'Well, if you have no weapons then they'll have pikes. They can use them,' Thomas said. 'Did you get supplies of food in?'

Father Kenyon avoided answering the question. 'I don't want their blood on my hands, Thomas. I won't ask them.'

'You promised half the county would be ready for this fight. Don't tell me that was a lie!'

Father Kenyon shook his head. 'We're not ready. The time is not right.'

Jane took a step forward. 'When will you be ready, Father?'

'I don't know. Maybe when this great hunger is over,' the priest blustered.

Jane looked at her friend. 'My priest in Galway told me that the Bishop has admonished the priests there to not get involved in political activity. If they did, then they'd be suspended from their parish.' She pointed a finger at the priest.

'Have you been admonished, Father? Is that why you're not ready to fight? Have you been suspended by your Bishop?' Jane heard her voice rise almost into a shriek and she took a deep breath and swallowed.

'That's got nothing to do with this,' the priest shouted.

'There's your answer, Thomas. He's been threatened by his Bishop. We'll get no help from him. He's a coward.' She was calmer now that she knew.

They turned and left the priest at the door and climbed up on the trap. The poor pony looked as dejected as they felt.

'Where to now?' Jane asked.

'We'll make our way to the others. They're all meeting in The Commons, a village near Ballingarry. It's about thirty miles or so.'

* * *

As they got nearer to Ballingarry, Thomas told Jane to go on alone. He scribbled a quick note for her to give to Smith O'Brien saying that they had failed with Father Kenyon. 'I can't go back empty-handed, Jane. I need to make another try at raising an army. I'll go south, and see who I can find.'

'Let me come with you,' she said.

'No. I don't know what I'm going into, but one thing is for sure, I don't need to worry about your safety. Go to the meeting and tell them to wait for me. I'll bring an army!'

He smiled. They both knew he'd struggle to raise an army if the Roman Catholic Church had told the faithful to stay at home. But he had to try. He took the pony and trap and headed south while she walked for five miles until she reached The Commons, a village near the small townland of Ballingarry.

She delivered Tom's note to the leader, Mr Smith O'Brien. He said nothing as he read it, then thanked Jane.

* * *

The place was full of a rag-tag of people, mainly families with children, who had come to join the rebellion. Jane was thankful she had not brought Jamie and the boys along with her, but they would have fitted right in. By evening, the volunteers numbered five hundred and Jane saw they were all up for a fight. That is, until the meeting began.

William Smith O'Brien spoke first. 'We are ready to fight for a free Ireland. But we need to be armed and provisioned.' He raised his voice. 'I want you all to go home. We'll wait here for you to gather up provisions, bring enough food for four days, and arm yourselves. If you can't get hold of a gun, then bring a pike.'

The silence that fell over the crowd was soon filled with mutters of disbelief.

The people Jane saw in front of her and around her, had not eaten a decent meal in the last three years. A crowd of ragged, starving men, women and children, they would fight, right enough, but food and arms were out of their reach.

Overnight, the volunteer army dwindled to fifty men and a few women. Between them they had a dozen pistols and as many pikes. All of them, including Jane, were hungry. They needed Thomas Meagher to get there soon, and with an army of rebels.

* * *

The next day, a sunny Saturday morning on the 29th of July, a contingent of Irish Constabulary rode through Ballingarry and stopped at the barricade blocking the road. The ragged volunteer army fired some shots and chased them across the fields until they saw the policemen take cover in a farm-house a few miles away from the village.

In this way, the 1848 rebellion began.

When the chasing volunteers caught up with the policemen, Jane heard children screaming from inside the house.

The rebels surrounded the house and shots were fired from both sides.

An hour later, a stocky, black-clad woman came hurrying along the road towards them. 'What are you doing here, and who is in there with my children?' she asked.

Smith-O'Brien answered her. 'We've started the rebellion, Missus. There's Irish Constabulary in there.'

'Jesus, Mary and Joseph! Get away out of that with your rebellion. I have to get inside to my children. Move out of my way there!'

The woman pushed past Smith-O'Brien and opened the gate to the garden in front of her house.

Jane saw a rifle poking out of a window and ran to catch up with the woman.

'Where are you going?' the woman asked her.

Jane was almost too embarrassed to speak. 'I'll go in with you. I came to join the rebellion. To make Ireland free,' she said.

'Well, one thing is for sure, you're in the wrong place. Not in my garden, or my home. Get yourselves off up to Dublin Castle if you want to fight, not here in the middle of the country!'

'There are ten thousand soldiers in Dublin, and as many

again in Cork. We have to start somewhere, Missus. I'm sorry,' Jane said, then added. 'I think this is all a mistake.' Speranza's words echoed in her mind. *I guarantee your soldier, Owen Doran, knows more about how to organise and fight a rebellion than these young, privileged men.*

By now they had reached the front door. The woman shouted. 'You in there! I want to get in to my children.'

The cries of her young children intensified.

The door opened a crack and an officer motioned her to come in. Having come this far, Jane followed her.

'Who are you?' An officer asked.

'I'm Mrs McCormack. This is my house and land and these are my children. Where are they? What have you done to them?'

The officer looked at Jane.

'Jane,' she said. 'I'm with the Missus.' She couldn't think of another thing to say.

Then she was inside a house full of screaming, terrified children and surrounded by a dozen, armed police officers.

'Get over there, and you, missus, shut those children up!'

Their mother took her children upstairs into one of the bedrooms to comfort them.

* * *

The firing started again. Jane edged out of the room, ran into the hall and up the stairs to the front bedroom. She looked out of the window and saw Smith O'Brien and his men only yards from the house. They were crouched down behind a low stone wall. Most had pistols and fired at the house. One of their companions tried to join them and was shot. He fell, and lay not moving.

Smith O'Brien called out to the policemen in the house. 'Men, I don't want any more bloodshed. Lay down your arms and we'll talk.'

Jane crept down the stairs and tried to overhear any conversations between the policemen. One was arguing for surrender. 'We'll not hold out much longer.'

Another, an officer, raised a finger and pointed at the man. 'O'Farrell is on his way to call for help from Cashel. They'll be here in a few hours. We've got ammunition, and that lot won't get in here.'

Jane had to get out of the house and join the rebels. She slipped along the hall to the back door. The door was barricaded, but there was a small scullery with a sash window. She pushed the window up and climbed out into a walled yard. She hopped over the low wall and ran around the perimeter to meet up with Smith-O'Brien and his men.

'They won't surrender. They're waiting on reinforcements from Cashel,' she said.

'How did you get out?'

'The back door is barricaded. I got out through a small window.'

'I'll go and try to talk to them again,' Smith-O'Brien said. 'We've lost one of our men and I don't want to lose any more.'

'What will we do now?' Jane asked him. 'Will you surrender?'

'No.' He looked exhausted. To Jane, the leader of this rebellion, William Smith O'Brien, a Member of Parliament, and the son of a baronet, appeared to be totally lost for what to do next. His suit, shirt and cravat were covered in dust from crouching down in the road and his curly hair was in disarray. He spoke in a cultivated English accent. 'We'll have no choice when the reinforcements get here. I'll keep on trying to get them to throw their arms down. Then we can claim a victory.'

'Can we hold on until Thomas gets here?' Jane asked.

'He'd better get here soon.'

'He'll come. The children are in a bedroom upstairs with their mother. They are safe enough,' she said.

They crouched down and made their way to wall at the front of the farmhouse.

A few of the policemen in the farmhouse had begun shooting at them from the front windows. They picked off another volunteer who had been standing right next to Jane. He fell dead beside her.

'Get down, Jane!' O'Brien yelled.

She picked up the rebel's pistol. It was still loaded, but she couldn't get a look over the wall for the shooting from the house.

* * *

An hour passed. It appeared to be stalemate. The policemen were trapped in the house, but equally the attackers, the rebels, were pinned down behind the stone wall in front of the house and couldn't advance.

Smith O'Brien continually called out to the police officers in the house. 'We'll give you safe passage. Throw down your weapons!'

The only response was more gunfire. The police seemed to have plenty of ammunition.

Jane heard sounds out on the lane behind them.

Meagher had arrived. His news was not good. 'They're not ready to fight.'

233

* * *

Later, reinforcements trotted across the fields to the rear of the house, and they were not rebel volunteers but the police from Cashel.

'Look!' she whispered. Fifty mounted Irish Constabulary men trotted towards the rebels. They heard cheers from inside the farmhouse.

It was all over.

Smith O'Brien shouted. 'Everyone! Save yourselves.' He threw his gun down and held his hands up in surrender and stepped in front of the mounted soldiers.

Meagher had tears in his eyes. 'I'm sorry, Jane. This is the end of it. I want you to get away from here.' He hugged her. 'You're a brave girl, but don't sacrifice yourself for this. Run for your life!'

'We'll go together.'

He shook his head. 'I'm a wanted man. You get away, please! The pony and trap is up the lane, take it and get yourself to Galway.' He wiped his tears away. 'This is just the beginning of the fight, Jane. People will see that Ireland can be free one day. Please God, we'll see it in our lifetimes. And you'll be able to say you were here at the start of it. Stay free!'

She left him there and went around the shed, then along the hedgerow and into the adjoining field.

Behind her she heard gunshots and shouted orders.

The men in the house, many of them Irishmen in British uniform, cheered at the defeat of their own countrymen. She kept moving.

She only had get to the pony and trap and drive away.

She could hardly believe the rebellion was over. It had failed, leaving, two men dead. Her boots crunched on the stony path. To think it ended like this.

Blackbirds in the hawthorn trees sang a sweet song to accompany her along the lane, then suddenly stopped. In that silent space, a step sounded behind her. She slowed, and cocked her head to listen; looked up and saw two blackbirds fly off across the field. Then set off again.

26

After the Rebellion.

Jane moved forward and felt a hand grab her hair. She turned to see who it was. 'No!' she screamed.

It was Smullen, in his Irish Constabulary uniform.

'Well now, I wonder why you weren't rounded up with the rest of them.' He smirked, as if he knew he had her.

She stayed silent, for there was no-one around to help her. Her muscles tensed, ready to run or fight him off. She spat in his face.

'Bitch!' Smullen yelled. 'I should have finished you off when I had the chance.'

He had one hand on the back of Jane's head and he clutched a fistful of her hair tightly. He caught her hand in his and dragged her away from the house.

'It'll be no use me arresting you,' he said. 'Then I'll have to put up with you shouting about how I shot your stupid cousin.'

Jane clenched her teeth to not cry out for the pain in her head. Was he going to kill her? There was nothing else he could do. He needed to keep his secret safe. He had murdered once before, she was sure of that now. Was she to be next? She tried to catch her breath, but gasped in pain. Will it end here on a back lane in Ballingarry?

'I'm only sorry I didn't do this two years ago,' he growled. Then he stopped and turned to look her in the face. 'And then, do you know what I'll do?'

She looked into his mad eyes, saw the sweat on his face, and knew instantly. 'Say it.'

'Them two Keating orphans will follow you to the grave. I swear there won't be a Keating left on the face of the earth. And if your soft friend, Fahy, asks any questions, believe me, he'll go the same way.'

He dragged her further along the rutted lane.

'They'll find you, if you kill me,' she said. Little by little a thought came to her. He daren't kill me. He's got too much to lose.

'Don't be so sure. They didn't find me after I shot your brave cousin, Brendan, now did they?'

'You won't kill me, you're all talk. I know for a fact you're an informer.' She dragged her feet and looked for a chance to escape. They were now at the top of the rutted track; further down, she saw some trees in a small woods. It was the only place to hide.

Jane had one hand free. She slowed and he stepped up beside her then she glanced across at him. She had put the dead rebel's gun in her pocket earlier. It was that or take the risk of him killing her. He could throw her into a ditch and there'd be no more about it.

* * *

She caught a glimpse of sudden movement behind Smullen,

heard a hard knock, saw Smullen's eyes roll up in his head, then he fell to the ground. Her legs gave way under her and she collapsed beside him.

'Are you alright, girl?'

The breath had been knocked out of her and she couldn't answer at first. It was Mrs McCormack, and she knelt beside Jane and peered into her eyes.

'Ah, sure you're grand! Come on. You need to get up.' The woman helped Jane up off the ground.

'You saved me!'

'I was up in the back bedroom and I saw him follow you. I thought, he's up to no good, the way he crept along behind you. So I got my saucepan and came to find out.'

'You heard what he said, about me and my cousins?' She coughed and tried to catch her breath. Her scalp stung from where he'd pulled her hair out.

Mrs McCormack smiled grimly. 'Oh, I heard him alright. What'll you do now? He's not dead, and he'll not give up on you, I'd say.' The widow kicked Smullen's foot. He groaned and sighed, but remained unconscious.

* * *

Jane was silent for a few moments. The two women stood over Smullen's body and looked at each other. Time paused, the breeze dropped and the songbirds were silent in the trees above them.

She knew exactly what to do. She'd known it for a while, just hadn't said it.

The woman smiled at her. 'Well?'

Jane swallowed hard and took a deep breath. 'I've got friends in America, and the money to pay for our fare.' She leaned forward to embrace the woman. 'Thank you,' she whispered. 'You saved my life! You took a big risk for me.'

'Sure, he didn't see me. I'll come back here in an hour. If he's still unconscious, then I'll get some help for him. I'll say I found him. What can they do to a poor widow woman?'

They linked arms and walked along the lane.

Mrs McCormack sighed. 'I've been thinking for a while now of getting out of here, myself. Today has made my mind up for me. Those police officers wrecked the place. They tore everything asunder. That's my home, and taking my children hostage! Sure, the poor things were terrified in there. They could have been killed with all that shooting going on.'

'I heard one of the police say that you were a widow.'

'I've been on my own for a couple of years now, since poor Donal died. He wouldn't want me to live like this. As soon as I get the fare together, I'll take them out of this madhouse. There has to be some place better for our children to grow up in.'

They reached the pony and trap and embraced again. 'Please God, we meet up in America,' Jane whispered.

'Don't worry about that one back there. What did you say his name was?"

'Niall Smullen.'

'Where will you go now?'

'I'm going home to Galway to collect my cousins, Sorcha and Jamie. Then we'll leave.' Just saying the words made it true. But there was another question lurking in the back of her mind. And the others? She shook the thought away.

'If he asks, I'll tell him I saw you heading off south. You need to go.' The widow pointed along the twisting lane. 'Follow along here for a mile, until it runs out. Then cut north across a couple of fields; that'll bring you to the Dublin road. Cross over it and head north-west past Lough Derg and Portumna. The road west will bring you home.'

Jane repeated the directions then turned to hug Mrs McCormack. 'You saved my life! Thank you.' She climbed onto the trap, waved goodbye to the widow and made her escape. The pony trotted up the narrow track and across the fields.

Jane headed towards home for the final time.

* * *

She drove the pony and trap north and followed the Widow McCormack's instructions. She drove all that evening and through the night.

At dawn she stopped at a stream to wash her face and hands. The pony needed a rest and she unhitched it and let it graze for an hour. They both had a drink of cool water from the stream. She saw a sign for the town of Portumna ahead, but didn't stop. She was in County Galway, at last, and breathed a sigh of relief at being halfway home.

She let the pony walk the rest of the way. It took most of the day, but by the time they reached Athenry, she knew she could walk home, so she unhitched the trap and left it on the side of the road. Neither she nor the poor tired pony had any further use for it. She followed the coast road in the twilight. She'd had plenty of time to think on her journey.

* * *

It was almost midnight by the time they arrived on the Long

Walk in Galway, and Jane was exhausted and starving. The poor animal was limping, head down, after days on the road. But they were both free and clear of the Ballingarry rebellion.

She led the pony into the back yard of the cottage and took off the bridle, made sure he had water and hay. 'Thank you,' she whispered, and rubbed his shoulder. She unlocked the door into the kitchen, re-locked it behind her, kicked her boots off, and went through to her bed and lay on it.

The lonely hoot of a night owl echoed through the shuttered window. She blessed herself and said a prayer for the two men who had been shot dead that day at Ballingarry.

Sleep wouldn't come, tired as she was, for Smullen's words resounded in her head. 'Them two Keating orphans will follow you to the grave.'

She got up and sat at the kitchen table and made a promise to herself. 'He won't get the better of me. This I swear.'

Much later, she slept until dawn.

27

Galway, Monday, 31st July 1848.

J ane must have fallen back asleep. She had dreamt that Owen had come back to her and was knocking on the door and calling her name. 'Jane, Jane! Are you in there? Wake up!'

She woke, still dressed in the clothes she had worn for the last five days. He's here. 'Yes! I'm coming, *mo ghrá*, my love.'

The knock sounded again. She sat up in the bed. Her hair was tangled around her face and her body ached from the miles she had covered in the last few days. The muscles in her arms were stiff from hauling the reins, and urging on the poor pony. Her feet were sore from walking the last miles home in the dark to reach her cottage beside the River Corrib.

'I knew you'd come back to me!' She stumbled into the kitchen and unlocked the door. She saw only Fahy and looked past him for Owen. 'No,' she whispered. 'It was only a dream.' Tears flowed down her cheeks and she looked at her friend who looked ill with worry. He had lost weight in recent weeks and his gaunt and lined face showed the strain of last few years.

'Jesus, Jane. You had me worried there. I tried all day

GALWAY, MONDAY, 31ST JULY 1848.

yesterday, but there was no sign of you.' Fahy must have seen the state she was in, for he added. 'Did I wake you?'

She stepped back from the door. 'You did. Come in.' She had been so sure it was Owen calling her name. The buttons on the front of her dress must have come undone while she slept and she fastened them and followed Fahy into the kitchen.

'There's been rumours all over the town about an uprising in Kilkenny,' Fahy said.

'It was outside Kilkenny. I was there, in The Commons near Ballingarry, in County Tipperary.'

Fahy muttered something under his breath.

'Give me a minute, I need a drink,' she said, and picked up a bucket and hurried out to the water pump in the back lane. The morning was overcast and heavy. Thunderstorms weren't far off by the feel of the sullen air. When she got back to the yard, Fahy was waiting for her beside the pony.

'Who's this fella?'

'He brought me home.' She poured some more water into a stone trough for the pony to drink. Then dipped a mug into the bucket and swallowed down a big drink. Fahy waited while she gathered up handfuls of cool water to splash on her face and eyes.

'I'm starving, Fahy. I've eaten hardly anything for days.' She went into the kitchen and collapsed onto a chair. The drink of water had steadied her and she dried off her face and hands with a cloth.

'I'll start a fire and cook up some oatmeal.' Fahy said, and set to work and lit the fire with kindling and bits of peat turf. When the flames sparked into life, he put oatmeal and water in a pot to boil. 'It'll be ready in a few minutes. Now, will you tell me what you've been up to?'

'The rebellion failed. They've all been arrested. Tom and Mr Smith-O'Brien, all of them.' She blew out a breath and didn't attempt to stop her tears.

'Christ! What the hell happened?'

'They fought with some Irish Constabulary men, two rebels were shot and killed, then, after a few hours, police reinforcements came and, it was all over. I got away. Even though that rotten Niall Smullen did everything he could to stop me.' She closed her eyes at the shocked expression on her friend's face.

'He came with the reinforcements from Cashel. There must have been fifty or more of them. It ended quickly. I was just about away when he caught me. Mrs McCormack, the woman who lives in the farmhouse, sent him flying with a belt of her cooking pot.' Jane felt a laugh bubble up and let it out. 'She crept up behind him. Hah!'

Her smile faltered and she pressed her hands on the table. Her fingers were scraped and sore from climbing over stone walls. Her scalp burned where Smullen had pulled out chunks of hair. She had no strength left in her to move out of the chair. She caught the sour smell of sweat off her body and longed to have a wash and change into clean clothes.

Fahy caught one of her hands in his. They sat in silence for a few minutes. Jane tilted her face to look at her old friend and saw tears in his eyes.

'He'll come after you again, would you say, Jane?'

'He threatened the children, Fahy.' She pressed her lips together and stared into his eyes. She didn't say, *and you.*

'Are you going to leave?' he murmured.

By now she had begun to compose herself and nodded. 'Yes. But I'm not running away. I've helped the Young Irelanders take the first step. I'm proud of that, Fahy. We're up against an empire. Sure, you know that. And half the country is starving. I swore never to leave Ireland, but I see now, that this is not the time to fight. That day will surely come, and, please God, it will be in my lifetime. Then I'll come back.'

Fahy squeezed her fingers. 'I have no doubt of that, girl. And Jamie and Sorcha?'

'We'll go together. They're my family now. Will you come, too, my friend?' She paused and saw the answer in his eyes.

He shook his head. 'I still have work to do here. As long as I get money from America, I'll keep the soup kitchen going. Soon, God willing, we'll get a crop of potatoes and eat our fill.' Fahy put his hand in his pocket. 'Here, you'll need this.' He placed her last gold nugget on the table.

She nodded her thanks and they sat and looked at the gold.

* * *

The pot bubbled on the stove. 'That porridge will burn if you don't dish it up!' she said, and then they both laughed.

'You'll have to eat it with salt. There's no milk here.'

'Just put it in a bowl and let me at it!'

Fahy put the bowl of porridge in front of her and she blew on the spoon to cool it. 'Ah, that's lovely.'

When she had eaten her fill, she sat back and looked at her friend. 'Thank you for your help, all this time. I'll need it again, later today. I have to tell Father Hanrahan and Mrs Flynn, and the other children. Will you meet me at the presbytery this afternoon?'

'I will. I'll leave you to get sorted out. I'll come back later and make the soup.'

Before he left, Fahy brought in another bucket of water and

put it to heat on the fire. Jane sat for a while and studied the water as it warmed. Bubbles rose slowly through the pail, then began to move faster. She sat, as if mesmerised, waiting for the water to come to a boil.

The words from the Bible flitted through her mind. 'For everything, there is a season. A time to get and a time to cast away. A time of war and a time of peace.' Bubbles roiled and burst on the surface of the water. She breathed out a long sigh and blinked away tears. 'It's time to cast away.'

She scrubbed her muddy boots outside in the yard and left them to dry by the stove. Next, she stripped off her filthy dress, her shift and drawers and washed herself then dressed in clean clothes. She brushed her hair, taking care not to touch her scalp, and tied it back with a thin ribbon. She left her dirty clothes in the kitchen; Fahy could get rid of them for her.

Finally, she packed the rest of her belongings. At the bottom of her travelling bag she found Annie Power's 'Commonplace Book.' She had meant to give it to Marsh's library in Dublin, but now it would go with her. She opened it and read about Annie's harrowing journey through Quebec and Montreal on her way to New York. 'Annie, I'll follow your route and we'll get there safely, please God.'

She picked up the gold nugget. Mr Duffy had been right to tell her to keep one back. It was the best of the gold, too. She rubbed it, the smooth, gleaming ridges. Even in the dim light of the kitchen, it exuded an ancient radiance. This would be the saving of her. She had wanted to use it to put as a deposit on the newspaper in Waterford, but now, there was another use for it. 'Thank you, Sally and Jimmy.' She had helped to save her Aboriginal friends in Melbourne. Now their gift would save her.

She put the gold nugget in her pocketbook, picked up her bag and left the house. There wasn't much time, and she had things to do.

As she left the cottage, Fahy came back to start up the soup.

'Will you come out to Saint Vincent's when you're done?' she asked him.

'I'll see you there later,' he promised. She gave him the key to the house.

* * *

First, she went to the newspaper, and told Una and Paddy of her plans to leave. Una asked her to write up a report on the uprising and promised to publish it. While Jane wrote the report, Una sat beside her at the clerk's desk and wrote up a letter of reference for Jane's work at The Galway Star.

When that was done, Jane searched through the newspaper archives for an advertisement she'd seen a few weeks ago. Old copies of the newspaper were stored in a big cupboard in the corner of the office. She had to scan through the last three editions before she found it. At the time, the name of the ship had caught her eye.

'Here it is!' She showed it to Una and read it aloud.

Out of Limerick for Quebec

To sail on Wednesday 2nd August, 1848

The Splendid, First-class Belfast-built Ship

Jane Black

T. O'Gorman, Commander

This fast sailing ship is now discharging her cargo of timber and refitting to leave for Quebec.

She will be fitted up with every attention to the comfort of Passengers who will receive the usual allowance of Provisions and Water during the passage.

Application to be made to Captain O'Gorman on board ship, or at the offices of

Francis Spaight & Co, Ship Agents, Limerick Quay.

Or

John Daley, Shipping Agents, The Long Walk, Galway.

July, 1848.

She said goodbye to Una and Paddy and hurried along to the bank. She only glanced over her shoulder the one time. If Smullen came after her then she'd deal with him. No use worrying until it happened. Something told her she was right to think of him as a bully and a coward, but she kept an eye open just in case she was wrong.

Inside the bank, she laid her bank deposit book on the counter in front of the teller, and looked at him in silence, then she placed the gold nugget on the dark oak surface where it glimmered against the grain of the wood.

She rested both hands on either side of the last piece of her gift from Sally. 'I want to change this into sovereigns. Can you do that for me?'

The bank teller reached out and touched the nugget with a finger-tip. 'Oh, that is a rare sight. I'll just take it and ask the manager.'

'Leave it there. I'll bring it to him.' The last person to touch it, apart from herself and Fahy, had been her Aboriginal friend, Sally, in Melbourne.

'Yes, Miss. Of course.' He drew his hand away and went to find the bank manager.

She picked the gold up and held it in her hand and felt it slowly warm to her touch. 'I'll never forget you, Sally,' she murmured. She was saying goodbye to the last of the gold that tied her to Melbourne in New South Wales.

The clerk was back in a couple of minutes. 'Please, come with me.'

She followed him to the manager's office and again showed her bank book and the gold.

'I see you deposited more gold in Dublin, last year.' The manager looked very like the Dublin bank manager. Smartly turned out in an expensive tweed suit with a high starched collar and a silk cravat.

'Yes. Mister Gavan Duffy helped me open the account. You know of him?' The bank manager nodded.

'His name is there.' She pointed to the cursive handwriting on the first page of the small leather-bound book. 'I need to change this gold today. Can you do that?'

'Of course. I'll weigh it and then we'll know the value.' He dismissed the teller and went to a cupboard to take out a small brass weighing scales. He set up the scales on his desk.

He looked at Jane warily. 'May I?'

She stopped a smile and nodded. He placed the nugget on the tray and added tiny weights to the opposite tray. 'There, we have the balance.'

Jane added up the weights and nodded in agreement.

At the end of the transaction, she had thirty-five pounds. She put twenty of the heavy gold sovereigns into her purse and wrapped the remainder in a small leather pouch that she put in the bottom of her bag.

After shaking hands with the bank manager, she headed towards the Long Walk and the shipping agent's office. The heavy clouds from earlier had cleared away leaving a sunny morning and the few trees along the paths rang with birdsong. She was alert for any sign of Smullen, but he was nowhere to be seen. If he had to return to Cashel with the rest of his unit of police officers, he might not be back yet.

She reached the Long Walk and strolled along the side of the Corrib. The Spanish Arches had been built hundreds of years ago and would still be there when she came back to Galway. 'If I ever return,' she murmured to herself. It was now early afternoon, so she'd need to get a move on.

Several homeless people sat in the shelter of the Arches and she was at a loss to know what to do, if anything. The sovereigns in her purse weighed on her. She had to use them to save herself, but stopped and bent down to speak to a young man in a doorway. 'Do you know there's a soup kitchen up past the bridge?'

He nodded. 'I've had my soup there already. Thank you.'

'Where are you from?' she asked.

'Here in the town. I was in the workhouse, but I couldn't stand it in there.' His eyes were large in his gaunt face and his head drooped. 'At least I can breathe fresh air. And the soup is better out here than in that place.'

She handed him a silver shilling. 'Good luck.'

* * *

Thankfully, there were no other people in the ticket office.

'I want to buy a ticket for Quebec on the Jane Black, from Limerick. It's sailing tomorrow. Is there a second class cabin to be had?' She had made up her mind that if she had to go through Quebec, then she'd not risk spending weeks in steerage. She remembered reading Annie Power's account of her journey, and wanted to avoid that at all costs.

A second class cabin ticket was fifteen pounds for Jane and the two children. When she saw that it would only cost half that for the three of them to travel in steerage, she was tempted, but decided not to risk it.

She would make good use of her gold and pay for a cabin for herself, Sorcha and Jamie.

She decided to leave five pounds with Father Hanrahan to help with the children. That left her fifteen pounds. She guessed it would be more than enough to rent a place for them in New York and see them through the first month or two. She'd have a job by then.

The afternoon was warm and sunny and she slipped off her shawl and looped it through her bag, as she walked out the road to the presbytery. Blackbirds and thrushes sang in the dark green hedgerows she passed. Tiny buttercups and daisies seemed to dance on the grass verges. She spotted two red squirrels darting up the trunk of a hazel tree.

Thoughts of never seeing this place again filled her with sorrow. Her father's grave and the headstone she had placed on it would record the presence of her family for years to come. One day, maybe she'd return.

She'd miss Father Hanrahan, Mrs Flynn and the children. She persuaded herself that they'd be fine. Fahy would see them right and she'd leave them some money and send more when she could. The ache in her head told her there would be no good outcome to this.

28

To Limerick, 1st August 1848

F ahy had reached the presbytery before her. The soup
kitchen was all done for the day, and now it was early
evening. Jane hugged Sorcha and Jamie, she felt their
arms around her, and kissed their soft cheeks. 'Have you been
good while I was away?'

The four of them walked to the chapel. Sorcha clung to Jane.
'Don't go away again, Jane. I don't like it when you're not here.'
The child's worried face wrinkled as if she were about to cry.
Jane smoothed her hand across Sorcha's hair. 'I won't leave
you again, *acushla,* my darling.' Jane made a silent promise to
herself, she'd not make her little cousin cry, ever.

'Father has some important news for you,' Jamie said, and led
the way from the door of the church along the aisle towards
the altar. The place was strangely silent. Jane expected the
children to be on the move, but they stood or sat quietly. The
two large statues of the saints, one on either side of the bare
altar, towered over the children.

Father Hanrahan walked up to the pulpit and Jane glanced
at him. What on earth could be more important than her news

of the rebellion?

The priest pointed to a pew for Jane and Fahy to sit next to Mrs Flynn, who sat unmoving.

'Thanks be to God and his Blessed Mother,' Father Hanrahan said. 'You got back safe and sound. We were worried you'd be arrested, and then where would we be?'

'Well, I'm here now, Father, and the rebellion is over.' Jane looked sideways at Mrs Flynn and noticed that she held a handkerchief in her fingers, as if she had been crying. The housekeeper avoided Jane's glance. The air in the church smelt thin and stale; the light from stained glass window above the altar seemed to have dimmed in the few moments she had been in the church, as if a cloud had momentarily covered the sky outside.

It seemed as if everyone was holding their breath. Billy and Shay leaned against the chapel wall with their heads down. Liam sat alone, his arms clasped around himself as if to protect his body. He swung his legs and waited. Maria moved over to sit next to her brother and brought her dolly with her. The twins, Lucy and Grace, sat on the other side of Mrs Flynn, and Sorcha joined them. They had been waiting for Jane to come back from her rebellion to tell her that their little world had collapsed.

Father Hanrahan began to speak again. His hands trembled as he brushed his fine white hair back from his face. 'I'm sorry to say this, but I have been instructed by my Bishop to retire. He said there's not enough people left in the parish to keep the church open. And, due to my ill health, he has found me a place in a monastery in Galway. I explained to His Excellency that this will leave Mrs Flynn and the children homeless. But . . .' His voice tailed off and he closed his eyes.

'Oh, Father! Nan!'

Mrs Flynn spoke to Jane. 'The Bishop says we have to move to the workhouse. I went to see to the Master on Friday. He said he'd make room for us, because the Bishop has asked him to, but they are over-full as it is.' Her voice cracked, the dark circles beneath her eyes dominated her narrow face and made her appear older than her years.

Billy spoke up. 'Not me. The Master said they'll send me to Australia.' His voice was matter-of-fact, as if he were trying to be brave, but Jane saw fear in his tense young body. He seemed set to run away, yet she knew there was nowhere to run to.

Jane shook her head. 'That can't be right, Billy. They wouldn't do that. Would they?' She looked at the adults and got her answer. Billy O'Reilly had just turned thirteen.

'They'll send me to New South Wales, because I'm old enough to work and there's no jobs here.' Billy explained.

Jane saw tears in Mrs Flynn's faded brown eyes. She had heard of such an apprenticeship scheme for orphans. The Union Workhouse would send the older boys away. There was no work anywhere, and no money to keep young people idle in the workhouse for years.

Maria ran over to Shay, her brother, and caught his hand. All of this was news to her and, at seven years old, having lost both parents, she opened her mouth and let out a wail. 'They won't send you, too, will they? If you leave me and Liam, who'll look after us?'

Shay Cleary was six months younger than Billy O'Reilly. Jane was almost certain the Workhouse Guardians would send the two boys together.

Jane was speechless and breathless. Time stood still.

* * *

A candle had been left burning on the altar, and the flame began to gutter out and cast moving glints of light on a picture of the Holy Family. Jane stared at the painting on the church wall. Most of the colours had faded, but the Virgin Mary's cloak was still the same vivid blue as the summer sky outside, and the halo painted around her young face and head blazed with golden shafts of light.

She looked at the children and adults. 'No, you won't go to Australia, Billy. You're still a child. I won't let them send you.'

Father Hanrahan and Mrs Flynn both had their heads bowed as if defeated and unable to solve this new problem. Jane looked at Fahy, who stayed silent. Did he know about this? She couldn't tell from his grim expression.

'No,' Jane said again. 'Fahy, I need to speak to you, outside.'

* * *

They stepped out into the bright evening air. 'It's not right, girl, I know it,' her friend said. 'But what can we do?'

'I won't let them send Billy to New South Wales. I'll take him with me, on my ticket. It will only be a couple of pounds extra.' She took a few paces up and back along the path. 'Fahy, I can't take everyone, much as I'd like to.'

'You don't have to take everyone, Jane.' Fahy reached out a hand to her, then let it drop, as she turned and paced again along the path.

'Listen, you told me the rent's paid on the cottage up to Christmas. Is that right?' he asked.

'Yes, and you know you're welcome to stay there.'

'Then instead of the workhouse, why don't Mrs Flynn and the other children come with me? They could have the bedroom and I'll sleep in the kitchen. What do you think of that?'

By the time he had finished speaking, Jane had reached him and put her arm around his neck. She rested her head on his chest and wept. She felt the pressure of his arms around her and after a while she managed to stop crying. She used her hand to wipe her face. Her eyes were swollen almost shut and her voice cracked when she spoke.

'I'll get more money, or I'll save up and send it to you.' She could hardly speak for the weight of sorrow that enveloped her.

Each side of the path they stood on was sheltered by old hazel trees with knotted greyish-brown bark. The many spreading branches were filled with deep green leaves and evening sunlight cast twilight shadows on the path and on them. Dormice scampered around the base of the trees, gathering in fallen hazelnuts to store for the coming autumn and winter.

'Will we go in and tell them?' Fahy asked.

Jane watched a couple of squirrels race up the tree trunks. What will they have to live on for the years and years it will take for this disaster to end; when she had taken the last of her gold with her to America?

She took a deep breath and felt herself relax. At that moment, she made her decision. 'I have a better idea, Fahy.'

She saw him study her face, then his expression cleared, as if he had read her thoughts, and he nodded slowly. He smiled at her. 'Yes.'

The chapel was in silence. It seemed they hadn't moved,

they all waited for Jane and Fahy to come back.

'No-one is going to the workhouse, that's my promise.' Jane turned to Billy O'Reilly. 'Billy, you're not going to New South Wales. This morning I bought tickets on a ship to America. I want you, and the rest of you, to come with me and Jamie and Sorcha. We'll go together. What do you say?' She looked at each child, Billy, Shay, his brother, Liam and sister, Maria, and the twins, Lucy and Grace. Billy spoke first. 'Yes!' He leapt into the air and whooped with delight.

Jane looked at the faces of the children who had seen Billy's reaction and understood they, too, were going on an adventure. Jamie and Shay punched the air. 'Yes!' Then both shouted in English. 'We're off to Amerikay!' and laughed with delight at their cleverness.

Sorcha ran over to Mrs Flynn and hugged her, then turned to Jane. 'What about uncle Fahy and Nan?'

Jane reached out her hand out to Mrs Flynn. 'Nan, will you come, too?'

The older woman shook her head. 'I don't know if I can leave Ireland.' Then the girls, gathered around their Nan and hugged her. 'Say you'll come with us, Nan. We need you,' Lucy said.

At that, Mrs Flynn reached out and squeezed Jane's hand in hers. 'I'll come, and gladly.'

Once she had made her decision, Mrs Flynn appeared full of energy. 'We've got things to do. I'll go and put the kettle on first and we'll have a cup of tea!' With that, the children's Nan hurried out of the chapel to the presbytery to get them all a drink.

Fahy explained to the children and Father Hanrahan, 'I have work to do here with the soup kitchen. And I have Jane's cottage to live in, so don't worry about me.'

To Jane's eyes he was also trying to to hide his relief at not having to take on the responsibility for five children and their Nan. She hugged him. 'I'll see Finn in New York, and we'll be sure to send you money to keep the cottage and the soup kitchen going as long as it is needed. But promise me, when this is over, you'll come to us.'

'I will do my best,' Fahy said.

She turned to the children and asked again. 'What do you say? Will you come and live with me and Nan, Sorcha and Jamie, in America? You can all go to school together.'

The children shouted 'Yes!' Worried looks had been replaced with big smiles and hugs. Billy and Shay started up a game of hide and seek and they were all off to play.

Father Hanrahan smiled. 'I'll be happy knowing you are safe in America. The monks will look after me. Go, with my blessing.'

* * *

When all the tears were dried, they ate supper together. Father Hanrahan had just one more task to do. To say a mass for the safe journey of the emigrants.

Candles gleamed and Father lit some incense, and a smoky cloud of ancient spices filled the church. Jane knelt on the altar steps, whispered her confession and the priest blessed her and absolved her of any sins. She remembered her parents and her brothers; prayed for Sorcha and Jamie's mother and father; blessed herself in memory of her daughter and her best friend, Annie Power.

She was surrounded by those she loved and who loved her,

both the living and the dead.

She took Holy Communion and offered it up for the souls of her dead, the sliver of the crisp Host, dipped in consecrated wine, warmed her tongue. She swallowed and felt at peace.

The priest said the final words of the Latin mass. '*Ite missa est.*' He held his hand up for attention. 'I have just one more thing to say to you. Especially for Jane, who has had many trials in her young life. And for you children, who've lost your parents and siblings.'

He switched to speak in English and read from the Old Testament Book of Ecclesiastes. 'For everything there is a season, a time for every purpose under heaven.

'The most important lines for today are these,

"A time to cry and a time to laugh,

A time to grieve and a time to dance."

'Jane has cried many tears over the loss of her dear mother and father, her brothers, her child, and Brendan and Aoife, and her friend, Annie Power.

'Today, Jane, and all you children, it is time to laugh and to dance. In years to come, when you are all together in America, may you remember this day and have many more joyful days.'

And they did indeed spend a couple of hours that evening, dancing and dreaming about the future.

* * *

They left the church at dawn on Tuesday, the first of August. Jane thought back to that day in March, 1846, when she had left for Waterford. Father Hanrahan had blessed her and Mrs Flynn had given her some bread and cheese and apples in a bag for the journey. This time she wasn't going alone; she had an entire family with her.

As for Constable Smullen, she wasn't afraid. If he caught up with her, then he'd have to follow through with his threats. And he'd get no peace in the town after. No, he might be a murderer, but he was also a bully and a coward.

They set off for Limerick. Fahy had brought along the pony, so the ass and the pony could take turns to haul the cart. Billy and Shay took advantage of this and rode the pony bareback beside the cart.

* * *

It was a fine day for the journey. Jane and Fahy took it in turns to drive. They followed the road south, heading for Limerick on the River Shannon.

Later that morning, on the road, Billy turned to call back to Jane who was driving the cart. 'I forgot to tell you what Owen said.'

'What do you mean? What did Owen say, and when?' Jane asked. He slowed the pony to let the cart catch up with him. His dark eyes flashed a smile.

'Before he left, he came out to the church. He told me to tell you he'd be in Boston, waiting for you, if you ever got to America. He said he was getting a job in the police and if I came, he'd get me one, too, when I'm old enough. You'll find him there.'

'Billy! Why didn't you tell me?' She heard Fahy and Mrs Flynn gasp and laugh together.

Billy shrugged. 'I forgot.' He clicked on the pony and raced off along the road, his black curls bounced on his shoulders, Shay holding on tight behind him.

* * *

Late on in the evening, just as the full moon rose, they saw the ship, the Jane Black, at the quay in Limerick. Jane had no trouble changing her cabin ticket for one in steerage for all of them. There wasn't much difference in the price. The shipping agent assured her that the conditions in steerage were hygienic and comfortable.

Thoughts of baby Margaret, her mother and father and brothers had flitted through her head on the journey to Limerick. But now, they were welcome thoughts. She was no longer frightened of their ghosts. This Great Hunger would end one day, but she would never forget her people. Soon, she and Mrs Flynn would make a home for her new family in America. Jane would turn eighteen in October.

In her heart, she was certain that this rebellion had only been the first step on the road to an Ireland free of the British Empire. A free country, for Irish men and women, no matter what their language or religion. If America had broken away from the British Empire, then so could Ireland. She was just as sure that she'd have to live a very long life to see it happen.

She thought of Annie Power who had made the journey before them, with her brother and sister. 'I'll find Finn and Katty, and tell them how you inspired me, my friend,' she whispered, as she stood at the ship's railing and glanced back at her homeland.

The children stood close beside her and she turned with them to face the ocean and the western horizon. 'We'll start a new life in America,' she promised.

The wind was fine for a fast crossing to Quebec. The ship weighed anchor and the sails unfurled and filled with air.

29

Afterword

The Potato famine, fevers and evictions continued throughout 1849 and 1850. The west and the south of Ireland suffered from continuing lack of food, disease and land clearances. Many abandoned their farms and headed to America, never to return to Ireland. Many of those brought their hatred of the British government with them.

The trials of Thomas Francis Meagher and the other leaders took place in October, 1848. Meagher was sentenced to be hanged, drawn and quartered for treason. This sentence was commuted to transportation to Tasmania. He gave a speech from the dock in the courthouse in Clonmel, about his love for Ireland.

'No, I do not despair of my poor old country, - her peace, her liberty, her glory. For that country I can do no more than bid her hope. To lift this land up. Make her a benefactor to humanity, instead of being, as she is now, the meanest beggar in the world, to restore her native powers and her ancient constitution. This has been my ambition and this ambition has been my crime.'

Charles Gavan Duffy had been found not guilty but his newspaper, The Nation, was shut down in August, 1848. Eventually, he, too, left Ireland.

* * *

It took another hundred years before Ireland was 'officially declared a republic in 1949, following the Republic of Ireland Act 1948.'

https://en.wikipedia.org/wiki/Republic_of_Ireland

The End.

About the Author

I retired from working in Further Education some years ago. As a gift to myself, I enrolled on a Masters degree in Creative Writing with the Open University in 2019 and began to write.

I am married to Michael. Our three children are married with children of their own. I adore my six grandchildren.

I enjoy travelling in my spare time, especially to Ireland, to visit my daughter, Fran, her husband and children, and to research settings for my novels.

I am second generation Irish and, although I spent many happy years living in Ireland. I now live in England.

My passion is researching and writing about nineteenth and twentieth century Irish history, especially women's history. My novels all have women as the main protagonists.

I began my writing with this a trilogy of historical novels about women and girls, starting with the Irish Famine in 1845.

The first book *'Daughters of the Famine Road'* was published in March 2022. **https://rotf.lol/Famine-Road**

The second, *'Daughters in Exile,* was published in October 2022.

https://amzn.to/3F34hMw

This is the final novel in the trilogy: *'Daughter of Éireann'*

All of these novels are on Amazon, in e-books and paperback. If you have read and enjoyed this book, I would be very grateful for a review or rating on Amazon.

Please check out my website, www.Bridgetsjournal.com (see link below) to read about the strong women who inspired my characters and how my imagined characters, and their historical counterparts, survived a brutal Famine.

You can connect with me on:

🌐 https://www.bridgetsjournal.com

🐦 https://twitter.com/bridgetw1807

Subscribe to my newsletter:

✉ https://www.bridgetsjournal.com/contact

Also by Bridget Walsh

Read the first two novels in my Irish Famine trilogy and see how Irish women fought to survive a terrible Famine.

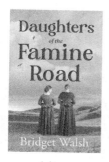

Daughters of the Famine Road

When they meet, Jane and Annie have much in common. As young Irish women in the 1840s, they both know the value of family, home and friendship. Even more importantly, they understand the need to survive against a backdrop of famine, disease and cruel colonial rule. With Ireland crumbling around them and peril at every turn, can these tenacious women overcome the arc of history and create a better life?

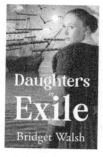

Daughters in Exile

Annie and Jane leave Ireland at the height of the Famine. Annie takes her brother and sister to their aunt in New York. She is determined to help other young exiles like herself. Jane, now a convict, is transported to New South Wales. Vulnerable and alone, she vows to meet Annie again, and dreams of them both returning home to Ireland.

This is the second in a historical novel trilogy that takes the reader on the journeys of both young Irish exiles. Will Annie evade the gangs in New York and save others like herself? Can Jane make her dream come true in these harsh colonial times?